I0725324

THE SEER

SENTINELS OF MAGIC BOOK 3

T.M. CROMER

PROLOGUE

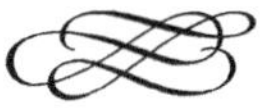

OCTOBER 31, 2327 - EARLY MORNING...

Sunlight streamed through the branches, creating shadows on the face of the headstone. It was newer than most in this cemetery; clean, polished, and carved from marble streaked with aquamarine veins. The color choice had been Bloodstone's request. Subtle. Striking. Not quite what anyone expected, like the woman herself.

Damian stood silently, staring at the name etched in stone, with his fingers curled loosely around the edge of his coat, holding the edges together. The morning was chilly, but the cold couldn't touch him. Those blessed with magic easily regulated their body temperature without excess clothing. Yet he still preferred the feel of a soft sweater against his skin and a peacoat to cut the wind, allowing him to concentrate on things other than warming his cells.

No, the ache in his chest had nothing to do with the weather. It had everything to do with saying farewell to another friend's memory. In this case, multiple friends, all the Sentinels he'd come to love. But first, he needed to say goodbye to her.

Taryn Marie Stephens.

His sister-in-law and the woman who helped him bring down a corrupt organization.

He grinned.

Those bastards had messed with the wrong woman. Gone after the wrong man, too. The one she'd loved with all her heart, and who had loved her in return.

Damian inhaled, then exhaled slowly.

Goddess, the memories cut deep some days, and perhaps this morning he was a little more melancholy than usual, but he'd been too busy wrapping up the loose ends of his life. His beloved daughter and heir, Sabrina, had little left to do when he crossed over within the hour. After today, he was free of his Aether responsibilities. He could hardly wait to reunite with his wife's spirit, to be reborn with Vivian by his side. The years had been endless since her passing, and he missed her dreadfully.

Movement in his peripheral caught his eye, but he didn't need to turn. He already knew who was there, lurking in the shadows.

"Word on the street and under the ocean is that you're calling it quits today, Aether."

Damian grinned at the man's annoyed tone. "The word is correct."

"Well, that's some shite. Am I supposed to be the only immortal left now? Do you know how bloody boring it's going to be?"

"Oh, I'm sure you'll manage, my friend." He met Bloodstone's moody sea-green eyes. "Besides, I'm tired. After all these centuries, it's hard to do the math anymore. I have no idea how old I am."

"I'm going to call BS. And did you miss the word 'immortal'?"

Damian chuckled. "I'm passing that mantle on to Beastie. I've left instructions for her to annoy you and not let you sulk in your grotto."

"Bastard. At least tell me she knows how to play chess, or I'm liable to rip this damned amulet from my chest and head into the Otherworld with you."

"She learned from the best," Damian quipped.

"That would be me, and I know I didn't teach her."

They grew contemplative as they stared at the names etched in stone.

"I'm glad we chose to trust each other that day, Dethridge. Legacy is better for it."

"He was the man to thank." Damian nodded, indicating the name displayed on Taryn's matching tombstone. "If he hadn't brokered the peace between us, we'd have been on opposite sides of the fight."

"I'd like to think we'd have come together eventually. The cause was just."

"Yes." He couldn't disagree.

Silence stretched between them. The kind that only came between men who'd fought together, lost too much, and said most of what needed saying years ago.

"Do you think about her as often as I think about Viv?"

There was no need to clarify who. The Siren prince never wavered in his love for Taryn.

"I think of her daily." The confession was wrung out of Bloodstone, and the husky note in his voice struck a chord in Damian's heart. "She surprised me," the man said. "Not many people do."

"She turned out to be a helluva head council member, didn't she?" Damian said.

The question was rhetorical; the only answer could be "yes." Taryn, heavily involved in rebuilding the new Legacy council, became the magical community's fiercest advocate. Under her tutelage, members young and old had learned to set aside their prejudices and embrace their fears, working through potential problems before they could escalate. And somewhere in her free time, she lent her voice to Fintan's, and the two created achingly beautiful music. Their three diamond and two multi-platinum albums were a testament to how much the world loved the duo.

The Siren prince grinned, casting one last glance at the Seer's headstone before sauntering away. But not before saying, "Don't think I'm after forgiving you for taking the easy way out, Dethridge."

Damian expelled a soft huff of amusement. Bloodstone wasn't fooling him. They'd often discussed reincarnation over a glass of brandy while playing a game of chess. The Siren prince's incarnation as Fintan had been his most talked-about.

"Try not to burn the place down," Damian called back.

Fintan Sullivan.

The Seer.

The person always quick to answer a summons and provide future intel when needed. When Damian had first met him, he'd been reserved, grumpy, and suffering unbearable pain, tortured at every turn by his "ancestors" all in the name of preserving an organization that should've been dismantled a century ago. He'd had his revenge in the end.

CHAPTER 1

PRESENT DAY...

Fintan Sullivan hated his gift. He always had. Having the sight was a fecking bastard, and he'd prefer not to see the future if he didn't have to. Mainly, it was why he avoided anything and anyone unrelated to his employment with the Authority. He didn't want to know if the guy next to him on the street was about to drop dead of a heart attack or if the woman behind the counter at the shop was cheating on her hard-working husband. He tended to keep to his family's grounds unless required for some magical deed or another.

But when the Aether called, you answered.

As the balance between good and evil in the world, Damian Dethridge was a law unto himself, acting as judge and jury for those who stepped out of line. No one wanted to be on the man's bad side. Also, he was Fintan's boss.

He sighed heavily as he double-checked the building's number and walked up the path to the Victorian house with the black wrought-iron fence. Already, he despised the place. Its overall vibe screamed old. Not as ancient as some of the homes he'd seen in Europe or even his own family's Irish estate, but creaky enough that a few spirits likely lingered in the American mausoleum in front of him.

His ultimate demise lay on the other side of that wooden door with its stained glass.

And her name was *Taryn Stephens.*

The visions had told him as much. Not just today but nearly every day since he'd met her twenty-four years ago. A nightmarish premonition stuck on repeat. But suffering wasn't new to the Irish.

"Feckin' second sight," he muttered.

She also happened to be Damian's sister-in-law.

From behind him, the slapping of soles against the walkway caught Fintan's notice. He glanced over his shoulder and frowned when he saw the Guardian, Draven Masters.

"Draven? Sure, and what are you doing here, man?"

"When the Aether calls, you come running, *cher.*"

Fintan snorted. "Yeah, and didn't I have the same thought just minutes ago?"

"Why are you standin' out here? Shouldn't you be in there?" Draven possessed a raspy, leftover-old-Louisiana accent, the only true hint of a heritage he never spoke of. His past was tucked in a lockbox and only he held the key. Although Fintan had caught glimpses, he didn't know the gritty details leading up to the Guardian's defection from the Authority. But he could guess. Things at that fecking place were in turmoil and had been from the moment a rogue member went after Damian's beloved daughter, Sabrina.

"Fate, visions, and my ultimate demise," Fintan replied dryly.

One side of Draven's mouth kicked up, and humor lit his warm, whiskey eyes. "Sounds like a woman."

"It is."

"Why am I not surprised?"

"What the feck are ya meanin'?" Fintan demanded, not truly

irate but stalling for time. If it required getting into a heated debate rather than walking through that bleeding stained-glass door, he'd do it. His people preferred fighting to exploring their inner feelings, and he was onboard with it. He abhorred heightened emotions.

"You'll not get a rise out of me, *cher*. I've been summoned."

"I hate it when you do that," he grumbled. Deflecting was his specialty, and having it used against him was irritating.

"What?"

"*That.* Skirt a volatile situation as easily as ya do, ya scut!"

Draven laughed, and the sound was pure magic. Low and throaty, but leaving one in no doubt his amusement was real. "You're tryin' to fight me so you don't have to deal with one petite female? She doesn't seem threatenin' to me."

"You'll be after tellin' me why, ya will. And how you know Taryn." Fintan *was* annoyed this time. He may not want her for himself, but he sure as feck didn't want to see her hook up with Draven. The thought of them together was acid searing his soul, and it burned hotter than expected. Imagining someone else touching her, hearing her laughter, and being the recipient of her affection hollowed him out. If his friend had designs on her, Fintan wanted to know.

With dark-blond brows drawn together in confusion, Draven shook his head.

"Give in now, Fintan. You're head over heels."

He didn't bother to deny it, not when the truth was a rising tide he couldn't hold back.

"I didn't say I *don't* care about her," Fintan grumbled. "Just that I don't *want* to care about her."

"She's your *ultimate demise?*"

"Aye."

Draven clapped him on the back and grinned. "What a way to go, *cher*! What a way to go!"

"Sure, and I never got a clear vision of the future with her or why," Fintan mumbled as he scratched his chest and stared at the offending door.

"What's all this?" A gravelly male voice asked from behind them.

He didn't turn around. He'd known five minutes ago Trevor Blane would be joining their group. Next would be Alexander Castor, then Creed Calder. Only Jordan Brothers would be late to this pointless meeting of the Aether's.

"Our man Fintan is stallin' for time. He doesn't want to face what's on the other side of that door." Draven smirked triumphantly when Trevor chuckled.

Fintan never wanted to plant another person a facer as badly as he did his long-time friend. He didn't dignify Draven's response with a reply. Instead, he charged toward the fecking door. When he raised his hand to knock, it swung open, and the one person he wished to avoid stood there with a welcoming smile on her too-grand face. Her aqua eyes shone brighter than jewels, and the breeze kicked up, as if waiting to caress her, and tossed her titian- and mocha-brown hair with its white-blonde highlights.

He scowled.

She ignored his ire.

"Fintan. Just the man I was hoping to speak with," she said with a peek over his shoulder at the others. "Hi, Trev. Soleil's in the greenhouse if you want to stop before breakfast. Damian is running a little late. Baby Nate was fussy."

"Sure, and did we need a rundown of his bleedin' problems?" Fintan grumbled. "The man could've texted and delayed the feckin' meeting."

"Don't mind him, *cher*. He's been in a bad mood since birth." Draven pushed past him and kissed Taryn on the cheek. "Thank you for lettin' us know."

Her responding grin was like pure sunshine illuminating the faerie-blessed green fields of *Éire*, and it caused Fintan's heart to pound harder. The urge to turn and run was hard fought, and despite his misgivings, he crossed the threshold of her home.

The ancestors had something to say about it, and his body seized.

When Fintan regained consciousness, he was lying on the floor, and half the household, along with his fellow Sentinels, were peering down at him. It took a precious extra minute to realize his head was cradled in Taryn's lap, and she was stroking his hair back from his hot forehead. The realization lit a fire under his ass, and he jumped to his feet so fast it was sure to insult her.

TARYN SIGHED IN DISAPPOINTMENT. NOT AT FINTAN. HE WAS doing what he'd always done when it came to avoiding her. No, the frustration was directed at herself. Once again, she'd let down her guard, and Fintan Sullivan had stomped all over her tender feelings. The jerk couldn't scramble away fast enough.

For the span of a heartbeat, she met his tormented gaze.

And wasn't that the problem? When he wasn't eyeing her like she was about to steal the silver, he looked at her like he wanted to eat her up. His intense expression put naughty thoughts in a girl's head and fed her dreams. It also made one wonder what kept them apart when his desire was apparent for all to see.

He still possessed a rockstar quality after all these years. His stance, seemingly casual, was commanding, and his body—oh, Goddess that fucking body!—had muscles to spare. Though not overly tall, he was built like a prizefighter with biceps putting a spinached-up Popeye to shame.

"May I speak with you in private?" she asked him.

"No!" His cheeks flushed, and he actively sought someone to rescue him. It tumbled Taryn back to when, as a famous musician, he'd required security to keep over-eager fans at bay. "I mean, I've no time. The, uh, the Aether..." Trailing off, he cast a desperate glance at Draven as if expecting help from his direction.

The Guardian enjoyed being contrary for the hell of it, and instead of tossing out a lifeline, he crossed his arms and raised a brow. The gesture earned him a scowl from Fintan and a laugh from Castor, who had entered the room right after Fintan dropped to the floor.

Castor, ever the charming rogue and gallant to every female he met, offered a hand to help her stand.

Her cheeks warmed as she realized she hadn't moved from the floor where Fintan had left her. No, like the love-starved fool she was, she sat, gawking at him and wishing things had turned out differently.

Way to go, Taryn.

With an irritated huff, Fintan knocked Castor out of the way and hauled her to her feet. His touch electrified her, and she sucked in a breath. For an unguarded second, his tortured sea-green eyes drank her in. But he recalled his abhorrence for her, and his iris color darkened as his face hardened.

"Stop wearing your feckin' heart on yer sleeve, Taryn Stephens," he growled in a low voice. "You're always doin' that, ya are, and it's bleedin' embarrassing for both of us."

Her heart, like her face and body, went cold, and she shoved past him. Before she could make good her escape, Creed Calder caught her in his arms and tucked her protectively against his chest.

"Do you always have to be such an animal, Fin?" he snapped. The air grew thick with tension as the two men glared at each other.

"The only person whose behavior is embarrassing is yours, Sullivan," Castor added sternly with a challenging look for Fintan. "She's being nothing but kind to a dour little prick."

Taryn was torn between crying and defending him. He didn't

deserve to be piled on, but then again, neither did she deserve his constant scorn. Their romance had been magical until the day he'd ghosted her. She'd spent years trying to forget him and those unimaginable weeks together. There were entire days she didn't think of him once. All that changed two years ago when he entered her orbit again, uncovering the feelings she'd long believed buried.

But she did neither, cry nor defend him. He was a big boy and could fight his battles himself.

Taryn patted Creed's chest—a mighty fine one—and drew away from his sheltering embrace.

"Thank you," she said, giving him a grateful smile and extending it to Castor. "You've both been very kind. I appreciate your defense, but there's no need to exchange blows with Fintan. You might break your knuckles on his hard head."

Okay, so yeah, her comment was petty, but so was his.

Avoiding a backward glance at the cause of all her woes, she gave a regal nod and hurried toward the library—her sanctuary in a world gone mad.

She'd barely settled in when Fintan entered, sucking all the air from the room and her lungs.

"I'm after apologizing to ya," he said, proverbial hat in hand.

"You're *after* doing it, or you're *actually* doing it?" she asked coolly. "Because they aren't the same thing."

"I'm *doin'* it," he replied, sullen despite the overture.

"For which incident?" Tapping her finger on her chin, she affected a contemplative air. "Ghosting me after telling me I was the one? Hiding every time I visit your cousin, Brenna? Treating me like I have the plague when I was only trying to protect your thick head from the marble floor?"

He smirked at "thick head," and Taryn wanted to throat punch him.

Instead, she ignored his teenage humor and continued roasting his hurtful actions. "Or this latest one? Treating me like one of your overzealous groupies from your stupid boy band days?"

Fintan scowled. "It was never a boy band. Let's make that clear."

"Hmm, really? Five guys dancing in sync during the heyday of the boy-band era? Don't kid yourself, Fintan. It was totally a boy band."

"You'll take that back, or you'll be sufferin' me wrath," he warned.

Her laugh was genuine. "Your wrath? And what's that? You'll sing me to sleep or make predictions until I run away screaming?"

"Sure, and ya think it's a joke, but I'll be tellin' ya the prediction is real, and you're to be—"

He gulped and dropped his gaze.

"Don't stop now. You're getting to the good part." She jumped up and stalked to him, somewhat satisfied to see the wariness cross his reddening face. "What prediction, Fintan? What do your all-fired important ancestors have to say about my life that I give two shits about?" she taunted.

"Don't mock them or the visions, Taryn," he warned with an ill-at-ease glance skyward. "It's not the craic."

"No, it's not funny, and neither is your behavior toward me. So do us both a favor and shove your apology up your ass, okay?"

His handsome face was a foot above hers, alerting her to the not-so-subtle changes time had wrought. Where once his visage bore that of youth and eagerness—perhaps excitement at a blossoming career—now, it was a chiseled monument to his complex adult life. All the engaging energy of a burgeoning artist had disappeared behind a rock-solid mask of disillusionment and surliness.

"What happened to you?" she asked softly. "To that sweet, kind guy I met who was thrilled to sing to the masses?"

"He discovered what he was," he said, equally as soft and a

helluva lot more tormented. "He has a monster waitin' inside to wake and gobble up innocent little girls like you, love."

"Are we speaking literally or figuratively? Because from where I'm standing, it's figurative and something you can control."

"It's not." His irises darkened further, and she could tell by the deepening color that he was hurting. An excellent barometer for a witch's feelings was the changing shades. "It's quite literal, and I can't control him. At least, not around you."

CHAPTER 2

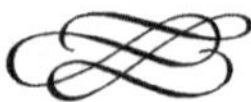

Throughout the meeting with the Aether, Fintan's attention strayed to Taryn, and he considered the wrongs he'd perpetrated on her. She'd carelessly listed them as if they meant little to her, but the deep grooves around her down-turned mouth and the lack of sparkle in her normally bright eyes spoke of a different story.

Positioned across the table from him, she did her level best to ignore him and avoid the curiosity of everyone else. Their volatile relationship was cause for speculation, and nothing was worse than a bunch of bored men without amusements to occupy them.

Fintan had embarrassed her, though he hadn't meant to.

Or maybe he had.

But he'd only erected and maintained the wall between them for her protection.

"Who are you kidding, Sullivan? It was to protect yourself." Alexander Castor's voice inside his mind jerked Fintan's head up and around.

Panicked, he looked at the Sentinels present. Draven's

watchful expression held a hint of pity, while Creed and Alex still expressed ire for Fintan's earlier behavior. He'd forgotten he wore the fecking tanzanite ring, allowing for unspoken communication with his fellow team members and giving them access to any unguarded thoughts.

"Aye, and maybe it was," he admitted inside the confines of their silent coms. With a glare at the others, he yanked the communicator off his finger.

What the hell had they heard when he'd been speaking to Taryn in the library? He attempted to recall what he'd been thinking at the time. Other than admiring her fiery fighting spirit or being willing to promise the fucking moon and stars if he could touch her once more, there wasn't much.

Yeah, he'd give his left nut to have a normal life with her.

"Fintan?"

He nodded when Damian Dethridge addressed him directly. Cursing himself for not paying attention, he shrugged. "Sure, and I've been mullin' over a vision I saw earlier," he replied, feeling like a disobedient schoolboy caught daydreaming. "I wasn't listenin'," he admitted.

Amusement danced in Damian's dark obsidian eyes, and Fintan fought the urge to squirm. If anyone knew what was going on in his brain, ring or no, it was the Aether.

"I had asked if you'd mind working with Taryn to discover the origins of the necklace she found. It's Celtic in nature."

His first instinct was to shout, "Feck no!" Luckily, he held it in check, and his curiosity won out.

"Necklace? What's that, then?" he asked.

Creed snorted, Draven grinned, and Alex laughed.

"His mind was on other things," the latter said. "I can't wait to see how this one plays out."

"Feck off, why don't ya?" Fintan growled. "Get your own house sorted before ya take a wreckin' ball to somebody else's, yeah?"

"I don't need his help, Damian," Taryn inserted quickly. "I'm sure Sabrina may have insight, or I can speak to Mackenzie Thorne."

Fintan breathed a sigh of relief. If he could avoid touching the object, certain to have a history he wanted no part of, while escaping the forced proximity to Taryn, he'd consider himself fortunate.

Damian grimaced. "I'd prefer not to bring Mack into this if we can help it. She's a new mother, and the less hassle or drama we bring to her door, the better. As for Beastie, we can ask, but she may experience the same aversion to touching it as I had."

Aversion?

Before Fintan could ask, Damian added, "I'd like to see Sullivan give it a go first."

And so saying, the Aether crushed his dreams of avoiding entanglement. Due to the timing of his vision in the foyer, he suspected he knew exactly what trinket they were discussing.

"Don't ever touch the bloodstone necklace, or it will send you down the path toward your eventual ruin and loss of power," the ancestors had intoned in their creepy-as-fuck way while imprisoning him in a trance.

The group was awaiting his response, and Fintan reluctantly nodded. "I'll have a quick look and tell ya any impressions I receive, but I'll not be touchin' it or hangin' about for research."

Taryn took exception and sneered.

"If you don't want to work with me, that's fine. I can take a hint." She stood and addressed Damian. "I'll go get it. Maybe there's someone his royal highness will actually speak to."

Fintan jumped up. "Taryn, love, I—"

"Fuck *off*, Fintan." The water in a pitcher at the center of the table swirled and dipped in the center, creating a mini maelstrom. Steam rose from mugs scattered about the table's surface like geysers, and those closest leaned backward to avoid injury. Taryn's rage had sparked to life, and she never appeared more beautiful than she did at that moment. "Just fuck all the way off already!"

Her voice cracked on the last word, and it echoed in the chambers of his heart.

The pitcher upended over his head, leaving him standing in shocked silence and looking for all the world like the eejit he was. Yet, he didn't care one whit about any of it. His focus was locked on her ramrod-straight back as she stalked away, and he experienced the certainty of love. If that fecker Cupid were standing in front of him, grinning like a fool and polishing his nails on his giant diaper for a job well done, it would come as no surprise to Fintan. Because the pain in his chest was as sharp as an arrow's tip, and his desire to chase after her was too over-powering to ignore, he gave chase.

He'd only taken two steps when Damian's laughter-filled voice reached him. "You may want to let her cool down a bit, Sullivan. If not, she's liable to host a lobster boil in the swimming pool with you at the center of it."

"Sure, and those are wise words, Dethridge, but I'll not let another minute go by without her knowin' it wasn't her I was objectin' to."

"It's your funeral," Castor said cheerfully. "Who has a mirror? We should scry. The fireworks are bound to be entertaining."

"Feck off," Fintan called back as he jogged for the door. The squish and squeaks from his shoes made him wince. Or maybe it was the laughter of the people behind him. His supposed friends, who claimed to have his back.

"Bastards," he muttered.

In the hallway, he snapped his fingers and dried his clothes, then toed off his soggy shoes. To calm his rioting emotions, he inhaled deeply before searching for Taryn.

Fintan found her pacing the library and cursing him with every breath. Leaning against the doorframe, he remained silent, letting her vent. He admired her creativity, especially regarding which part of his anatomy he could stick the necklace.

"You seem particularly obsessed with shovin' things up my arse. Should I be worried, then?" he said.

Additional color surged into her cheeks, and she resembled one of Soleil's prized tomatoes.

"You weren't meant to hear any of that."

Her haughty tone was as amusing as her colorful language, and Fintan grinned.

Lifting her chin, she glared. "You're a contrary ass!"

He nodded. "I am at that."

"Why are you here? Shouldn't you be running as fast and as far away from me as possible?" she asked, with attitude to spare. Her stance was packed with challenge and daring as if she hoped a motherfucker would.

"Aye, I should."

But I can't.

"Why can't you?" she asked.

He frowned.

"Can you hear me?" He thought the question but didn't speak it aloud. His heart clunked painfully in his chest, and he hoped to hell that he was mistaken about her new ability.

"Yes, you asked if I can hear—" With wide eyes and hands over her mouth, she paled and stared at him in horror.

She'd guessed what it meant.

Fintan straightened from the wall.

"Can you hear me?" Her thought was edged with a healthy heaping of desperation. Even though she hadn't spoken out loud, her dismay came through, giving the voice inside his head a squeaky pitch.

Fintan closed his eyes and hung his head.

"You know what this means, don't you, *aoibhneas mo croí?*" he asked her.

"I know what I don't want it to mean," she retorted.

He snorted a laugh, amazed he could in such dire circumstances.

Jaysus! Fated mates with the one woman destined to destroy him. Oh, how the gods must be enjoying the results of their sick humor.

"I would never do anything to destroy you, Fintan," she said with undeniable sincerity. "And I don't want to be fated mates with you or anyone."

Liar.

Color flooded her cheeks as her conscience called her out.

Sighing his resignation, he approached her.

"I never thought it would be intentional." He brushed the soft underside of her jaw with his thumb. "Never in a million years would I believe it."

"Why would you? And why avoid me?" she asked, unable to disguise the hurt in her voice. "I'm a big girl. I was then, too. At any time, you could've said I wasn't who you wanted as a girlfriend, and I'd have walked away. Like I intend to now."

His heart contracted painfully. "Sure, but I'd have been lyin'. And that's the one thing I won't do."

"I don't understand." She searched his face as if expecting to find answers to all her questions.

"I'm not sure I do, either," Fintan admitted. "I've wanted ya from the first, and that's the honest truth of it. But on the last night we were to meet, the night I didn't show up, my uncle died."

"Oh, Fintan! I'm so sorry. But why didn't you message me?"

"I couldn't. They wouldn't let me."

"Who?" Her scowl was fierce, as if she was prepared to battle an army on his behalf. "Who wouldn't let you?"

"The ancestors."

CHAPTER 3

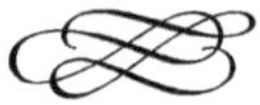

TWENTY-FOUR YEARS EARLIER...

Fintan glanced out over the sea of faces, staring up at him and his four bandmates in wide-eyed wonder. Excitement thrummed through the crowd, feeding the energy in the room. Most were non-magical, but scattered among them were the witches and other supernatural beings of the world. His voice was unique and packed venues, earning them top dollar and contracts out the arse.

He didn't care.

Not about the business end of things, nor the money. That was their drummer's gig. He was the brain and promotional genius behind their success. Well, his hard work and Fintan's talent.

He maintained his music was intended for the masses, for anyone who appreciated his unique brand of poetry in the form of lyrics and harmony combined.

One stood out.

A shining star in the black night sky that drew his notice and spiked his interest. Her aura was as multi-dimensional as her hair color, with its dyed red and orange streaks. With no past relationships to go by, Fintan didn't know much about love, but he was damned sure struck dumb in her presence.

The instant when their gazes collided, he forgot the song lyrics. Fortunately, they were mid-chorus, and the guys picked up the slack. And when the set was over, he didn't care that his bandmates had a go at him. He was obsessed with finding the girl he'd lost his heart to.

"Did ya see her, then?" he asked Donal, his bassist.

"Who?"

"The *cailín* down front with the large eyes and wild hair."

Donal laughed and slapped him on the back. "Sure, and they all have large eyes from where we're standin', man." With a dismissive shake of his head, he leaned halfway over the bar and ordered a pint from the server, flirting with the woman beside him all the while.

"He's right," someone said behind him.

A sense of rightness washed over him. His ears instinctively knew the sound of *her* voice. He turned, and the crowd around them faded like evening mist chased by the morning light, leaving only her.

"Sure, and what's he right about, then?" he asked with a face-splitting grin.

"There were a ton of women with large, admiring eyes staring up at you," his dream girl said, raising her voice to be heard over the pub noise. "And a few other *large* assets, as well."

"I'm only interested in one of those women," he assured her.

"Oh? Should I leave so you can find her?"

He leaned forward, speaking right beside her ear. "If you do, I'll be after chasin' ya and bringin' ya back."

Her smile, brighter than the sun sparkling on lake water and twenty times as warm, rewarded him.

"You're pretty smooth," she said. "Must come with the territory."

He considered her comment as he sipped his drink. One

would assume, as the lead singer in a popular rock band, he'd be a lady's man. Yes, he had the looks to back up any play he cared to make, but random hook-ups had never appealed to him. How did he tell her that inside, he was a jumbled mess of insecurity?

All because of her.

"I'm not, though." He gave her a self-deprecating smile. "I'm what you Yanks would call a 'hot mess.'"

Her eyes flared wide as she grinned up at him. "Consider me intrigued."

"Yeah, me, too." Fintan lifted a hand, stopping just shy of touching her flawless skin. "May I?"

She nodded after a moment's pause, and he stroked her silky smooth cheek, tracing her jawline, then cupped her neck to draw her close.

"What's your name?" he asked.

"Taryn. Taryn Stephens." Her voice had a sexy breathiness that he fucking adored.

"Well, it's nice to meet ya, Taryn-Taryn Stephens. I'm Fintan Sullivan."

Her laugh bordered on a giggle, and though he despised giggling girls in general, coming from her, the joyful sound wasn't annoying.

"You identified yourself at the beginning of your set," she said.

He shrugged, having forgotten anything that came before spotting her in the crowd. "And now the introductions are out of the way, can I snog ya, then?"

"Snog?"

"Kiss. I've a powerful need to kiss ya, love."

Again, she hesitated before nodding, giving him a shy smile in the process.

That bashful gesture created a burst of happiness in his chest, yet his stomach tightened. A knowing washed through him, alerting him that this meeting was big and its importance would carry through the rest of his life. But the impulse to press his mouth to hers, to taste her contagious merriment, was greater than all his wayward feelings combined, and since he had her permission, he wasted no time leaning in.

Their lips met. The explosion of light behind his eyes jolted him. But the sense of rightness he'd felt when she first spoke returned to embrace him, and he cupped her face with both hands, pressing into her as she gripped his waist.

"Get a feckin' room," Donal shouted, giving him a shove and laughing at his own idiocy when Taryn's beer spilled down the front of Fintan's trousers.

"Are ya a bleedin' eejit, Donal? Where the fuck's your brain, man?" Fintan growled. He'd long since had enough of the guy's antics. Once they'd gained a small measure of fame, Donal became an obnoxious dryshite.

To Taryn, who looked thoroughly dismayed, Fintan apologized. "It's sorry I am, love. Are you all right? You didn't get hurt by his eejit move?"

He would've sworn hearts entered her eyes as she smiled in her sweet, unassuming way. "No. I didn't get hurt. Would you like me to, um"—her gaze locked on his crotch—"take care of that?"

Fintan almost swallowed his tongue and, had he been able to speak, would've asked just what she intended. They were interrupted when the bartender tossed him a towel.

"Dry that up, and don't be acting the maggot in me pub, yeah?"

"Aye, Bridget. It won't happen again," he said, bending to soak up the mess on the floor.

As he returned the towel, the fiery redhead gave him a sharp nod before winking at Taryn. "Be careful, girl. Most of the men in these parts are only after a ride. Don't be losin' your heart to one such as these, yeah?"

"Ach! Now, why would ya be sayin' such a thing?" Fintan

pretended to cover Taryn's ears, then lifted one hand to say, "We're not all heartless rogues, love."

With a snort, Bridget gestured to the stage. "Break's over. Get your arse back up there. Your newest fan can sit here and keep me company."

"Sure, and don't be fillin' Taryn-Taryn's ears with shite about me," he warned with a wink.

"Go!" Bridget ordered, but laughter lurked in her command.

Leaning in for a quick kiss, he met Taryn's sparkling aqua eyes. "You'll stick around?"

"Yes."

"Grand. The next one is for you."

As he turned to go, she gripped his wrist. "Wait! It looks like you peed your pants. You can't go up there like that."

"The lighting is low, and—"

He made a strangled sound when she cupped him through his jeans. With berry-red cheeks, she whispered, "Come to me."

Brains scrambled, cock thickening, and agreement only a heartbeat away, Fintan opened his mouth to speak. But she withdrew her balled fist and placed it flat over the mouth of an empty glass. All the liquid that had been soaking his pants filled the mug, leaving his clothing bone dry.

Heat climbed his neck when she shot him an amused look.

"I know what you were thinking, but I'm not *that* easy," she said pertly.

"I never thought you were, Taryn-Taryn," he assured her, somehow knowing in his heart of hearts she wasn't the type to hook up with a random stranger, lead singer or no. He tucked a strand of her wild mane behind one ear. "But a man can hope, yeah?"

Her laughter followed him to the stage, or perhaps he imagined it did, but when he sought her out across the room, he experienced vertigo. His entire world was turned inside out in an instant.

PRESENT DAY...

TARYN HAD HEARD TALK OF FINTAN'S PSYCHIC GIFT IN RECENT years, particularly "the ancestors" part. The facts from Damian were that the Sullivan line produced one male per generation to receive the ability, and those controlling bastards directed his every movement.

Was it as simple as Fintan doing what he was told back then? Now, too? If so, did she want a man who wouldn't fight for her above all else? What was the alternative? Was he supposed to give up his magic for her? Definitely not. But goddess above, she wanted him to say he would, and not because she required it but because he desired her more.

She'd never ask him to, though.

"I know you wouldn't, *aoibhneas mo croí*." He tucked a strand of her hair behind her ear, reminiscent of the night they'd met.

And for the span of a heartbeat, she let herself believe he might still choose her. It was easy to convince herself that he might already have. Taryn could embrace delusion as well as anyone. Yet harsh reality had a way of intruding, especially in her world.

She sighed and shook her head at her foolishness. "You're privy to all my thoughts now, aren't you?"

"Aye. I am."

"Will I never have another one that's purely my own?" she croaked.

"Ya will, once we find the switch and turn this off."

For a cocksure man, he didn't sound convincing.

She threw up her hands. "Awesome. This is going to be great fun."

"Isn't it, though?" His frustration was as great as hers.

And she tried not to feel bad for him as she fought against

thinking anything at all. It wouldn't do to let him know how much he still affected her all these years later.

The side of his mouth quirked up. "Sure, and you affect me, too. Ya always have, Taryn-Taryn," he said huskily. "But we can never be, yeah? The ancestors have stated you'll be my downfall if I'm to love ya."

A chill penetrated her soul. His voice was gentle, but the rejection landed like a blade on bone.

"I'm sure they have nothing to worry about." Her tone was glib and at direct odds with how she was feeling. Searching for another topic, she glanced toward the table. "The amulet I found. Why don't you want to research it with me? Is this about me or the object?"

"Both."

She sucked in a breath, too surprised to form a response.

"Being around you is torture when I can't touch ya," he replied. His sincerity seemed real, and she nodded, backing around the coffee table to allow him space.

"It's sorry I am to have hurt your feelings, all the same."

"I'm an adult, Fintan. I'll cope." Her tone was as brittle as her heart.

"Are ya rejectin' the apology, then?"

"No. Not at all. I'm merely telling you that I stopped letting careless men hurt me decades ago." She recalled the day she'd been left standing at the train station, waiting for a gorgeous, talented singer to return after they'd spent a life-altering two-and-a-half weeks together. The rain was relentless as she'd lingered for hours, a soaking-wet, pathetic castoff, for a man who didn't have the courtesy to inform her he wasn't coming. "You were one in a succession of assholes, Fintan. The only thing that makes you special is that you were the first."

Although he didn't show it, she felt his internal wince.

Good.

She paused, waiting for him to argue. To say she was wrong and that she still mattered.

He didn't.

"Next time, be defiant enough to inform a woman you're not interested enough to pursue her." She reached for the box containing the artifact. But when she shifted to show him, his face had paled.

"Fintan?"

"Aye. I'm grand." He swallowed, never removing his horrified stare from the box. "Sure, and where did you say you found the necklace?"

"At a yard sale. Why?"

"It's the downfall I was tellin' ya about."

She shoved it under the sofa cushion. "Get out! Get out now!"

His gaze snapped to hers, and in the next instant, he was laughing.

"Why are you lingering? Are you nuts?" she screeched.

"Aye. But we're not in one of those action films you love so much, and it's doubtful the feckin' thing will explode."

Taryn stalked forward and punched his arm. "You're such a dick."

His irises had lightened, making his twinkling humor more prominent and, sadly, more alluring. His husky laughter eased the tension in her shoulders. But she didn't join in his amusement. Not right away. Laughing felt like surrender, and she wasn't ready to let her guard down with this mercurial man.

"Okay, so maybe I overreacted," she admitted with a sheepish shrug.

He held his thumb and index finger up. "Just a wee bit."

They stared at each other, caught up in the magic, similar to their initial meeting in Ireland.

The memory of their first kiss drifted back to her...

"And now the introductions are out of the way, can I snog ya, then?"

"Snog?" she'd asked.

"Kiss. I've a powerful need to kiss ya, love."

The memory affected them both. With the same intensity he had in the pub, Fintan tipped up her chin and brushed her nose with his. Desire, both his and hers, grew thick in the air, enchanting and drawing them together. If an inch of space existed between them, it wasn't by design.

"Sure, and I still have that powerful need, Taryn-Taryn. It's likely to never go away."

His voice was a mere whisper, but it thundered in her chest. Every intimate memory they'd shared surged to the surface: music, firelight, the feel of his bare skin on hers, and the weight of him cradled between her thighs. Chasing those memories was the ache of everything left unsaid.

Goddess, she was a fool, because here she was, ready to rush back in, if only to recapture the unique feeling of being alive only Fintan could spark within her.

Sucking in her breath, she tilted her head to receive his mouth.

But the kiss never came.

CHAPTER 4

"Sorry to interrupt."

Fintan snatched his hand away and tucked it behind his back as he shifted to face Taryn's sister, Josephine.

He was thankful she'd arrived when she did, or he'd have done something incredibly stupid.

The sudden slap against the back of his head was unexpected, and he cast a scowl over his shoulder. Before he could ask, Taryn's thoughts on the matter rang through loud and abundantly clear.

"Kissing me is stupid? You're an asshole!"

Fuck!

He'd forgotten about their new connection.

"I'd like to forget it, too," she muttered, shoving past him. "What's up, Josie?"

Her sister's gaze swept Taryn's face and locked on him. A slow smile curled her lips.

"Well, well, well. This is interesting."

"Why?" Taryn snapped. "You *interested* in stealing another boyfriend?"

Hurt flashed in Josie's amber eyes but she quickly replaced her pain with a mask of indifference.

"Rumor has it he's not that into you, kid," she said with a one-shoulder shrug. "I was just coming to tell you that Damian and his team are waiting for your little bauble."

With a finger wave, she turned on her heel to leave.

"Taryn. Your sister's not the enemy here," he said through their private link.

"I know," she snapped. *"But that doesn't give her the right to be mean,"* she added silently.

Josie spun back, fiery and in high dudgeon. "Look, I'm only relaying a message here, okay? Don't shoot the messenger because you're in a nasty mood."

Taryn dropped her head in her hands, missing her sister's tormented expression.

"It's past time to forgive her, aoibhneas mo croí."

"I know that, too, Jiminy Cricket."

He snorted, fully aware she did. Yet knowing and doing were oceans apart, and her unease screamed she wasn't ready to dive into those waters without a life preserver. Josie was a damned shark when she had a mind to be, and he suspected Taryn avoided her, preferring to keep her hide intact.

"Mend the rift, love," he urged.

"I hate being wrong," she said.

"We all have to take our lumps, Taryn-Taryn."

Lifting her head, she heaved a sigh so heartfelt that Fintan wanted to hold her and apologize to Josie on her behalf.

"I'm sorry, Jo," she said. "The 'I know' wasn't directed at you, and neither was my nastiness. Or it shouldn't have been."

With a wary look and a deep frown, the titian-haired beauty studied Taryn. "No one else spoke, T."

"Not aloud, anyway." She gestured with her thumb. "Looks like we're fated mates, and Fintan gets to live in my head from here to eternity."

Taryn's words were meant to be flippant. But his throat tightened with the weight of the truth. This wasn't a freak accident. Their bond was forever, whether they wanted it to be or not. Hearing it out loud felt more crushing than expected, and Fintan hated to be vulnerable.

Josie's first reaction was an unhinged jaw. Her second was laughter, and she doubled over, holding her stomach.

"What the hell is so damned funny?" Taryn demanded.

Across the room, the fish in the tank sped up as if they had somewhere to be.

"Unless you're after boilin' your aquarium pets, I'd say to simmer down, yeah?" Fintan suggested.

"What?"

He pointed to the tank.

"Crap. Right. Thanks." Taryn waved a hand toward the water, and her finned friends resumed their leisurely travels. With crossed arms, she tapped her toe. "Why is it funny, Jo?"

An affectionate smile transformed Josie's visage, taking it from alluring to breathtaking. Although Fintan could appreciate her loveliness, her beauty didn't have the power of Taryn's engaging smile or her naughty grin when amused.

Reaching back, Taryn gripped his hand and squeezed.

"Thank you."

"For what?"

"For finding me the attractive one."

He frowned, uncertain why she lacked confidence in herself. *"Are ya mad, then? Of course, you're the attractive one!"*

She sent him a sweet smile over her shoulder and released his hand to approach Josie.

"I was worried you wouldn't find someone, T. That you'd closed yourself off after the incident with Morcant," Josie confessed.

Fintan shuddered.

To this day, whenever he remembered the Arcane Devourer

and his hold on the Stephens family, Fintan wanted to smash things. Taryn had fallen for Morcant after he'd disguised who and what he was—a weapon of chaos for a manky bastard at the Authority. It still rankled.

"Sure, and can we never say that fucker's name again?" he asked. "It feels like the devil's dancin' on me grave whenever I think of him."

Taryn nodded. "Same."

"Sorry," Josie said with a grimace. "No one is happier he's dead than me, though."

"Well, maybe there are a few, yeah?" he said. Damian's daughter had been Morcant's prime target during that fiasco. But the girl had outsmarted him and everyone involved. To this day, Fintan thanked the Goddess Anu for the girl's clever brain and Oracle gifts. Had Morcant achieved his goal of appropriating the Aether magic he sought, they'd all be living in an unimaginable hell.

Josie smiled, but her amber eyes were troubled, and he felt a stirring of sympathy for all she'd gone through. She'd been tricked into a bond with Morcant, gotten shot, and—worst of all—suffered her sisters' disdain when they believed she'd stolen Taryn's boyfriend as some sick lark. For all her biting sarcasm, Josie had scars no one saw. She carried her shame in silence, hoping someone, *anyone*, might notice and tell her she would eventually be all right.

"You'll find your happiness where ya least expect it, Josephine," he said with all the assurances a Seer could offer. The future's outcome was never one hundred percent set in stone, but this, he felt confident enough to tell her.

Her hope flared to life but as quickly died out, and she shook her head. "I don't deserve it, Seer. But my sisters do." With a careless shrug, she looked between them. "You're different around him, Taryn. More alive somehow. Maybe you should explore—" She grimaced as she noted Taryn's distasteful expression. "What? Did I put my big-ass foot in it again?" With an impulsive hug, Josie said, "I'm sorry I can never say the right things around you."

She hurried from the room, leaving them in awkward silence.

Taryn's arms remained stiffly at her sides, and Fintan ached for her. Yes, Josie had meant well, but it wasn't something she was prepared to hear.

"You've never not been the liveliest version of yourself to me, Taryn-Taryn," he assured her.

His words had the opposite effect than he intended, and her expressive eyes dulled.

"But you still don't want me enough to fight for me," she stated flatly, holding up a hand when he would've objected. "The facts are, you ghosted me back then and ignored me in the years between when you could've sought me out. And more recently, whenever I visit my friends at your estate, you avoid me by hiding."

"Brenna's estate," he corrected. "I'm a lowly caretaker."

She stared at him, not allowing him to joke his way out of the situation he found himself in, as was his way when grunts didn't work. The weight of her words was a heavy burden.

Ghosted.

Ignored.

Avoided.

He'd never considered it from her angle. Yet standing here, observing her granite-carved expression, he couldn't deny it. He was a fucking arse.

Fintan sighed heavily. "Aye. I ghosted ya, but the reasons were as valid when we first met as they are today. But it doesn't mean I don't want you more than I want to breathe my next lungful of air, *aoibhneas mo croí.*"

"Right."

He hated her dismissive tone, but when he would've responded, she spoke over him.

"Let's get the necklace to Damian."

The fucking bloodstone necklace! He'd forgotten about it.

"May I see it first?" he asked.

"I thought you said it was a tool in your downfall. Like me." She frowned as she shot a glance toward the sofa cushion. "Maybe you shouldn't be in the room with it and me simultaneously."

"I'm not sure it works that way—ah!"

The pain in Fintan's head was searing, and he dropped to his knees. In the far reaches of his mind, where he'd retreated for the oncoming vision, the sound of Taryn's cry drifted to him. His subconscious was aware of her falling into him and of the two of them tumbling to the floor. Yet as he struggled to return to her, to help, he was drawn farther into the ether.

"Tayrn!" he shouted, straining to reach her through their connection.

No answer.

His panic grew. What had they done to her?

"She can't hear you, Fintan, me boy."

He spun around, searching for his Uncle Peter, whose voice he recognized. The standard rippling sea of black nothingness stretched out before him, and he wanted to scream his fury but refrained. Any cry would echo and cause untold assault on his eardrums. Stuck in a weightless state with no directional sense, he floated and awaited the ancestors' directive.

None came.

No unified omnipresent voice like usual.

"Where is she? Where's Taryn?" he demanded, waiting for them to join him from the other dimension or afterlife or wherever the fuck they resided. They hadn't seen fit to tell him in the twenty-four years he'd been a slave to their vision quests. He cursed his stupidity at allowing himself to be duped and for playing along.

What if they'd abducted her spirit? Or killed her for his

disobedience? Could they do it? Was her death to be his undoing? It certainly would be if it were his fault. Maybe because of their new link and the vision state brought on by his uncle, they had somehow imprisoned her soul, causing her to float in endless nothingness.

"Your girl is well, but listen to me now, yeah? There's not much time before they discover..."

A lengthy pause frayed his nerves. *"Discover what? Uncle Peter?"*

"Feck it all! Put on Bloodstone's necklace, boyo, and never take it off."

"But it's to be my downfall, the ancestors—"

"Lied," his uncle snapped. *"Now quit dickin' around, Fintan, or another will take what's yours. Wake and claim your prizes."*

"Prizes? Plural?"

But before Fintan received his answer, the buzzing of their connection grew deafening. If he could've, he would've slapped his hands over his ears, but in his limbo state, all he could do was suffer the pain as it transformed into a high-pitched squeal.

Soothing fingers stroked his brow, and healing energy flowed from warm fingertips to his brain, calming his neurotransmitters and allowing him to focus again.

"Taryn!"

He shoved the Healer away to sit upright. After locating her sisters hovering beside Damian's shoulder as they fretted over an immobile Taryn, Fintan crab crawled the short distance.

"What's happenin'? She not answerin' me!" He spun back to plead with the Healer. "Jordan! Do to her what ya did to me. Hurry, man! The pain is ungodly."

As the young Healer assisted Damian, Fintan questioned Josie. "How long was I unconscious?"

"Long enough for you to be missed and us to get a Sentinel Healer here."

His heart pounded too fast and way too hard. The thundering pulse rose into his throat, making it difficult to swallow. Or perhaps it was the lump of self-recrimination choking him. If she was hurt because of him…

Helplessly, he waited, alternating between being furious at himself, the Sullivan ancestors, and Damian for allowing him anywhere near Taryn. When she recovered, he'd put enough distance between them that it never happened again.

"Bloodstone's necklace."

Peter Sullivan's words echoed in his head, and Fintan glanced toward the cushion where Taryn stored the bleedin' thing. His uncle had said "Bloodstone's" and not "the bloodstone" as Fintan mistakingly believed it to be. Uncle Peter had given him an invaluable clue about the piece's provenance.

Did he dare slip it on without permission? What would it do to him? *For* him? Instinct had him pocketing the amulet, and the instant he did, Taryn's eyes snapped open to focus on him.

"Give it to Damian to destroy," she ordered in a voice not her own. "Give it to him or face our wrath."

CHAPTER 5

Five days had passed, and the bleedin' necklace was burning a hole in Fintan's pants pocket. He'd ignored the order to give it to the Aether, knowing his ancestors were using Taryn as a mouthpiece. But he couldn't ignore them for long. Odd, though, how in the time since he'd been carrying it on his person, they'd yet to summon him. He'd assumed they'd be as ruthless as usual, causing him untold pain whenever he dared to question their edict.

Still, caution urged him not to wear it as instructed by Uncle Peter. Too many things felt off about the entire incident, and until he had a handle on what the amulet could do, he wasn't taking any chances.

First, the urgency bothered him.

Why the sudden push to ignore his destiny?

Second, was the secrecy.

Why, when presented with the opportunity to tell him about the history, didn't his uncle take it?

As Fintan strummed his guitar and gazed out over the peaceful gardens of the Sullivan estate, he considered all the possibilities of the jewelry. As hard as he'd tried, he failed to dig up fuck all on Bloodstone or the bleedin' necklace. No one in his immediate circle had heard of it. He feared contacting Taryn was his only option.

His frustration was great in every way that counted.

Awareness rippled through him as the house alerted him to a visitor's presence. But had the magical notification not happened, he'd have known who was on the other side of the twelve-foot hawthorn-wood door. Pressing his forehead to the hard surface, he fought the desire to run or bash his brains in until forgetfulness came. Instead, he swung the door wide as Taryn reached for the knocker.

"Oh! Uh, hi," she stammered.

Her confusion was understandable. Fintan never answered the door if he knew she was visiting. In the past, he would inform Brenna or Eoin of her approach and disappear into the bowels of the estate, never to be seen again until she departed.

He stepped aside to allow her entry and looked his fill as she gestured to his guitar.

"You still play?" she asked in that breathy way that shot straight to his cock.

"Did ya think I wouldn't?" he asked dryly.

Her cheeks flushed becomingly, and he soaked in the sight, filing the memory for a later date.

"The world as a whole wondered when you disappeared from the music scene," she said.

"The world or you?"

"Both."

Though she knew the way to Brenna's wing, she followed him down the hallway and into the sunroom.

Fintan didn't object as he once might've.

"Surely you read all the reports?" Taryn asked. "There were rumors you'd died in a fiery crash or lost your vocal cords to some dreaded disease, like cancer."

"But you didn't believe them," he stated matter-of-factly.

After she perched on the loveseat, he sprawled in the chair opposite and propped his guitar on his thigh. Resting his head against the cushion, he observed her. In the brief time they'd dated, he loved watching her animated face as she gabbed on about whatever interested her.

"Ya had to know what I was back then, yeah?" he asked.

"I recognized you were a fellow witch, but I hadn't heard the term Siren before." She shrugged and met his curious regard. "I did wonder, though. There were anti-witch factions still at large, and I worried about you being caught in their trap."

"I'd have saved you the worry if I'd have known about it," he assured her.

Her lips twisted in a bitter smile, and the sight caused Fintan's gut to clench. His "ghosting" had hurt her far more than he'd realized. Hurt them both.

"Having learned of a Siren's ability to lure magic from others, I'm curious. Is that why you stopped singing? Are males of your kind known as Sirens, too?"

He considered her question as he fiddled with the tuning pegs. "No to the first, and yes to the second. I stopped because of Uncle Peter and this feckin' Seer nonsense. When he died, I was the one cursed with his gift. Can ya imagine me onstage, droppin' to the ground when a vision struck?" Fintan snorted with wry amusement, recalling his career with more than a little sadness. At odds with his need for privacy was the enjoyment he'd received performing.

"And yeah"—he locked eyes with her—"the males, rare though they be, are Sirens, too. They're far less dangerous than the females of our species until they turn evil."

"Turn evil?" Her brows clashed, and confusion filled her lovely visage. "I don't understand."

Fintan saw no reason to hold back the truth. If she wished to be so bold, she could easily ask Damian about his kind. Hell, she probably had.

"I'd have thought Brenna would've told you about our Aunt Odessa."

"Not all of it," she said. "She only mentioned she'd worked for her, in passing, and it wasn't pleasant."

His cousin's conflict with Odessa's Succubus was personal, and if she didn't wish to share, he'd not dishonor her by telling tales behind her back.

"If I steal another's magic through seduction, using my musical gifts, I'll become an Incubus."

She shook her head, and her frown deepened. "I've heard the term in passing, but I thought they were something the fantasy world made up."

"No, *aoibhneas mo croí*. They're very real. And they've an insatiable desire for sex and power, not carin' who they destroy to get it."

"But your cousins aren't evil, meaning they haven't stolen any power. What makes you believe you would?"

While it was true Narissa and Brenna were possessed of an ironclad will, Fintan wasn't. He was weak. And because of that weakness, he'd buried himself at the estate and enchanted the landscape to hide for the last two and a half decades. If the temptation were removed, his chances of remaining human were greater. Even as he had the thought, his gaze dropped to Taryn's full lips. The pull to seduce her was more fierce than any he'd experienced. Having her here, in his safe space, sheltered from the world, was intoxicating. If he could keep her here forever, he would.

"Sexual desire, whether it be a man's or a woman's, is biological, Taryn-Taryn," he said in a soft, hypnotic voice. As he spoke, the tendrils of his power emerged and drifted through the air between them. It enveloped her, caressing her aura and stoking her barely concealed desire for him. "It stems from a need to procreate. But for my kind, the drive is greater than all that." He strummed a haunting note, drawing it out longer than humanly possible. Lowering his voice, he said, "It's a necessity."

He felt the second her passion sparked to life, and she shifted in her seat. Her breaths were little more than pants as her head fell back and her eyes closed. If he wanted to give her an orgasm with just his music, he could, but the risk of taking what she wouldn't freely give—her magic—was too great.

The chord he struck was discordant and an assault on their ears. He dropped the guitar onto the seat beside him and rose.

"I'll tell Brenna you're here," he said coolly, prepared to hide from Taryn for the remainder of his life if he had to. There was no way in hell he'd hurt her if he could help it. And that's what stealing from her would do: remove not only her abilities but her life force with it.

"You wouldn't," she said, barely above a whisper, halting his retreat.

"What?" He spun back.

"You wouldn't steal from me or kill me. I know that, Fintan."

Sudden, uncontrollable rage filled him at her inability to grasp the seriousness of what he was, what he could do to her if left unchecked.

"Fuck if you know anything about me, Taryn Stephens! You with your basic witch ways and your feckin' sad eyes!" He stormed back and knelt before her. Roughly grabbing her hips, he dragged her to the edge of the cushion before parting her jean-clad legs to press his pelvis to hers. "Do ya not think I feel your lust? That me monster isn't excited by your wish for me to fuck ya every way to Sunday and beyond?"

He fisted her hair and forced her closer until their chests collided, and she was panting in earnest. Fear or desire, it didn't matter because both turned him on and, in doing so, turned her on through their bond.

"And this"—he ran his nose along the throat he'd exposed,

breathing in her addicting pheromones—"this *thing* inside me, strugglin' to break free? Yeah, it grows stronger every fuckin' time you come 'round, swishing that grand ass of yours."

Tugging her head back, he met her shimmering eyes and felt remorse for his aggression. Yet he needed to prove his point. She was no match for his strength or effortless ability to take what his Siren craved.

"I could make ya come with a song, love. Five notes at most. And it would be too late for you to protect yourself from my Incubus. Protect us both. Because I want ya more than I can put into words."

Contrarily, she licked her lips and looked intrigued. "Five notes?"

With a snort of disbelief, he released her and stood. "You're feckin' mad, you are. Stay away for your own safety, Taryn-Taryn. I'm beggin' ya."

As Fintan strode from her, Taryn whooshed out a breath. The idea of a five-note orgasm wouldn't leave her after he implanted it into her brain. How did a Siren make someone come with just their voice? Was that why Eoin was always smiling around Brenna? Why Narissa strutted with such confidence?

When Fintan had strummed his guitar and spoken to her in his husky, hypnotic voice, he'd awoken a vicious need inside Taryn. One that wouldn't quit until he satisfied it.

Was it intentional? Had he done it to prove a point only to forget to shut it down? Would sex with him today be better than their first time together?

"Fuuuuccccck!" His shout rang out, and he strode back into the sunroom an instant later. "Ya can't be havin' those thoughts while you're here! Get out!"

Lifting her chin, she dug deep for courage in the face of his furious scowl. "It's not your house, Fintan Sullivan. It's Brenna's."

Dismay chased shock across his divinely handsome face.

Yes, she could understand why all his gorgeousness, along with his Siren's song, could send a woman straight to her knees, either to beg for sexual favors or give them.

One of his dark brows shot up, and an intrigued light entered his stormy eyes. His sensual mouth kicked up at the corner. "It's temptin' to see you on those grand knees, *aoibhneas mo croí.*"

Heat spread from her chest up her neck and scorched her face.

Their stupid mental link was going to get her in deep shit if she didn't learn to turn it off.

"Aye," he growled. "The deepest shite imaginable."

But his gaze had softened, and the fierce man from a moment ago looked regretful.

"I'll try to keep my thoughts to myself," she promised.

"Sure, and that would be best." He turned on his heel to leave but paused. "It's sorry I am if I scared you, Taryn-Taryn."

"You didn't. Not really."

Fintan grunted in his standard grumpy fashion before striding out the door.

Next on her agenda was to find a way to block their thought exchange. Maybe Brenna could help, and if not, she could go to Damian as a last resort.

"Fintan?" she whispered, imagining him in her mind's eye. Not the angry, resentful version, but the grinning young man, with his mischievous dancing eyes.

The buzz of their link grew louder, and she assumed he could hear her.

"I didn't mean to provoke you or your Siren. I'm sorry, too."

Radio silence.

Well, she tried. Standing, she crossed to his beloved guitar and stroked her fingers along the wood's grain.

"I miss your music," she telegraphed. *"I never got the chance to tell you, but I was your biggest fan. And the world is worse for not experiencing your beautiful songs."*

"Thank you, Taryn-Taryn."

She closed her eyes in relief, strangely grateful he'd chosen to respond. *"When you're willing, we should discuss the necklace. I found out a few things—"*

Like a fucking wraith, he appeared, triggering her scream.

"Dude! What the fuck? I thought you'd left." She placed a hand over her pounding heart and glared. "Not cool."

His engaging grin was reminiscent of their first meeting, and Taryn's lungs squeezed, making breathing difficult.

"Yeah, and you should've led with the information about Bloodstone's necklace," he said.

"You never gave me a chance." She inhaled a steadying breath. "Ready to listen?"

He plopped down and drew the guitar in his lap as if it were his talisman against her particular brand of sorcery. "Aye."

CHAPTER 6

"*B*loodstone's necklace, as it's known, belonged to Ardghal"—Taryn mistakenly pronounced it ARD-gall—"Sullivan."

"It's AHR-dahl. The G is silent, and the D begins the second syllable, *aoibhneas mo croí,*" Fintan corrected, unable to contain his grin. He'd frequently hidden and listened to her slaughter the Irish language in conversations with Brenna and Eoin. Later, after she'd left, he and Eoin would craic on about the women's attempts. Never within Brenna's hearing, because they were considerate of her feelings.

Taryn waved a hand as if the name were of no importance. "Potato, potahto. But his nickname was Bloodstone, and he was the first Seer."

Fintan set the guitar aside and straightened. "Sure, and where did ya learn this?"

"Alastair Thorne is armed with an incredible arsenal of journals, and his son, Nash, has access to all sorts of artifacts at Thorne Industries. Nash is one of the most knowledgeable people I know, next to his cousin, Spring."

Nash, Nash, Nash! Sure, and didn't she sound infatuated?

Fintan took exception. "Are ya in love with the man, then? If so, I'm after tellin' ya—"

"Where the hell did that come from? Do you have a screw loose?" Fire burned in the grand eyes she rolled. "Nash is crazy about his wife."

He zeroed in on what she didn't say. "Yeah, but you're not denyin' it, are ya? People can love from afar."

Like him.

She sent him a sharp glance, and Fintan's stomach dropped when he remembered she could access his thoughts if he didn't keep them locked behind a wall. Disillusionment or disappointment pulled her mouth down at the corners, and she looked away.

After carefully erecting a block, he considered his options. He could tell her the truth about his feelings, or he could let her believe he pined for another. The second was safer and would avoid entanglements, but he hated her haunted expression.

Still, Fintan remained quiet.

"You're an idiot," she growled. "Back to the necklace… Like I said, Bloodstone, as your ancestor was known, was the first Seer. It's rumored that he traded part of his soul for the ability, but nothing exists in writing. For all I know, those tales were made up to scare his enemies. However, based on what I did find, he used his psychic visions to determine the outcome of battles. And he *always* won."

Though Fintan had never heard of Bloodstone or the man's history, instinct told him that Ardghal had done more than use his psychic ability to predict winners of war games. He'd bet his favorite instrument that Bloodstone the Badass had used his voice to lull enemies into a trance before he sicced his murderous Incubus on the lot of them. And if that was the case, why had Uncle Peter encouraged Fintan to find and wear the necklace? What magic did it hold?

As if the bleedin' thing could access his thoughts, it warmed to the point of discomfort, and Fintan's desire to remove it from his pocket was great. If Taryn weren't present, he'd have done it, only to avoid having it so close to his person.

"What does a piece of jewelry have to do with the man himself?" he asked her.

"That's just the thing. No one knows. But the ancient bloodstone was believed to have formed from the spilling of Christ's blood. It's said to provide protection and keep evil at bay." Excitement shone in her eyes. "And now that I've given it more thought, and considering what you are, what if Ardghal's stone was charmed? Maybe it kept his Siren locked away, and if that's true, maybe it could do the same for you!"

"Aye, but not the Siren, I'm bettin'," Fintan mused aloud. "The Incubus."

Her brows snapped together, and she looked decidedly uneasy. "I'm not sure how that could happen. I mean, if like you said…" She swallowed as heat rose in her cheeks, causing a lovely glow to her smooth skin. "Like the, uh, the notes… your, uh, monster…"

He almost laughed at her uncomfortableness, hearing exactly where her thoughts had gone. "Monster? I've never had a woman call me cock—"

She jumped up. "I'm done here."

Fintan did laugh then.

"You're a contrary prick, Fintan Sullivan," she snapped. "One minute you're growling and threatening to consume me, and the next—"

"Not you," he said sharply, climbing to his feet and approaching her. "Your power. And I'm the one consumed, Taryn-Taryn. Sure, and I thought I'd made it clear this thing inside me wants you. It nags me day and night, tauntin' me. Tellin' me to seduce you and have it all."

He drew out the pendant and dangled it in front of her. The

stone was oval-shaped inside a larger metal disc, and its color was a deep forest green with specks of red, orange, and copper. But the smaller center section leaned toward opaque, and it chilled Fintan to behold it. Many had claimed his eyes became a cloudy white during a vision.

As if enthralled, Taryn reached for the amulet. Electricity arched from the center and zapped the fingers she extended. With a pained yelp, she fell backward onto the sofa and thunked her head on the wooden back. Her eyes rolled back in her head, and she sagged to one side.

"Jaysus! Taryn!"

Jumping into action, Fintan flung the necklace and dove for her, searching for a heartbeat. He thanked Anu when he found one.

"Jaysus," he muttered again.

After easing her onto her side, he touched the wound, finding an egg-sized lump and pulling back a blood-coated hand.

"Fuck!"

A touch of his Tanzanite ring opened the line of communication between him and Jordan Brothers, but before he could do more than speak the man's name, the ancestors rattled his cage, and he fell across Taryn.

Once again, he found himself in the black void with omnipresent voices echoing around him.

"You disobeyed, Fintan Sullivan!" they intoned as one. *"A price must be exacted."*

"Fuck off, ya fuckin' wankers!" he growled. *"I'm tired of your shite. Wake me so I can attend to Taryn."*

But they didn't. They held him in limbo as he screamed and shouted his rage, leaving him to worry about her fate. He only prayed Jordan had understood who called him and had gotten to her in time.

Taryn stared down at Bloodstone's necklace, afraid to pick it up. Two hours had passed since Jordan and Damian had arrived and healed her, but Fintan had yet to wake. The answer lay in the amulet. She'd stake her life on it.

Damian had claimed he wasn't worried. Indeed, he seemed confident Fintan would awaken when he was good and ready. They'd left with orders for her to call if he didn't come around by evening.

During the first hour, she saw the wisdom of their caution, but now, not so much. Through their link, she was subjected to Fintan's blinding fury as he screamed dire threats at his ancestors.

It did no good.

If the electrified amulet was really the key, she didn't relish touching it again. Her brain had been scrambled the first time her head connected with the sofa's wooden scrollwork. Still, she didn't see where she had a choice. He'd go insane with his mind imprisoned as it was.

But perhaps that's what his sadistic ancestors wanted.

Maybe she should ask Brenna to put the necklace on?

Yet if it had been intended for Fintan, what damage might it do to his cousin? His next hoarse cry cemented her decision, and she raced through the house, searching for her friend.

"Brenna!"

With each empty room she encountered, Taryn grew more despondent and fearful for Fintan. It would be just her luck Brenna and Eoin popped off for a weekend getaway on some remote, sunny island.

"For fuck's sake, Brenna! Where are you?"

As she was hauling ass through the kitchen, she jerked to a halt. Water was her element, and Taryn cursed herself for not thinking of it before. She rummaged through the cupboard to find what she needed. After placing the large metal bowl in the sink, she filled and carried it to a seven-foot prep table.

"Show me Brenna," she commanded.

The liquid swirled, becoming cloudy before displaying a mirrored surface. The result was a sheet-draped Brenna posed suggestively while shooting a laughing glance over her shoulder.

"Expand the scene. Where is she?"

The water rippled once, and the view zoomed out, displaying the inside of Eoin's studio. The man himself was wearing only a pair of sweats, and although he was in the act of painting, there was little doubt his wife's scantily clad form aroused him.

"Shit."

Taryn hated to interrupt, but necessity wouldn't allow her to wait.

A secondary idea occurred to her, and she hoped she could pull it off.

"Show me Ardghal."

Inside the bowl, the liquid swirled, sloshing over the sides. It finally settled, reflecting an image of Fintan, sleeping in his bed.

"Okay, not what I was expecting or hoping for," she muttered.

After swiping her hand across the bowl and dumping the liquid in the sink, she raced for the door, halting just shy of crashing into the man blocking her exit.

"Creed!"

"In the flesh," he said dryly.

"I, uh, what, um, why are you here?" Taryn glanced behind him, hoping to extract herself politely to find Brenna, but unsure she should leave the man wandering around alone. "Are you looking for someone?"

"Fintan. And you're nervous. What's going on?" His tone had hardened along with his visage, revealing that, at the man's core, he was no-nonsense and ready to take immediate action when a threat arose. Other than the knowledge Creed Caldwell was formidable when riled, she knew nothing about him.

Her worry for Fintan overrode her caution. "The ancestors pulled him under hours ago, and he hasn't woken up yet."

"Did you phone Damian or Jordan?"

"They arrived here and checked him for signs of serious injury, but didn't find any. Damian feared permanently destroying Fintan's link to the ancestors if he pulled him out, so he's taking a wait-and-see approach. I'm to let them know if he doesn't wake up soon." She clenched her hands, feeling helpless and afraid for Fintan. "I'm worried, though. His screams are echoing in my head, and that's new."

Creed scowled. "What the fuck are you waiting for then? Let's go!"

"Where?"

"To get the other Sullivans. Maybe they know what to do."

Taryn halted him. "That's why I was in the kitchen. I was scrying for Brenna." She pointed in the opposite direction. "They're in Eoin's studio."

"And Narissa?"

Did she imagine his voice was grittier than normal? "I don't really know her. I'd only met her once at Damian's when Morgan—uh, *Morcant*—attacked, and I don't know how to contact her."

"Okay. I'll call her. You get Brenna. Then we'll meet..." Creed's brows met. "Where's Fintan?"

"His room."

"Which is?"

"Oh. I'd forgotten you've never been here before. It's in the north wing, top floor."

"I've been here plenty, but this place is the size of a fucking mausoleum," he said with an irritated glance around. "I've never ventured above the second floor and haven't felt the need to seek out Fintan's bedroom."

Taryn would've laughed if she were in a joking mood.

They separated, with Creed heading for the gardens and her going toward Eoin's studio. When she reached her destination, she hesitated. Goddess, the last thing she wanted was to discover them getting busy. But she didn't see where she had a choice.

Fintan's bellow echoed loudly inside her mind, removing any hesitation. Taryn gasped and fell against the studio door, holding the frame for dear life.

His pain was great. She reached through their link, praying to ease his suffering in some small way, and was promptly electrocuted.

A scream was torn from her throat.

Within seconds of her shout, the door was yanked open, and Taryn sprawled at Eoin's feet. He looked none too happy she'd disturbed them. But his scowl immediately shifted to concern, and he wrapped an arm around her as he helped her to her feet.

"Taryn? What's happened, love?"

"Fintan—*ah!*" Piercing pain shot through her skull, forcing her to clamp her head in her hands. She expected her brain would explode at any moment, or at the very least, an aneurysm.

"Fintan?" Brenna snapped her fingers, and by the time she'd reached them, she was fully clothed. Based on her forbidding expression, she was prepared for an epic battle. There were a handful of people she adored in addition to her husband, and Fintan ranked at the top of that list.

"What's happened to him?" she demanded.

"He's trapped in his mind." Taryn panted through the agony of another shockwave. "The ancestors..."

"Where?"

"His room."

Brenna touched her with one hand and clasped her husband's wrist with the other. Taryn's cells warmed to the point of burning, but cooled as soon as they landed in front of Fintan's door. Group teleports caused additional friction and were much more uncomfortable than a single-person jump, though still tolerable.

Through the wooden panel, Fintan's cries sounded as if they

were ripping his insides out, and Brenna wasted no time charging to the rescue.

Taryn's ability to concentrate on anything but the searing pain was nil, and she sagged against the wall.

Creed and Narissa's bickering heralded their arrival, but the instant she saw Fintan, Narissa left off arguing and rushed to his side.

"What the hell? This has never happened to him before," she said, her brow knitted with confusion.

Taryn's stomach sank. "That's what I was afraid of."

Had she caused this? Was she truly to be his downfall?

CHAPTER 7

"I'm not positive, but I think it happened when he took off Bloodstone's necklace," Taryn told them. "We were downstairs, discussing its origins. He lifted it from his pocket, and when I tried to touch it, I got electrocuted."

"Holy fuck," Creed swore. "Is that what happened to him, too?"

"I don't think so. When Damian and Jordan woke me, I spotted the amulet across the room, like Fintan had thrown it away," she said.

Narissa watched her narrowly, then glanced at Fintan before nodding. "It seems like the sort of impulsive gesture he'd do. Don't stress it, sugar."

Her voice was heavily accented, as if she'd lived in the Deep South for her entire life, making the endearment sound like "shoog-ah." Hers was the type of slow-rolling speech that transformed guys into insta-gentlemen, who opened doors, tipped their imaginary hats, and believed she was a helpless "little lady," needing their manly assistance.

But they'd be wrong.

No more powerful female existed except a goddess or an Aether. Taryn had learned that, when in full form, Siren magic rivaled a Guardian's. As the perfect mimics, they adapted to fit in —speech included—wherever they settled. Narissa was no different.

"A chameleon-like safety measure," Brenna had once told Taryn. "It has kept my kind safe for hundreds of years. Most aren't aware they do it, and the accent adaptation comes naturally."

Taryn had assumed it was a pitch-perfect thing. Talented singers possessed a discerning ear, but many ordinary humans couldn't carry a tune in a plastic shopping bag.

"He's still as salty as ever," Brenna said after double-checking Fintan's pulse and ducking his flailing arm. "Where's the necklace now?"

They all gave her the standard *Are you loony?* look, but then sought the answer from Taryn.

"I wasn't about to touch it again, so I assume it's still on the floor. Damian seemed to forget about it before he left." She shrugged. "I—"

Her brain felt as if some sadist was digging around with a hot poker, and she screamed as she dropped to her knees.

"Shit!" Creed sat and drew her close, stroking her temple and rocking her like a small child. "Concentrate on my voice, sweetheart. Can you do that?"

Taryn whimpered, unable to stem the excruciating onslaught.

"Focus and do as I tell you, okay?" He gave her a light squeeze when she nodded. "Excellent. Now, you're about to become a virtual bricklayer. In your mind's eye, picture an endless stack of masonry bricks. Got it?"

"Yes," she whispered through her agony. "But what about Fintan? I can't leave him alone in there."

"You don't have a choice, sugar. You're likely to go full-on bonkers if you don't." Narissa squatted beside them. Humming in a low, sultry voice, she stroked Taryn's cheek repeatedly. The Siren's divine-smelling perfume was citrusy, layered with subtle notes of vanilla and gardenia. It rose like an invisible mist, blending with the haunting melody and wrapping around Taryn to soothe her worry.

"I know my cousin, and he wouldn't want you to suffer," Narissa assured her.

"But—"

"No buts," Brenna said before adding her voice to Narissa's song.

Creed gave her another light squeeze. "Taryn, in front of the bricks is a bucket of mortar and a trough. As quickly as you can, begin building a wall as tall as you can imagine." He positioned her hands as if she were doing the physical act. "Slap, smooth, block. Slap, smooth, block. Slap, smooth, block."

He continued the hypnotic rhythm with gestures and verbal guidance.

Under Creed's instruction, Taryn built the wall between her and Fintan, but her already fractured heart was cracking, and no amount of mortar would seal it back up. When the wall was as high as it could go, and Fintan's voice was the faintest echo, she pulled away.

"I'm okay." She straightened and gave them a tight smile. "I think I've got control. I just wasn't expecting his pain..."

"I wish I could say I understand, but my telepathy experiences are limited to the Aether's group rings." Creed helped her to stand and handed her off to Narissa. "To clarify for anyone not in the loop, these two were bonded last week and now share one brain," Creed said with a commiserating look for Taryn. "Sorry about your bad luck, sweetheart."

She sputtered a laugh as she brushed her hair from her face. "Yeah, so far, it hasn't been a picnic. Not with Fintan and not with his fuckwit ancestors who apparently love to torture him." To Narissa, she said, "I'm fine now. Thank you."

"You should prop up your feet and let me conjure you a mojito. I've got a feeling you need one after all that."

Narissa tried to guide her to a chair, but Taryn drew back.

"No, thanks. I appreciate your kindness, but I can't leave him like that," she said with a grateful smile and a worried glance at Fintan. "It was awful, and his screams…" She shuddered. "I don't hear them as loud anymore, but I don't think I'll forget the agonizing sound anytime soon. If this is normal, I can't understand how he hasn't tried to sever their hold."

"I don't believe it is." Narissa cast a worried look at Creed, then clasped Taryn's hand. "Show me this necklace, please."

"It's in the sunroom. I'm afraid if I try to lead you there, I might get lost," she confessed.

"No problem, sugar. Brenna and I know this monstrosity of a house well enough." Narissa and Brenna shared a smile. "Maybe not as well as our caretaker there"—she gestured to Fintan—"but well enough to get you where you need to go."

"I don't understand."

Brenna flicked Fintan's foot as if he were a pesky little brother. "He keeps any hidden passageways secret, and it's highly annoying."

"Why am I not surprised there are hidden passageways?" Creed muttered. For a lingering moment, he and Narissa locked gazes and smiled, but then he glared and presented his back to her.

Taryn sent her a questioning look, to which the other woman grimaced and said nothing. Clearly, these two had history, and she'd love to know what it was. But the timing was terrible. She needed to learn more about Bloodstone and why his enchanted necklace could electrocute people.

"It was right there!" Taryn cried.

The others looked at her like she'd lost her freaking mind, and she didn't blame them one bit. After the fuss she'd raised, it would be natural for anyone to believe she was deranged.

"No one else can enter the house, sugar. Not without alerting us and shaking our teeth loose. I've only experienced it once, quite a few years back now, when an enemy of Mama's entered the place." Her sultry eyes flared wide, and she grinned. "The ground shook, and the place lit up brighter than a Macy's Fourth of July celebration in New York."

"But what about Creed? He came out of nowhere," Taryn pointed out.

His dark brows shot skyward. "You think I took the damned thing?"

"No! Oh my god, no. I… Look, all I'm saying is that you entered the house, and no one knew you were here. That must mean the early warning system is off, right? How did you lower the wards?"

"Well, I can't be considered an enemy of anyone residing here." His eyes were troubled as he watched her, and he sent an inquiring glance at Narissa. "But she has a point. Fintan always greeted me at the door. Today is the first time I entered and roamed about alone."

"Oh, dear." Brenna wrung her hands until Eoin curled an arm around her waist. "Fintan gets irritated when strangers wander about. Not that anyone can find this place without an invitation, or that strangers arrive on our doorstep. Who would want to? I mean—"

Eoin kissed her, effectively stopping her nervous babble. He drew away with a grin. "Better?"

"Much," Brenna sighed, beaming at him like he hung the stars. "Thanks."

"It was entirely my pleasure." After gracing her with a sizzling look hot enough to cook steak, he faced the others. "We need to figure out who can enter the house without setting off the wards, yeah?"

Brenna hustled to a nearby table and returned with a pencil and one of Eoin's sketchpads. His brows shot up, and she laughed. "To make a list," she said.

Taryn bit the inside of her cheek to stem her laughter. Her friend's secretarial instincts were strong. She had spent years in servitude to her horrid Aunt Odessa as an administrative assistant and general flunky.

"It's ingrained at this point," Brenna said with a shrug as if she guessed why Taryn found her list-making behavior amusing.

"Aye, but did ya need to use my sketchbook?" Eoin retrieved a notepad and traded her for his precious drawings.

"Sorry." She put the lead tip to paper. "Okay. Who's first?"

Creed rattled off the Sentinels under Damian's command. "Don't forget to add the Aether and his kid to the list."

"Got it. Who else?" Brenna asked.

"Clearly me," Taryn said as she attempted to recall who'd been present whenever she visited. "Oh! Your family, right, Eoin?"

He nodded briskly, reading over Brenna's shoulder as she jotted more names. "Add Ronan and me da, love."

"Like I could ever forget Ronan," she said with an eye roll.

"Don't be lustin' after me brother-in-law, woman. You won't like the consequences if Dubheasa finds out. She's a might jealous, she is."

"More than you?" Taryn taunted with a teasing grin.

"She's got those Guardian powers now, so I'm not intendin' to test her." The twinkle in his emerald eyes belied his serious tone.

"I'll take my chances," Brenna replied dryly. "Who else?"

Taryn hated to bring it up, mainly because she didn't care to know—or so she told herself—but it had to be asked. "What about any steady girlfriend of Fintan's? Is he likely to allow his, um, lovers to…" Her embarrassment set her face ablaze, but thankfully, they ignored her discomfort to focus on the question.

"If he had hook-ups, I've never known about them. He's insanely private." Narissa shrugged. "But even if he were entertaining lovers, he wouldn't allow them full access to the place."

Feeling somewhat relieved to learn he wasn't going steady with anyone, Taryn nodded and stepped away from the group. What did it matter whether he had a revolving door of lovers or not? He didn't want her as one. Not in any significant way. And the damnable part of it was their ridiculous mental connection.

"What about Aunt Odessa?" Brenna asked in a worried voice. "Do you think she can access the house?"

"There's only one way to find out, honey," Narissa stated. Her grimness prodded Taryn to turn around. Their gazes locked. "You don't know her, but the rest of us do. She's not a particularly nice person. In fact, she's downright meaner than a rattlesnake and ten times as lethal."

Stomach churning with dread, Taryn asked, "Do you think she did something to Fintan?"

"I wouldn't put it past the hateful heifer, but I can't see how she'd get the best of him when she's never been able to before."

"Would it help if I went with you to see her?" Taryn would rather stay with Fintan, but she didn't understand how she'd do him any good at this point.

"No. Absolutely not." Narissa focused on Creed. "I intend to leave Brenna and Eoin here to protect Fintan should he need it. Will you guard the property?"

After a visible internal struggle, he agreed, and her shoulders sagged in what Taryn assumed was relief.

"What do you want me to do?" she asked.

"Go home, sugar. There's nothing more you can do here, and your place is probably the safest for you."

Rejected again. Why did she feel like crying at being

dismissed from Fintan's life again? Why did she care after twenty-odd years?

Before she could leave, Creed clasped her hand and squeezed. "She'll stay. Right now, she may be the only one able to reach inside your cousin's mind if needed."

The tsunami of gratitude she felt for his understanding nearly took her out at the knees, and she tightened her grip.

Narissa dropped her gaze to their joined hands. Any of the woman's deeper emotions were masked, leaving Taryn to wonder what she thought of Creed's protectiveness. "Sure, sugar. Whatever you say."

The sharp tap-tap-tap of her retreating heels on the marbled floor echoed in the still room. Weirdly, they all released a collective breath.

"I don't think she was too happy," Brenna said in a low voice as if fearful Narissa might overhear from wherever she'd stalked off to.

"She'll get over it," Creed said coolly. "She always does." He softened when he looked down at Brenna's lovely face. "Will you and Eoin be so kind as to watch over Fintan? He's one of the few friends I have left."

After they teleported away, Taryn locked gazes with Creed. "And then there were two."

A corner of his firm mouth kicked up. "We need to talk."

"About?"

He withdrew Bloodstone's necklace from his pocket. "This."

CHAPTER 8

"Dude! What the hell?" Taryn couldn't believe Creed could touch it, to say nothing of swiping it from under their noses. "When… How… What?"

Amusement filled his hazel eyes, and she was struck by how handsome he was. Of average height, he wasn't necessarily beefy or muscle-bound, but he was pretty damned fit, nonetheless. Taryn was sure if she got a glimpse of his abs, they'd be washboard, and his BF percentage was probably low single digits if it registered at all. His visage was an interesting mix of hardness and handsomeness that some would call chiseled. A hint of laugh lines bracketed his mouth and eyes, suggesting he'd once been happy but not anymore.

"Are you a jewel thief?" she asked, half-serious.

Since first meeting him, she'd played the guessing game with her sister Viv. No one knew much about Creed other than he preferred big cities and had never stayed in one place for long. If Damian knew about the man's past, he wasn't saying. He was annoyingly close-lipped.

Creed's laughter was rich and robust, like a vintage wine, and she glimpsed how he might've looked when his troubles were few. Had she met him prior to Fintan, she could've easily fallen for him. Hell, nothing was stopping her now except any residual feelings he had for Narissa.

"You and Narissa, what happened there?" she found herself asking.

All humor left him. "She betrayed me."

"Is she stupid?" she gasped.

In today's day and age, not much shocked Taryn, certainly not betrayal, but who the hell cheated on someone who looked like Creed? He possessed a rough-and-ready hot-biker vibe, and she, for one, loved a bad boy with a heart of gold.

"Wait," she said. "I'm assuming when you say 'betrayed,' it was an affair. Am I right?"

"No. Or not that I know of, anyway. In that regard, she was loyal." Absently, he rubbed his chest as if pain still resided in his heart. "She abandoned me when shit went down with the Authority. Hell, she may have been the one who turned me in. Who knows?" He spoke like it was all matter-of-fact, but there was an underlying hurt he couldn't hide, and Taryn was crushed for him. Granted, she didn't know the details of his banishment, but if Damian had allowed him into his inner circle, Creed couldn't be bad.

"But you suspect she did, don't you?"

"Yes."

"I'm sorry," she said, touching his arm. "Maybe you should talk to her. Find out for sure."

"It no longer matters. Narissa abandoned me when I needed her the most. I should thank her because it taught me a valuable life lesson."

Taryn released a bitter laugh on his behalf—and perhaps her own, too. Having been a dupe, she knew exactly how badly that shit hurt. She was nowhere near over it.

"Not to trust another living soul?" she quipped.

"Close enough. It felt a helluva lot worse at the time. I feel mostly numb these days," he confessed, in what she suspected was a rare bout of vulnerability for him.

"I wish I knew what to say to make it better." She eyed the amulet in his hand. "I'd give you a comforting hug, but the last time I got close to that thing, it nearly killed me."

He grinned. "I'll throw it out the fucking window if it means you'll rub that gorgeous body against mine."

Heat spread across her cheeks, and for a reckless moment, she considered flirting with him.

"Sure, and I wouldn't be doin' that if I were you, Taryn-Taryn." Fintan's comment was a surprise and nothing short of surly. His expression was forbidding when she glanced his way.

He looked like hell. Gray-faced and lion's mane hair a mess, he rested against the door jamb as if using it to prop himself up. And it seemed he needed it.

"Fintan!" When she would've rushed to his side, he shook his head.

"I'm grand, love. Don't fuss."

She did her damnedest to hold still when everything in her screamed to help him.

"Back to your question, wouldn't do what? Flirt or rub my body against him?" she asked. She hadn't meant for it to sound taunting, but what gave him, a man unwilling to stay in the same room with her for longer than five minutes, the right to warn her away from Creed?

His gaze turned solemn. "Either. You're the kind of *cailín* who demands commitment. You'll not be gettin' it from him."

"Or you," she retorted. "And you don't know me anymore, Fintan Sullivan. Maybe I'm just looking for a good time."

"I'm wounded you both think I'm a commitment phobe," Creed said dryly. Bunching up the necklace, he chucked it at Fintan. "I believe this belongs to you." With a half smile, he winked at Taryn. "Seems I'm not the only one hiding a past with the Sullivans, hm?"

"Nothing to hide," she replied with a single-shoulder shrug. "We met at one of his concerts. He pretended he was into me to get what he wanted, and then he ghosted me. Now, twenty-something years later, he's still an asshole."

"It wasn't pretend, and you know it," Fintan growled.

"Yeah, but maybe acting like Creed's the one with commitment phobia is hypocritical on your part."

"Time out." Creed formed a T with his hands. "First, to clarify, I am not a commitment phobe. I simply distrust people in general. Second, I need details about what went down. Fin never said." He glanced between them before focusing on Fintan.

"He was in a boy band," Taryn replied, unable and unwilling to keep from mocking Fintan. Sure, she was catty, especially when he looked like death warmed over, but his holier-than-thou attitude rubbed her the wrong way.

"Jaysus! For the last time, it wasn't a feckin' boy band!" Fintan staggered into the room and plunked down on the sofa. "Stop spreadin' that rumor, already."

She uncrossed her arms and felt his forehead. His skin was cooler to the touch than earlier, but he was still warm. "But it's so much fun."

"Will ya tell her, Caldwell?"

Creed shrugged. "We were young and on the heels of the boy-band craze."

"Aye, but we didn't jump around the feckin' stage, shakin' our arses like a bunch of—"

"Wait! I remember you!" Taryn gasped at Creed in shock. "The drummer!"

He grinned. "I can understand why you didn't put two and two together. You only had eyes for our lead singer."

"Don't remind me. Clearly, I chose the wrong bandmate."

"Clearly." Creed chuckled. "But I remember he was pretty

into you, too. To the point he'd refused to stay late for practice and was always disappearing to make a phone call."

"Yeah, but he turned out to be a royal dick," she replied, as she shoved away the warm feeling Creed's words evoked.

"Who ordered this feckin' shite? I'm right here, aren't I?" Fintan growled, looking like a sick, surly bear.

And she was relieved he was finally awake. Her stress level had grown by the minute, despite the wall she'd managed to erect.

"Oh, hush. It's not like I'm a Traveler and can change anything. When did you wake up?" she asked him, taking pity and changing the subject.

"Right before Eoin and Brenna arrived in my room." When she would've backed away, he gripped her forearm and kissed the inside of her wrist. "Thank you, Taryn-Taryn, for trying to help."

She yanked away, fighting the desire to scrub her wrist on her jeans. Yes, she'd experienced a thrill from the gesture, but it felt too reminiscent of their first few dates. Recalling that time hurt too much.

"Where did they go?" she asked instead.

"To make tea," he replied with a weary sigh. "Brenna's got an obsession for all the wee cakes and sandwiches."

"I'm aware. Okay, if you're in good hands, I'll head out." She'd barely gotten the words out when he lunged forward and dragged her onto his lap.

She squeaked with surprise.

"You'll not be goin' anywhere, *aoibhneas mo croí.* 'Tisn't safe for you out there."

"What the hell are you talking about, Fintan Sullivan? I'm perfectly fine—"

"Will you shut the feck up and listen to what I'm tellin' ya, woman? I had a vision."

She shut up. But only because he'd shocked her into silence.

Staring into his troubled eyes, she understood one thing. If there weren't a threat to her life, Fintan would've had her out the door faster than a witch denying she hexed her ex, even though his hair had mysteriously fallen out.

Taryn eyed Fintan's head for a bald spot and sighed when she didn't find one. She hated that he was perfect and impervious to her petty magic.

Sagging against him in defeat, she sighed. "What's this vision?"

OVER THE TOP OF TARYN'S HEAD, FINTAN MET CREED'S WORRIED gaze, and an unspoken understanding passed between them. They'd both protect her at the cost of their lives. Indeed, if they didn't, theirs would be short-lived anyway. The Aether would wear their femurs as a crown if she were hurt under their watch.

It seemed that in the short time Creed and Taryn had been alone, she'd wormed her way into his friend's heart. Fintan wasn't surprised. Her charm was effortless and addictive to the unsuspecting.

She poked him in the ribs. "Quit stalling. Tell us about the vision."

"I was standin' beside your grave as dirt was shoveled over your coffin," he said roughly.

Her body stiffened, and the blood drained from her face. "That's pretty fucking specific."

"Aye."

Creed sank into a nearby chair. "Anything leading up to it?"

"Not much. Just a general sense someone evil was targeting her."

Taryn swallowed hard and relaxed into him as if seeking his warmth. Holding her felt better than he remembered, and he rested his chin atop her silky hair.

"It has to be linked to Bloodstone's necklace. It's the only artifact I've been researching lately," she said. "Don't you think?"

"Aye, but why? Who would know besides the Sentinels that ya found it?"

Her brows met as she considered Fintan's question. "Just the Archive Keeper at the Witches' Council and Ryanne Thorne."

"Ryanne Thorne? That's not a name I'm familiar with. You?" Creed asked him.

"No."

Taryn curled her legs up and rested her head on Fintan's shoulder, and it felt natural for him to tighten his arms around her, cuddling her close. The scent of her freshly washed hair was a delicious mix of apples and cinnamon, reminding him of his favorite pie. Inside, his Siren stirred, tempted by her closeness.

"Don't do it," he warned the creature.

He must've been too forceful and telegraphed the thought to her via their link, making her pull away. The separation caused a literal ache in his heart, but he told himself it was for the best.

"That wasn't for you, *aoibhneas mo croí*. It was for my Siren." Why he'd felt compelled to say it aloud, he had no clue. Maybe it was the flash of hurt he'd witnessed or the whirlwind of insecurities dancing inside her head. "He's a feckin' gobshite who craves one thing."

"Got it."

Her stiff response told him she didn't understand. Not really. But he let it go. The distance would benefit them in the end.

When he met Creed's watchful gaze, he felt the weight of his old friend's disapproval.

Taryn steered their conversational ship back on course. "Ryanne is Nash Thorne's wife. I told you about him earlier, Fintan." To Creed, she said, "He's Alastair's son and now heads Thorne Industries. It's one of the Council's largest archives for documents and magical artifacts. Nash's knowledge is extensive, and what he doesn't know, his father does."

"So he's the Archive Keeper?" Creed asked.

"No. That's actually someone at the Council. I went there after I spoke with Nash and Ryanne."

"Sure, and ya could've led with that earlier," Fintan muttered. "You had me believin' you were in tight with the man."

"I only told you I spoke with him. You were the one who built it up to be more than it is," Taryn retorted.

Creed shot him an amused look, and Fintan flipped him the bird behind her back.

"Okay, so to catch up here, you two spoke about this necklace earlier, and she apparently mentioned Nash Thorne," Creed said. "You, dour-faced fucker you are, then lost your shit because she dared to voice another man's name in your presence." He glanced at Taryn before Fintan could protest. "*You* were electrocuted by the same necklace you were researching, making it seem you didn't know it held that party trick in its arsenal. Your morning concluded with Fintan falling into a three-hour coma and being tortured by visions and the ancestors. Have I got that right?"

"Pretty much." She smiled at Brenna when she arrived with the tea trays. "Lemon macarons! My favorite."

"What did we miss?" Eoin asked, sitting on the sofa across from Fintan and Taryn. "Should Narissa be here for this?"

Creed looked like he'd rather eat nails than include her, but he gave a short nod. His frown followed it up as he glanced at his watch. "Shouldn't she have been back by now?"

"Back?" Fintan felt a stirring of unease. "Where did she go?"

Brenna's expression held the same level of worry he had. "To confront Aunt Odessa."

"*Fuck!*"

CHAPTER 9

*N*arissa hated her aunt's home.

The place was filled with the ghosts of her victims, with the primary one being Narissa's mother, Doreen. There had been many instances she'd wanted to seek her revenge and end Odessa's life for what she'd done, but it would require her inner Siren to accomplish the task. If she managed so grisly a feat, she risked turning into the one thing she despised—a Succubus.

Like Odessa.

"What are you doing here, you ungrateful bitch?"

Narissa glanced at the top of the stairs where her aunt lurked with one fist clenched on her hip and the other leaning heavily on her cane. The woman appeared more frail than the last time they'd met, but she didn't have the resources to steal magic like she'd once had. Still, as an enemy, Odessa couldn't be discounted. Narissa, better than anyone, understood that looks were deceiving.

Shoving away her glumness over Creed, she stepped farther into the foyer.

"Well, ain't that the well-seasoned cast-iron skillet calling the kettle black, Auntie O?"

"What do you *want?*" Odessa's clipped words were laced with fury.

Narissa smiled at a job well done. Any chance for a dig, she'd take, especially if it meant the older woman might suffer a sudden stroke and end a chronic headache for the rest of the Sullivans.

"I'd hoped you might impart a little knowledge about a particular object."

A crafty light entered Odessa's cold eyes. "I give nothing away for free, as you well know."

"No, ma'am. You'll provide the information I seek, or it'll be Damian Dethridge asking the next time."

The hatred on her aunt's face turned her dissipated visage downright ugly. "You like to hide behind the shield of his name, don't you? Foolish child! He'll turn on you just like he does everyone, eventually."

"Well, bless your heart. You honestly believe that, don't you?" Narissa tsked. "Poor dear."

Odessa slapped the tip of her cane on the floorboards. "Don't you mock me in my own home, girl. I still hold power here."

"Power that you stole from others," Narissa snapped. "Don't think you're not on the Authority's watchlist. Step out of line one more time, and they'll execute you without remorse."

Although she paled, Odessa lifted her chin. "I don't give a fig for the Authority or the sycophants who work for them."

"Namely me?" Narissa taunted.

"Namely you."

They'd never gotten on, and their hatred of each other was one of the things that drove her to run away from the mother and sister she'd loved at such a young age. The oppressive atmosphere was impossible to bear.

"The feeling's mutual, you old sow. But I don't have time for your games. Fintan is suffering."

Odessa's beady eyes narrowed further. "Fintan?"

"Yes, you remember your nephew, no? The only other survivor of your siblings' children? No? Doesn't ring a bell?"

"I know who Fintan is, ya disrespectful shite! And don't be layin' the deaths of other Sullivans at my feckin' door!"

Narissa grinned. "Careful, Auntie O. Your Irish is showing. We both know how much you hate that."

Odessa had cultivated a British accent in her youth, hoping to appear more refined. She'd always hated that her siblings refused to do the same. But she'd outlived them all—Doreen, Megan, Finelia, and Peter. A few of whom she'd murdered. As far as Narissa knew, the only Sullivans left were Fintan, Brenna, and her, if one didn't count their odious aunt. And she didn't trust that Odessa wouldn't kill them if given half a chance.

Her aunt stepped forward as if to descend the stairs.

"Stay put," Narissa ordered. "You're not getting access to the ley lines. I'm in charge here."

Ley lines—the invisible pathways between ancient and mystical sites—held great power. Two of which crossed directly below Odessa's home. The Sullivan estate in Ireland boasted seven intersecting lines, which gave Fintan his early warning system should someone step on the grounds.

"I need my medication," Odessa said in a shaky voice.

"Nice try. I happen to know you carry it on you, and you're not due for another thirty minutes or more. Right, Mama?" Narissa turned her head to acknowledge her mother's spirit standing beside Odessa.

Doreen beamed at her. "You've the right of it, Nari, my love."

"Just say what you intend to say and get out of my home!" Odessa shouted.

The force behind her voice was as strong as a sonic boom,

and had Narissa not been a Siren, her eardrums would've shattered.

"Tsk, tsk. Control that temper, Auntie O. I'm not here to *say* anything. I'm here to learn what you know about the bloody stone necklace." Her misuse of the name was intentional. If indeed Odessa knew what it was, she would show her superiority over another's ignorance. But if she didn't know, then there was nothing further to be gained from lingering about, and Narissa could get back to her family.

"Bloodstone's," her aunt corrected. "The first Siren, and a mighty Incubus."

Narissa's stomach dropped.

Odessa was involved.

<hr>

FINTAN URGED TARYN TO HER FEET AND ROSE TO STAND BESIDE her. Her confusion was normal in the face of his reaction to Odessa. She'd not been privy to his visions, and he doubted she understood what his aunt was capable of.

"I need to go after her," he said, dreading the fact already. Nothing good ever came with setting foot in that cursed house of his aunt's. Many never made it out alive.

"Not alone, you don't," she said, stubborn chin in the air.

"I'll not argue with you, Taryn-Taryn. Stay here with the others. If I'm not back in thirty minutes, call the Aether and send him to Odessa's."

Fear lit her glorious eyes, and she shook her head. "I don't like it. You're too weak."

"I've a way to supercharge, so don't be worryin' about me, yeah?" But he fucking loved she still did.

Taryn shot Brenna a frustrated look. "A little help here, please."

"I agree with Taryn, Fin. Can you please take someone with you?"

"Other than another Sullivan, no one is strong enough to fight a Succubus." He shook his head. "It has to be me, all the same."

Creed stood. "I'll go."

"No offense, man, but you're as useless as tits on a bull in a fight with her. Ya don't understand what she's capable of."

"I'm stealthy, and she won't expect me."

"Like here, ley lines run under her house," Brenna said. "She'll know if you approach."

Eoin frowned. "Where did ya learn that, love? You didn't know what a Siren was two years ago."

"Gran's diary. The one she left for me has it all." She tilted her head as if trying to recall something. "She may have mentioned that necklace, come to think of it. Wait while I get it."

She was gone in a blink, but Fintan didn't have time to spare. The pressing need to get to Narissa was overwhelming his senses, making him dizzy. If he didn't get to her soon, the consequences would be dire.

"Send Brenna and Damian if I'm not back," he instructed Creed. "Don't come yourself."

Taryn latched onto his arm. "Fintan. Please, wait for her. That book might have something useful."

Sweat broke out on his forehead. He grew clammy, and his skin felt too tight for his body.

"I can't. I've got to leave right now." After prying her fingers from his arm, he lifted her hand and nipped her fingertips. "It's good to know ya still care, all the same."

"Pfft." But her expressive eyes said she did.

Leaning in, he claimed her mouth for a brief kiss. It was unsatisfying in its briefness because he couldn't spirit her away to his bedroom as his inner Siren demanded. Leaning close, he whispered, "Take care of yourself, Taryn-Taryn. I'd be wrecked if anything happened to you."

After brushing his knuckles along her jaw, he teleported away.

"This is bad. Like an asteroid two hours from striking Earth bad," Taryn said.

Fintan's brief show of affection had scrambled her brain, and she was nowhere near figuring out his new about-face. For the last few years, if they'd managed to find themselves in the same room, he'd practically hiss like a vampire encountering sunlight before bolting from the room.

She was developing a complex.

But the more pressing matter was his following Narissa into a precarious situation with no intel or backup. Fintan wasn't a spontaneous guy. From what little she knew about him these days, he preferred guidelines and a carefully crafted plan.

"Yeah, I don't have a great feeling about this. You?" Creed asked Eoin.

"No."

Taryn dropped onto the seat cushion, yelped from the small electrical shock she received, and popped back up. "What the… Holy fuckballs! He left the necklace! Why would he do that?"

"We don't know how it works, and he's strong enough without it," Creed assured her.

"But it's unprotected here. What if whoever is after me guesses we're alone and comes looking for it?"

"Who's after you?" Eoin demanded.

"We don't know," Creed said with a grimace as he scooted to the edge of his seat and reached for a tea cake. "It's a Fintan thing."

Eoin nodded as if it made sense, and perhaps for these two, it did. As for Taryn, she was less inclined to be blasé about someone wanting to end her life.

"When has he been wrong? Is he ever wrong?" she asked. It wasn't easy to keep the nerves out of her voice. When a fairly trustworthy psychic predicts a dire event, one should take heed.

Creed looked as if he were considering her question, but Eoin wasn't concerned.

"They'd have to go through the two of us to get you, love," he said, indicating Creed and himself. Brenna reentered the room. "Make that three of us."

"I'm not worried for myself," Taryn lied. "I just feel this necklace shouldn't fall into the wrong hands. Based on my research…"

"Sorry to cut you off"—Brenna waved the journal—"but Gran mentions Bloodstone."

"Where were you when I was deep-diving into its history?" Taryn patted the sofa next to her. "Quick, tell me what she wrote."

"Like the Seer ability, it passes to the only male heir. My grand-uncle, Peter, should've been the last to own it before Fintan." Brenna scanned the pages as she spoke. "According to Gran, it amps up the male Siren's magic, but she's not certain how. Other than the Witches' War, Peter never needed to use it. But she wrote that even then, he couldn't get it to work."

"Witches' War? That was forever ago. How did the thing end up at a garage sale?"

Brenna gaped at her. "That's where you found it?"

"Yes. I sensed the magic straight away, so I purchased it and took it to Damian." Taryn glanced between the others and shrugged. It was curious she was able to touch it the first few times, but maybe once its owner had reclaimed it, the stupid thing turned temperamental. "Damian looked, but refused to touch it. He said I needed to speak with Fintan, and I assumed he didn't know its significance."

Creed scoffed. "The man is hundreds of years old, serving as the balance between the magical and non-magical communities. If he said he didn't know, he's lying."

Racking her brain, Taryn attempted to recall. "If I remember correctly, he didn't actually say he didn't know. His words were along the lines of, 'You should contact Fintan Sullivan.'"

Brenna laughed.

"What's so funny?" Taryn demanded.

With casual innocence that fooled no one, Brenna studied the food tray and picked out a macaron. Before taking a delicate bite, she dropped her bombshell. "Whenever Damian or Alastair Thorne seeks to match people they care about, they pull the same trick."

Taryn groaned. Of course! Beneath those austere exteriors, the two men were romantics at heart. Damian's matchmaking would be sweet if the result weren't going to be so freaking tragic. One would think that an Aether able to see the future wouldn't be inclined to set her up for certain heartache.

"They're wasting their time. Fintan doesn't care about me," she said, trying to sound less woe-is-me and more practical.

"That's not what I witnessed," Creed said. "Not then. Not now. Our boy is crazy about you."

"You've heard the saying 'actions speak louder than words,' right?" She waited for his nod. "Well, his actions scream 'back the fuck off' at every turn."

A pained expression flashed across his handsome visage. "You're right. I'm sorry."

She shrugged and eyed the lemon macarons with regret. There was no time to enjoy her favorite cookies.

"I have to find him and bring him the necklace. I have a feeling he's going to need it."

"You'll wait right feckin' here like he asked you to do." Eoin shot her a no-nonsense look. "We live with the man, and I'll not be subjected to his bad-tempered ways."

"You're not the boss of me," she grumbled. But she didn't argue like she wanted to. Mainly because it wasn't fair to subject Brenna and him to Fintan's Grumbly Gus routine. "Okay, fine. But if they don't return within the allotted thirty minutes, we call Damian and rain hellfire down on Odessa. Agreed?"

CHAPTER 10

Fintan watched Odessa's house from across the street. His ancestors were active in his head, but they spoke in hushed whispers as if arguing amongst themselves. Ignoring them, he continued his vigil. At any second, Narissa might sashay her arse out the door, but he doubted she would. The niggling feeling she was in trouble wouldn't go away. Yet, walking in their aunt's residence without a clear idea of the future would see him dead.

Female Sirens were stronger than males, their song ten times more potent and alluring. In demon form, men had the advantage, but only if they were crafty enough. There, he'd freely admit if asked, women were more intelligent and diabolical, in general.

"What does Odessa want?" he asked aloud, hoping the ancestors would pull their heads from their arses and give him a clue. Odds were they wouldn't. They were undoubtedly still salty at him from the week's reprieve and his association with Taryn.

"Bloodstone's necklace." Uncle Peter's whisper brushed along his skin, raising the hair at his nape.

"And if she gets it?" he asked.

"My sister is a mad cow. She'll take it into her head to go after the big fishes: the Aether, the Death Dealer, the Guardians... you."

"And she'd likely win, yeah?" He didn't wait for an answer. They both knew an amped-up Odessa would kill him. "Is Narissa alive?"

"Aye, but she's imprisoned. Odessa utilized the ley lines and created a cage."

"How do I—"

"Do you frequently stand on the street and talk to yourself, *cher?"*

"Jaysus!" Fintan's heart was pumping so fast it could've performed a drum solo at a heavy metal concert. "Where the feck did you come from?"

Draven's smirk was annoying as fuck. "Your girlfriend called."

"She's not."

"I'll let Creed know. I believe he's interested if you aren't."

"Sure, and I'll rip his head from those freakishly broad shoulders and spit down his windpipe if he so much as looks at her."

Draven chuckled. "I'll be sure to inform him of your penchant for violence."

"Aye. You do that, ya scut." Fintan refocused on Odessa's Victorian house and noted the similarities to Taryn's family home. Perhaps his original distaste stemmed from knowing what lay behind the doors of the one across the street. "My cousin's in there. Trapped."

"Narissa's trapped?" Draven's tone sharpened, and he stepped forward as if to get a better look. "Creed didn't mention that little tidbit. He only said she was gone a long while."

Fintan tapped his temple. "Uncle Peter."

"What else did Uncle Peter tell you?"

"Odessa is a mad cow, and she's after bigger fish, like Damian, you, and me," he replied grimly.

"Did he say how we're supposed to retrieve Narissa?"

"No. Only that the ley lines created a cage. I was conversin' with him when you frightened years off me feckin' life." Fintan shot him a wry glance before returning his gaze to the house. "I've forgotten my ring, but now that you're here, you can try the link to Narissa, yeah?"

"Here." Draven slid the tanzanite ring off his pinky and handed it over. "Don't say I never gave you anythin', *cher*."

"Ah, the feckin' gift I've always wanted, it is. Where are you goin'?"

"To retrieve yours. Where is it?"

"My bedroom. Ask Brenna to find it."

Draven gave a single nod. "Don't do anything stupid while I'm gone. Rescuing one of you is challenging enough."

"Aye. I'll wait unless Narissa's injured. I'll not be leavin' her to Odessa's mercy."

"Fair enough, *cher*. I'll let the others know."

Fintan latched onto his wrist. "Not Taryn. I'll thank you to send her home, Masters. She's stubborn and after insertin' herself in the fray, but I'll not have her hurt because she's weaker than us."

"She can decide for herself, Fin. I'm not about to tell a capable female what to do or not to."

The rebuke in his friend's tone was telling, and he didn't love sounding like a sexist bastard. Yet the idea of Taryn being injured didn't bear thinking about.

"Draven?"

"Yes?"

"Be sure to cloak when you're comin' and goin'. It's better to keep Odessa guessin' about our numbers."

"Well, look at you, considerin' all the angles instead of chargin' in with fists at the ready!" Draven drawled.

"Sure, and you can feck all the way off," Fintan growled.

"For the record, your woman believed you'd take the intelligent route and think things through."

Warmth filled him, and he paused his surveillance to look at Draven. "She did?"

"Yes. Said you'd want a carefully crafted plan before going in. Looks like she knows you better than anyone, hm?"

PISSED DIDN'T BEGIN TO DESCRIBE NARISSA'S MOOD. ODESSA HAD tricked her, which was a rarity in itself. Stuck in a high-voltage prison, her only option for freedom was to shape-shift into her Siren. Yet doing so would make her vulnerable to her aunt's attack.

"I swear, this time, I'm going to snap your turkey-wattled neck, you beak-nosed—"

"Such language, Narissa." Odessa's disproving tone was followed by a tsk-tsk. "My dear sister raised you girls better than that."

"Don't you dare mention my mother, you magic-stealing, prune-faced—ahhhh!" The shock was instantaneous, and Narissa spasmed as electricity coursed through her body, mentally cursing herself for being caught unaware. She entered the house knowing Odessa wasn't to be trusted, yet she fell for her staged fall like an unsuspecting newborn.

"Manners, girl. If you fail to keep a civil tongue, I'll fry it out of your head."

As she lay on the ground, taking stock of all her limbs and praying to the Goddess she hadn't wet herself, Narissa swore a silent oath that she'd murder Odessa the first chance she got. No way was that horrid wench living to torture another person!

She swiped her wrist across her mouth and wiped away the drool. Simply performing the gesture fueled her rage, but she needed to keep her Siren contained. If the creature felt threatened, she'd emerge. Though she'd always suspected hers was stronger than Odessa's, they'd never been pitted against each other. And she was trapped at the moment, allowing her aunt the advantage and to syphon magic.

Her only hope was Taryn and Creed. They knew where she'd gone, and if she didn't return by nightfall, they'd send someone after her. Narissa didn't dare dream Creed would care one way or the other. Yet he answered to Damian, and he'd feel compelled to save her if only to stay in the Aether's good graces. It seemed Damian Dethridge was the only person Creed maintained a healthy respect for.

Creed.

She should've never distanced herself to keep her position at the Authority. All these years later, she still hadn't discovered who'd set him up to take the fall for the break-in at HQ. Perhaps their relationship had been unearthed, and whoever was responsible purposely kept her in the dark—if only to cover their ass.

"Why so sad, dear?" Odessa taunted. "Your cousins will come for you."

"I hope they don't. Then you won't get your hands on Bloodstone's necklace."

"You and Fintan were inseparable as children. You're the closest thing he has to a sister. He'll come," her aunt assured her, and the unwavering confidence scraped Narissa's nerves raw.

"Last I checked, he was in stasis, so it's doubtful." She shrugged and cast Odessa a pitying glance. "Your pathetic attempts to preserve your life are—ahhh!" Gritting her teeth against the pain, Narissa prayed she wouldn't stroke out or suffer a heart attack from so many electrocutions.

"Sadistic bitch," she muttered.

"Would you care for another jolt, girl?"

With a shake of her head, she moderated her tone and asked,

"Why do you want Fintan's new necklace? What good will it do you?"

A rare vulnerability flashed across Odessa's visage before she quickly pasted on her standard arrogant expression. "That's none of your concern."

"I beg to differ, sugar. It concerns me greatly since you practically hog-tied me and slapped butter on my backside for this little barbeque." She deepened her Southern drawl to annoy her uptight aunt. "Why, the only thing missin' is an apple between my teeth!"

Odessa's lips tightened. "My intent was never to torture you, but you can't keep your smart mouth shut long enough to see reason."

Narissa studied her for a long moment, for the first time seeing her aunt's underlying sadness. Having lost her only sibling, she was no stranger to grief and loneliness. Was that what Odessa was feeling? The pain of losing all her family and having no one left to care about her? She'd chased off Brenna a few years back, and living conditions had to have been terrible if her sweet-as-pecan-pie niece had bolted. A more loyal person didn't exist than Brenna.

"What is it you want, Auntie O?" Narissa asked tiredly, feeling three times her forty-seven years. She'd lost too much to their stupid Sullivan "gifts." Her twin, her mother, friends... *Creed.* Shaking off her melancholy, she sighed. "Tell me so we can be done with this. You want my magic? Fine. If you can take it without killing me, it's yours."

Odessa's shock held her immobile, and her response was drastically different than any Narissa might've anticipated.

"What the bloody hell is wrong with ya?" Odessa dropped her upper-crust accent and adopted the Irish dialect of her youth. "Are ya a feckin' eejit, then? Ya don't go offerin' your magic up— ever! And certainly not without a payoff, ya daft—"

Compressing her lips, Odessa clomped away, her cane tapping out her agitation.

"Sure, and that's one way to clear a room." Fintan's voice in her head surprised Narissa so badly, she almost did what her aunt's shock treatment failed to do and wet herself.

"Holy crispy critters!" she hissed.

"Keep your words contained inside your mind, yeah?" he warned.

"You surprised me. I thought you were in stasis. And don't forget, if she concentrates, she can tap into our thoughts. We all share a connection, sugar."

"Aye, I'd forgotten. And the ancestors decided they were done torturin' me for a wee bit." He paused before adding, *"Tell me what's happenin' with you. Has she hurt ya?"*

"Nothing too serious. Electric shock treatment by way of the ley lines."

His outrage curled her lips. Fintan would never admit it, but he had a hero complex. His biggest upset was if women and children were hurt.

"And why haven't the ancestors allowed you to access that same power grid?" he asked.

"Don't rightly know, but I suspect she's concocted some sort of spell to harness their magic."

"Uncle Peter just said it's why they released me. They didn't have enough to hold me and you at the same time."

Narissa snorted, then glanced at the doorway, hoping like hell her aunt hadn't heard. *"Then maybe you should come in here, sugar, and bust me out. The two of us in this little ol' cage would short-circuit their grid for sure."*

"It's not the worst idea, to be sure. Hang on."

Their connection fizzled and snapped before going silent.

"Fintan?" Why the hell was she worried about him when she was the one imprisoned? Still, he was her best chance to get the hell out of this creepy-ass place.

"He's fine, Nari," her mother said from beside her, giving her another fright.

For pity's sake, when had she become so jumpy?

"But I'll be urging you both to be careful," Doreen told her. "My sister is not in her right mind."

"I miss you so much, Mama," she whispered.

"I'm always around, my love. You've only to summon me."

But summoning required using her Sullivan gifts, and Narissa hated that side of herself. The constant battle to be perfect so she didn't take an irrevocable step and hurt another. Yes, she used her Siren for Damian, and for the Authority before him in her capacity as a spy. Yet never to steal. Never anything that would turn her into the horrendous monster her aunt now was.

Tears burned her eyes as she stared up at her mother. They'd missed so many years when she'd run away.

"Thirty. It's been thirty years since you've returned home," Doreen said, as if she'd plucked the thought from Narissa's mind. "I wish you'd stayed."

"But you're glad I didn't?" she hazarded a guess. She didn't want to tell her mother this haunted heap had never truly been her home. In all the time she'd lived there, she'd felt Odessa's ghostly victims lingering.

Her mother nodded. "She'd have found a way to drain you, too."

"So all this"—Narissa waved to encompass the cage—"is about gaining more?"

"Yes and no. She'll explain as soon as Fintan arrives."

Narissa's brows shot up. "I said he should join me. Should I not have?"

"I've already sent him an invitation, girl," Odessa said from the doorway. Fintan lurked beside her, none too pleased to be there. "He understands the terms."

"What terms?"

"For your release." Her aunt narrowed her eyes at Fintan. "He's agreed. No tricks."

"Aye, now release her," he growled.

"Not until I get Bloodstone's necklace. Until then, crawl back into the hole you came out of."

"No!" Narissa knew fuck all about the pendant, but if Odessa wanted the blasted thing, it couldn't be good.

"Too late, girl. Siren's creed, and a deal's a deal!"

CHAPTER 11

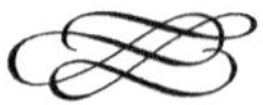

Whatever was necessary to free Narissa, Fintan would do. That's why, when Odessa interrupted his conversation with his cousin and telepathed a message, proclaiming a temporary truce, he agreed to enter her home.

"Fintan, no! She can't be trusted," Narissa warned, mouth tight with disapproval and pain.

His stomach clenched when he saw how exhausted and ragged she looked. Her eyes were dulled from the torture, and her luxurious blonde hair was lank, dampened by sweat. The clothes she wore were sweat-soaked and clinging, too. But mainly, she was pale from the abuse, and Fintan would move heaven and earth to get her out. It took a lot to bring down a Sullivan Siren, and utilizing the electrical ley lines feeding their estates was the perfect way. They were tied to the magic running beneath their homes.

Inside, his creature shifted, and Fintan felt its rage. His nature was to protect, not destroy, and if that enraged beast got loose, he'd decimate this entire place.

Odessa had a lot to answer for. But he'd give her the bloody necklace if it meant keeping her from killing Narissa, as she'd threatened to do.

"Sure, and all Sullivans are inclined to backstab when the mood strikes us." He winked.

Her expression fell, and tears gathered in her hurt-filled, blue-green eyes.

Uncertain what he'd said wrong, he frowned his question, but she shook her head and glanced away. She was smart not to reveal her weakness for their aunt to exploit, but he would've spared her feelings if he could.

"I'm offering the trade of your cousin for the Bloodstone's necklace in good faith, Fintan," Odessa said, eyes calculating, yet wary.

She feared him, and the why of it would be a grand question for Uncle Peter when the man contacted him again. But maybe he wasn't as good at hiding his anger as he imagined.

"What have you done to her?" he asked Odessa, though he already knew the answer. Still, he needed to stall until Draven's return. Likely, he'd bring reinforcements.

"I've been the perfect hostess." Odessa sniffed and raised her chin as if offended. "She can't be civil, and a lesson was needed."

Fintan twisted and gripped her throat in a move so fast that his aunt's cane crashed to the floor, and Narissa cried out.

His creature growled, clawing to find a way out. And because of the struggle, he squeezed harder than intended. "Hurt her again, in any fuckin' way, and I'll rip your black heart out through your feckin' throat," he snarled.

With her rheumy eyes bulging, Odessa gurgled her agreement.

He waited for her Succubus to appear, but it remained dormant, likely not viewing his action as an actual threat. Either the demon inside her had weakened considerably, or she possessed the ability to defeat him with little effort. Fintan preferred to believe it was the former.

Cautious and watchful, he released her, held up his hands, and stepped back. Although he half expected a retaliation, none came. Did that mean she'd used up her store of magic keeping Narissa caged? It bore further consideration.

"I don't have the necklace here," he said. "But I'll return with it after I see Narissa's taken care of."

"No. You'll turn it over before I release her."

He locked gazes with Narissa briefly, then he faced his aunt. "I'll not leave her here with you in this condition, all the same."

"You're in no place to bargain, boy. My home. My rules."

An idea tickled the back of his brain. If he could put himself in jeopardy, would the ancestors abandon her to save him?

He was about to find out.

"Aye, but you need the Sullivan ancestors to maintain your cage. What if I took them from you?"

Odessa's eyes narrowed. "If you could, you'd have done it by now."

"Sure, and I didn't think of it before. I'm slower than most. Just ask anyone."

Narissa released a weak chuckle.

"Then do it," Odessa challenged. "But then you'll be going back on our deal, and if you do, all bets are off, boy."

She had him by his bollocks, and they both knew it.

"If ya let her go now, you've my word I'll bring ya that cursed necklace," he growled. "On me life."

Odessa nodded, smiling with satisfaction. "That's good enough for me and the ancestors since you swore to it."

The cage containing Narissa disintegrated in a shower of sparks, and she curled into a ball to avoid getting burned. Fintan swore and dove forward to protect her as best he could. Behind him, Odessa's evil chuckle scraped his last nerve raw, triggering his Siren.

Narissa must've sensed the change and grabbed his shirt-front. "Don't! Don't you dare shift, Fintan Sullivan!" she ordered. "She won't be able to resist stealing what you have."

"She can't," he replied through gritted teeth. While he understood the wisdom of Narissa's words, his Siren was awakening. Taryn had nudged it earlier, and the situation with his cousin had amplified its need to escape. "She has to take it through sex, and I find her repellant."

"She has other ways, sugar. Remember the spell she cast on Brenna?"

He did.

Inside him, the beast roared its rage, beating the shit out of Fintan's insides as he struggled to retain control.

Narissa stroked his throat. "Finny, listen to me now." Her words were sing-song and hypnotic. "She has no power over our Sirens and isn't worth the cost to transform. Let's go home."

His skin cooled along with his temper, and the creature grumbled as it slunk back into its cave.

"Thank you," he whispered.

"Anytime, sugar."

Fintan helped her to stand, and when they faced Odessa, she wore an expression of concern. Not buying a second of it, he shifted to place himself between the women and then guided Narissa toward the exit. "I'll be back with your feckin' jewelry, but if you come after us or anyone we care about again, I'll fuckin' end you, yeah?"

Although she frowned, his aunt lifted her chin, proud and defiant to the bitter end. "I'll not come after you or her, and you'll need to be satisfied with my word."

"Not good enough," Narissa said, swaying into him but pausing their escape. "Brenna, the Guardians, the Aether, and anyone else we care about are untouchable, or you'll face the combined force of whoever is left of our family. Got it?"

"You're no match for me, girl. None of you are in your sorry states."

"The instant you step away from these ley lines, you're power ends, old woman," Fintan said. "Necklace or no, you can't defeat us in battle, so don't be startin' a war."

"THEY SHOULD'VE BEEN BACK BY NOW," TARYN SAID AS SHE PACED behind the sofa that tried to take her out earlier. Her blood had long since been cleaned from the wood, courtesy of Damian and Jordan, but she would prefer to burn the piece for good measure. Or perhaps it was her frustration welling. She needed an outlet.

"Stay calm, sweetheart," Creed said. Across the room, he sat at the piano, thumbing through a songbook. Periodically, he'd tickle the keys and grin before skimming more pages.

"How can you say that? Why aren't you worried?"

When he glanced up, his smile was reassuring. "I've known Fin since we were teens, Taryn. He's never gotten himself into a mess he couldn't get out of." Creed winked. "With one exception."

"Which was?"

"You."

"One, I don't like to be considered a mess. I mean, I am, but pointing it out might get you cut. And two, you're imagining things. Fintan and I were done over two decades ago."

Creed scoffed. "Keep telling yourself that, sweetheart."

She chose to ignore his teasing. Paused beside him, she listened as he played, curious about the current song he was drawing from the ivories.

"That's beautiful!"

"Fin is an exceptional songwriter," he replied, patting the bench. "Here. Now, sing."

"I'm not any good," she protested.

"Bullshit. Your voice is sweet but with an underlying rasp. If you had training, you'd be as good as Celine, Adele, or Christine Agu—"

A commotion in the foyer sent them running.

When they skidded to a halt, they found Fintan and Draven supporting Narissa between them.

Creed stepped forward, as if instinctively, before catching himself.

"What the hell happened to you?" he demanded.

Narissa's head came up, and the sheer exhaustion on her face spoke of her trials.

He swore.

Not waiting for answers, Taryn rushed to her and, drawing strength from her cells, transferred it through touch. A hint of color returned to Narissa's cheeks, and she smiled her thanks.

"That stream of swear words would blister a nun's backside, sugar," she said to Creed as he scooped her into his arms. "But no need to fuss. I've been through worse and came out just peachy."

"Shut up," he growled, charging for the stairs.

"Do we dare leave them alone together?" Taryn asked in an aside to Fintan and Draven.

"She'll eat him up and spit him out, *cher,*" the Guardian said with a chuckle. "But he's man enough to survive."

"He's awfully angry with her still."

Fintan's expression reflected surprise. "Sure, and how close did the two of you become while I was fightin' for me life?"

"Which time? With the ancestors or Odessa?"

His scowl rivaled Creed's. "Where's the bleedin' necklace?"

"You left it on the couch, so Brenna put it in the safe."

"I'll wait here while you retrieve it and then return with you, *mon ami,*" Draven told Fintan.

After he left, Taryn sank to the marbled step leading upstairs. "How bad was it? Narissa looks rough."

"From what I gather, Odessa tortured her with high-amperage volts of electricity that she drew from the ley lines protectin' her home."

"My god!" She pressed a hand to her stomach, hoping to calm her churning gut.

"Whatever god you follow, *cher*, he had nothing to do with it. It was all the work of an evil Succubus."

"I never should've let her go alone."

Draven squatted in front of her and tilted up her chin. "There's nothin' you or anyone else could've done to help her that Fintan didn't do. You were safer here, out of the fray."

"But—"

"No buts." His tone was rough and no-nonsense. "The truth is, you don't have the ability to confront an animal like Odessa Sullivan, Taryn. Don't ever believe you can and live to tell the tale. She's killed many who mistakenly thought they could."

"I hate being a simple witch," she said.

"You're far from a simple anythin', Taryn-Taryn."

She jumped upon hearing Fintan behind her. "You're like a damned wraith! Stop doing that!"

Both men chuckled, and Draven pulled her to her feet.

With an unhurried grace, Fintan descended the remaining stairs, halting before her. "Somethin's been botherin' me since I spoke to Odessa. She was too confident. Too knowing."

"Knowing? About what? The necklace?" Taryn asked. "Do you think she's stumbled upon information we don't have?"

He nodded. "Who was the person at the Witches' Council you spoke with about the necklace, *aoibhneas mo croí*?"

"He's a new hire named Micha Forsyth."

"Forsyth?" He didn't look pleased. "Ya said he was a new hire?"

"Yes. He was newly appointed by the Council to head up the archive department," she replied, glancing between Draven and him. "Why?"

Fintan avoided her question and addressed Draven. "Do you know anythin' about the man?" he asked sharply.

"I don't, but I've been avoidin' the witch community for decades, *cher*. It seems you do, though."

Taryn touched Fintan's arm but immediately drew away when his gaze grew intense. "What's wrong?"

"Nothin'." When she didn't readily accept his answer, he said, "A feelin' as if someone's been walkin' on me grave but nothing I can pinpoint or explain. The last name is one I'm familiar with."

"Uh… I, um, I can ask Alastair or Nash. They know everyone."

"Sure, and you're on again about the man!" The twinkle in his eyes contradicted his WTF tone.

She grinned, happy he wasn't truly jealous. "What can I say? The Thornes make beautiful people. As long as Ryanne doesn't mind, I'll look my fill."

"Oh, I'm jealous, Taryn-Taryn. I'll kill the man if he touches ya," Fintan replied through their connection.

"You forgot to block the ring's ability, *cher*," Draven said dryly. "Let's deliver the necklace and determine our next move."

"I didn't forget. Let my words serve as a warnin' to any man who tries to woo her."

Left with her mouth hanging open, Taryn didn't know what to say. Fintan's possessive routine was new and confusing as hell.

Draven glanced back, shooting her a wink.

"Am I in a fever dream?" she muttered. Why did he become territorial? And the better question was why she tolerated it? The about-face was baffling—for both of them.

"I love ya, Taryn-Taryn. I always have, and I'll not be denyin' it any longer."

"But the ancestors—"

"We'll find a solution, yeah?"

CHAPTER 12

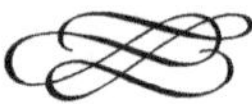

*T*ragically, Taryn didn't trust Fintan's willingness to vex the entities controlling his brain. She built the mental wall like Creed had instructed before giving way to her doubts. With Fintan's mission to deliver the necklace, he needed all his wits. Her skepticism regarding a relationship shouldn't weigh on his mind.

Left with nothing to do but check on Narissa and head home, she went upstairs—and promptly got lost. Wandering aimlessly, she checked room after room, climbing the tower until she stumbled upon the one she least expected to find again.

Fintan's.

She hadn't realized she'd ventured into the north wing. But maybe her heart was leading her feet instead of listening to her head. Her rebellious limbs took control and crossed the threshold to his room. The first time she was here, she hadn't given her surroundings much thought. She'd been too concerned for him. But how did she resist a peek into his space when it might give her insight into the man himself?

Decorated in rich navy blue with silver and black accents, it leaned toward gothic. The mammoth four-poster bed was made of the sturdiest wood, and without magical ability, the damned thing wasn't moving an inch. Although his room was the size of two of hers combined, it was sparse, hinting that Fintan preferred a minimalist lifestyle.

A bureau of drawers on the far wall sparked her curiosity, and she eased open the middle one to peer inside. Graphic t-shirts were neatly folded and coordinated by color, clarifying he was a bit of a neat freak, like she'd always suspected. Lifting one, she inhaled. The combination of wild prairies and ocean breezes greeted her nose. Did he hike? Spend time at the beach? How did the material still retain his unique scent after washing?

She rubbed her cheek on the butter-soft material, half tempted to steal it. Deciding to forego the larcenous life, she returned the shirt to its home and closed the drawer. Abandoning the bureau, she crossed to an antique writing desk. A half-composed song lay on top, and Taryn played the notes in her mind. The tune was haunting and would hit platinum status if he decided to make a comeback and release it.

Peering into the drawers, she found more handwritten music, all neatly stacked. The words were pure poetry and spoke to her battered heart. Who had the man become in the twenty-plus years since they'd met? The grumpy recluse or the romantic musician? She sighed and shoved the drawer closed, pausing when a framed picture slid into view.

Like a woman dying of thirst, she drank in Fintan's happy face. The wide grin, the sparkling eyes, the way he leaned into the person he was with. It took a few precious heartbeats to realize *she* was the one he held. That effervescent girl was someone she no longer recognized when she looked in the mirror.

"I love ya, Taryn-Taryn. I always have, and I'll not be denyin' it any longer."

Fintan's departing words rang inside her head, and she sat

down heavily on the bed's edge as she stared at the photo in her hands. Was this proof? Why wait a lifetime to say anything? And why speak up now when her ability to return his love was questionable? How was she supposed to trust he wouldn't leave her at a train station again?

"We were just kids, *aoibhneas mo croí*," he said softly from the doorway.

Caught red-handed, she gasped and flung the frame toward the head of the bed. "What are you doing back so soon?"

He laughed. "Sure, and it only takes a minute to hand over an object to a person you never want to see or speak to again." Fintan retrieved the picture and studied the joyful couple. With a sad expression, he said, "I'd have come back for you if I were able."

"You had decades, and you never did." Taryn felt exposed and brittle.

"Aye, but I never stopped tryin'." He tossed the photo, circled the four-poster, and cupped her jaw. "I meant what I said."

Knocking his hand away, she stood. "No. I've visited Brenna countless times, and every single one of those times, you scurried away." She swallowed her rising anger. No good would come of her raging this late in the game. "I'm not buying what you're selling, Fintan Sullivan. Go peddle it to someone else," she said tiredly.

"That's it then? You've—*argh!*" He paled and fell backward, clutching his head

"Fintan!" She dove for him with no idea what to do to save him, but willing to try anyway. When she reached his side, his eyes were opaque, and his jaw was slack.

"Shit! What do I do?" she cried as she cradled his face in her hands. The wave of energy almost knocked her on her ass, actually would have had she not been kneeling on the mattress.

He returned to himself with a string of curses. For a brief moment, his eyes were tortured as they stared up at her, and in the next instant, he was holding her in a bear hug as if he would never let go. She let the embrace continue until the tension left his body, then she wiggled to get free.

"I feel a bit suffocated here, Fintan."

"Jaysus! Sorry." Color stained his cheeks, and he looked everywhere but at her. "I didn't mean… I… you… the vision." He scrubbed his face with his palms. "Yeah, and I'll shut me gob now."

Leaving him in his shaky state would be heartless, and Taryn repositioned herself to kneel beside him, stroking his sweat-damp hair away from his temple. "What did you see?" she asked softly.

"More of the same. Things meant to torment and cause sleepless nights." His voice was raw, and it was easy to guess he hated being exposed as he was. Vulnerability wasn't the man's strong suit.

"You were standing over my grave again?" It hurt her to ask, but knowledge was power, right?

"Aye."

"So whatever happened today with the necklace didn't change anything," she concluded, falling back on her heels. Why she was calm was a mystery when her death couldn't be more certain, yet she wasn't afraid. Her fear had receded in light of the mystery surrounding the vision. Or maybe acceptance came with age. No one lived indefinitely, and to believe she was fated to have a long, happy life was arrogant.

His gaze locked with hers. "I'll do my fuckin' best to keep you safe, *aoibhneas mo croí*."

"Thank you for not promising to save me. I hate it when people do that. The Gods and Fates hold all the power over us, not men, despite their white-knight complexes."

"Sure, and sometimes those feckin' bastards can be reasoned with." A wry smile crooked his lips. "Other times, they need to be shown the error of their ways."

"The white knights or the Gods and Fates?" she asked with a faint smile.

"The whole bleedin' lot of them."

His warm smile, the admiration shining from his gorgeous eyes, and his blasted nearness all worked against her. Taryn wanted to give in to his magnetism, but down that path lay destruction. *Hers*!

"So everything went okay with Odessa?" she asked as she rose and walked to his writing desk. "Your fast return seems anti-climactic."

Fintan followed her. "She only wanted the necklace."

"Do you think it was wise to afford her that much power?" Taryn glanced up to see him watching her with something akin to adoration. Her heart rate doubled, hammering hard against her ribcage.

His lips twisted as if he possessed intimate knowledge of her uncomfortableness in his presence. Yes, she could leave, but the part of her that didn't want to was in control of her legs.

"No, but she'll need to unlock its abilities, and none of us know what it truly does, yeah?" Fintan shrugged, turning away to retrieve a guitar from beside the desk. He sprawled on the window seat, with his back to the attached bookcase, and crossed his ankles as he fiddled with the tuning pegs. Once satisfied, he closed his eyes and plucked out a tune.

She recognized it from the half-written song on the desk.

Opening his eyes, he met hers across the distance and began singing words he'd not written. By the end of the first line, she was sitting on the floor beside the bench. By the end of the second, her throat was constricted with all the heartbreak and regret she'd felt from their aborted relationship. And with the third verse, tears streamed uncontrolled down her cheeks.

He never broke eye contact, but his voice turned raspy, lending more emotion to the song. Doubtless, he was experiencing the same emotions as her. The truth was laid bare for her to see if she cared to.

"Is this the effect of your Siren," she asked, her mouth dry. "This stirring?"

He set the guitar aside, then joined her on the floor. Kneeling in front of her, he simply stared, making no move to touch.

"What stirring, *aoibhneas mo croí*? What is it ya feel?"

"The worst sort of regret and pain," she confessed.

"Aye. Maybe you've accessed my feelings on the matter, yeah? I've had nothing but regret from the moment I left you that morning with the promise to return."

Daring the one question tormenting her forever, she asked, "Do you think it would've been different if I'd gone with you instead of leaving you to deal with Peter's death on your own? That we'd have stayed together?"

"No."

His bluntness stole her breath, and she nodded slowly, willing her lungs to function.

"Not because of us, Taryn-Taryn. The ancestors wouldn't allow it, but I wish you'd have come with me anyway." A single tear trailed down his cheek, and Taryn caught it with her fingers. Fintan grasped her hand and kissed the moisture away. "I'll never be able to apologize enough. Yours wasn't the only heart broken that day, *aoibhneas mo croí*."

He didn't try to hide his pain, and she appreciated his honesty.

"So many wasted years, huh?" she murmured almost to herself. Dropping her hand, she rose. It helped, perhaps even healed her a little, to know he'd suffered. She wasn't being petty, but learning he'd truly cared made their brief love affair a lot less like a careless fling. "I suppose I should thank you for the truth after all this time."

"Will ya stay?"

Did he mean with him or at the estate? Strangely, she didn't possess the courage to ask.

"Either," he replied to her internal question, reminding her of their link.

Enveloping her hands in his, he looked up at her, compelling her to say yes. She wanted to, but she was also damned tired of making foolish mistakes when it came to men and her heart.

"It's not a good idea, Fintan."

His hopeful light died. He released her with a nod, focusing on the horizon outside the window. "Will ya check in with me daily until I can determine what the vision is about?"

"I can do that."

"Grand." Climbing to his feet, he raised his arm, palm up. "I'll take ya to Narissa."

"Oh! Right." She'd long forgotten her intent to check on his cousin and Creed. Placing her hand in his, she squeezed tightly. "Thank you for giving me a choice, Fintan. For not trying to force me to stay in some misguided need to protect me."

"Your destiny is your own, Taryn-Taryn. But if I can prevent the bleedin' Fates from hurtin' ya or help you figure out where the threat originates, I will."

As they traversed the halls, she gave in to the desire to lace her arm through his and hug this small part of him close. They'd reached the top of the stairs when one of the hottest men she'd ever encountered stepped into view.

Black-haired and hot enough to melt steel, he was tall, with wide shoulders and a killer smile. The man possessed a laid-back but powerful vibe that immediately gained one's notice. His midnight-colored gaze swept the length of her, and a lazy grin spread across his face when he saw them.

Her body went into gushy, schoolgirl mode, and heat swept through her, landing squarely in her cheeks. Pressing her hands to her face in a vain effort to cool them, she did the unthinkable and batted her eyelashes.

"Well, hello, love. Where's this one been hidin' you?"

Dear lord, he was sin in human form, designed to ruin lives.

Beside her, Fintan growled.

"I, uh… who… you…" Good Christ! She'd lost her wits and her ability to speak!

"Are ya feckin' bamming me with this shite?" Fintan snarled inside her head.

She winced and turned to glare. "Seriously, dude? Can I help it if he's a walking thirst trap for parched women?"

"Didn't I warn ya I'd kill a man?" he demanded.

"Of all the caveman bullshit to come out of your mouth, Fintan Sullivan, this is the dumbest!"

"The sexual tension between the two of you couldn't be sliced with the sharpest blade," the stranger quipped. "I'm not after stealing your woman, Sullivan. It just comes naturally."

Fintan charged.

CHAPTER 13

This chapter has been omitted for the standard reasons.

I'm curious, though. Have you guessed who the visitor is? If you've read Highballs & Hexes, I'm sure you have. ;) Might I suggest a bathroom break and snack retrieval despite your need to discover why he's arrived to taunt Fintan? No? Then carry on, dearest reader!

CHAPTER 14

The grin on Noah Riley's face was pure deviltry and required Fintan to wipe it off—with his fists. Jealousy and possessiveness clouded his mind until he couldn't think straight, fueled by his inner Siren's need to claim Taryn, to eliminate anyone who might pose a threat. His logical side understood he was being a ridiculous git, but ever since Taryn had been hanging around, the instinct-driven beast neared the surface and was dangerously close to taking control.

He had to hand it to Noah; the guy didn't back down. But then, as the Aether's long-lost brother with his own superpowers, the bastard was as hard to kill as Fintan. Noah took the punch like a seasoned boxing champ, proof the years as a pub owner had toughened him up.

Taryn's distressed cry pierced Fintan's fury haze a second before she launched herself at him and locked him in a chokehold.

"Fintan Sullivan! You stop this insanity right now! Do you hear me?" With her free hand, she bonked him on the head. "Ow! How hard is that thing you call a skull?"

Noah snorted, crossed his arms, and leaned back on the banister to enjoy the show.

Fintan wanted to plant the man another facer, but he had Taryn to contend with. "Calm yourself, woman. He's used to a bit of rowdiness now and again. Any man who runs an Irish pub can hold his own in a fight, or he won't be in business long."

She bonked him a second time before sliding down his back. The feel of her breasts against him intrigued the beast inside, and Fintan grinned when she lingered a few seconds longer than necessary. A quick glance at Noah told him the man hadn't missed a bleeding thing. Neither Taryn's indignation turned interest, nor Fintan's rage turned amusement.

"Is this foreplay for the two of you?" Noah asked dryly.

Fintan sensed the instant she processed the jest. Not only did she yank away from him, but her mind went into denial. And didn't that make him sad? When they first met, she would've been the first to laugh and quip something cheeky. The Taryn of today was reserved and slower to laugh.

The blame lay with him and all the arseholes who'd ever hurt her. She wasn't wrong to say he was the first in succession. Despite what she believed, he'd kept tabs on her over the years, and when needed, he chased away a loser or two. The others she wised up about and kicked to the curb. Thankfully, Josie and the Aether got to Morcant first. There was no prediction for how a scenario would end if Fintan had taken matters into his own hands. He'd likely be dead or drained, considering an Arcane Devourer fed on grief and negativity. Fintan had loads to spare, believing Taryn loved another.

To save her any embarrassment and the need to answer, Fintan hauled her into his arms and tucked her against his chest. "What are you doin' here, man? I thought we were to meet at your pub on Saturday."

"Wait!" Taryn drew back and stared up at him curiously, but

immediately punched him in the chest as if she'd remembered she should put up a token fight. "You're friends? You hang out?"

Her disappointment, filtering through their connection, was keen, and his Siren growled.

This time, he managed to keep his jealousy controlled... barely.

"If ya want to date the man, Taryn-Taryn, best keep those thoughts to yourself, yeah?" he said through their link. *"This monster inside has claimed ya for its own, and it's gettin' harder to deny."*

She gaped at him, and he gently tapped her mouth shut, releasing a resigned sigh.

"Build your mental wall before havin' such thoughts, *aoibhneas mo croí*," he said. "You may not care for me anymore, but I still love you, yeah? Your thoughts are hard for me to hear."

"I didn't say I wanted to date him. I don't know him," she shot back, looking annoyed.

And that's when it hit him—Noah's magnetism was intrinsic, like Damian's, inherited from their mother, the Enchantress. He didn't wield his sex appeal as a weapon with any intention of stealing women from others, although he very well could. Taryn had no control over her attraction to him.

"My niece, Sabrina, sent me with the Aether's blessing," Noah said. "There's something about your estate that doesn't agree with their magic, but I've been here before with no lasting effects, so..." He shrugged.

Taryn glanced between them with a tight smile. "Fintan, if you point me toward Narissa's room, I'll pop in to see her before I go."

"Across the landing and one floor up," he replied.

"Thanks." Her eyes weren't as bright as when they were younger or when she visited with Brenna, indicating she was unhappy to a large degree. And he only had himself to blame. There were so many things he wanted to tell her, but the timing was shite with Noah watching.

In silence, they waited until she was out of sight.

"She's the one you were referring to when you said you had your own fate to avoid?" Noah asked with an appreciative smile.

"Sure, and when did I tell ya that?"

"The day we met. And technically, you told Patrick O'Malley. I just happened to be present." Noah faced him. "What's going on, Fin? You look more vexed than normal."

Stalling for time, he asked, "What did your family tell ya?"

"Not much. They're reticent when it comes to spilling the future. Damian said you'd fill me in on anything you want me to know." Noah's dark eyes narrowed. "So spill."

"She found an amulet from my ancestor, and it may be the key to lockin' the others out of my head. But I traded it to save Narissa."

"Narissa? Your cousin?"

"Aye." Fintan nodded sharply. "Our feckin' aunt was torturin' her."

"Jaysus!"

"Yeah." It still made him sick to think of it. He hated how easily Odessa had manipulated them, and he vowed to be better prepared for her next trick. Doubtless, there would be one. The Succubus ruled her, and sentimentality had no place in its heart.

Somber, Noah slapped him on the back. "Let's get a pint. I think there's a helluva lot more to this story than you're telling me, and I want to know how I can help."

Ten minutes later, in an abnormal act for him, Fintan was spilling his guts. Normally, his emotions were best expressed in song, or preferably not at all, but Noah had an easy way about him. It could be the "listener" gene all bartenders possess, or it could be the result of over two centuries of a constantly changing world, but he relayed caring and concern with a simple look.

"Grovel," Noah suggested. "Find a way to lock your fucking

ancestors out and do what men have been doing to get back into their partner's good graces from the beginning of time."

Fintan laughed and raised his glass in a toast. "Feckin' grand plan if I could boot the bastards from me head."

"Have you considered asking the Aether to remove your magic?"

The question required serious thought, and Fintan gave it its due. Finally, he shook his head. "Sure, and it wouldn't feel right without my abilities. Not that I love them, mind, but because there's no one to pass them to. Brenna and Narissa would be vulnerable to Odessa now that she's got the necklace, and if she figures out how it works."

"Why can't your Seer ability pass to one of them?"

"They're female."

Noah's black brows shot up. "Wow! Sexist much, mate?"

"Fuck off! Ya know I didn't mean it like that." Fintan cast him a sour look. "It's the feckin' curse of the Sullivans. Only the male gets the sight, and seein' as I'm the only one left, that's me, yeah?"

Narrowing his eyes, Noah sipped his drink in quiet contemplation, and Fintan was happy for the companionable silence.

"Why?" Noah asked.

"Why what?"

"Why only the men in your family? Have your ancestors said?"

"No." Fintan was ashamed he never thought to inquire.

Noah sat forward. "If you were to die, would it go away?"

"Aye, I believe so."

"You once told me you inherited your power from Peter. Who did he inherit it from?"

Racking his brain, Fintan thought back. No clear answer came to him. Why hadn't he asked? He rose and crossed to the bookshelf. Without needing to search, he went straight to the book he was looking for, tugging it down to open the Sullivans' ceremony room. Noah was close on his heels.

Pillar candles rested atop sconces screwed into stone-constructed walls and flared to life. They created dancing shadows, lending to an eerie atmosphere, reminiscent of a dungeon. But Fintan didn't mind. Nothing here would harm him or his, not even the ancestors. It was one of two safe rooms where he could hide from any pain they chose to inflict. Except for rustic shelves on the far wall, a floor-to-ceiling scrying mirror, an old sailor's chest at the altar's base, and a pentagram on the floor, the room was barren.

"Nice place ya got here," Noah said dryly. "Where are the bodies buried?"

Other than a chuckle, Fintan didn't respond. He went straight for the grimoire. Although his cousins had access to its spells, they rarely needed them. The Sullivans' gifts lay elsewhere. The book, along with the Seer ability, was intended for the estate's caretaker—him.

Showing deference to the ancient spellbook, he stroked his fingers along the wooden embellishment on the leather cover.

"It resembles driftwood," Noah said with a quirk of his lips.

"True enough, but it's from the Goddess's tree of life, like your brother's."

"I've never seen the Dethridge grimoire. My father stole me away one night, supposedly to save me."

Fintan glanced up, surprised to hear his friend confess to part of his past when he was reticent before. "Yeah, and you were keepin' that one close to the vest, man."

Noah laughed, releasing the melancholy attempting to take hold. How Fintan sensed the moodiness, he could only guess. Perhaps, like Damian, Noah had the ability to alter the atmosphere with his stronger emotions.

"Show me the family tree," he ordered the thick tome.

The grimoire's heart—a rich, dark amethyst over three hundred carats of the highest quality—lit from within, displaying its many facets, and the leatherbound cover flipped open. Parchment pages originally crafted from animal skin flipped with blinding speed, stopping midway to reveal a list of names.

"Not what I bleedin' asked for, but grand, all the same," he muttered.

Noah's grin flashed, and he bent forward to read the list.

Peter's name appeared above Fintan's, but it was the penciled-in name *after* his that surprised him.

Micha.

No last name or indication of relationship.

"Who's Micha?" Noah asked sharply, sensing Fintan's unease.

"I don't know, but I'm beginnin' to suspect I have my long-lost brother skulkin' around." Striding to the mirror, he said, "Show me Micha Sullivan."

Smoke obscured the glass, and the candles flickered in warning. The only instances Fintan encountered resistance while scrying were Aether-related.

"What the fuck?" He shook his head and glanced at Noah. "I'm not sure how the ley lines will react to you when I draw from them. I'm after creatin' a powerful spell, so the decision is yours to stay or leave the room."

"I'll stay, and if it interrupts your spell, I'll step out."

"Aye."

> *"By candle's reflection, spells undone,*
> *Reveal the place of Micha Sullivan.*
> *No shield or ward shall cloud my sight,*
> *Bring forth the truth, restoring the truth by right."*

The ground rumbled, and the mirror cracked.

Still, no Micha.

Fintan's vicious curses were echoed by Noah, though his friend's resulted more from shocked wonder.

"Have you ever encountered the likes of this before?" Fintan asked him.

"No," Noah admitted grimly. "But I know who might've. Give me a minute to get Damian on the line."

Once he was alone, Fintan strode to the grimoire. "Find a feckin' spell to fix the bleedin' mirror."

CHAPTER 15

"What the fuck was that?" Creed asked from his place beside the window.

Taryn exchanged a concerned glance with him.

On the bed, Narissa struggled to sit up, and a look of determination replaced her worried expression.

"Don't even think about it, woman," Creed growled, pushing her back down. "You're not setting one foot out of that bed—*goddamn it!*"

Wincing from the force of his anger over Narissa disregarding his command and teleporting anyway, Taryn met his furious gaze.

"Maybe she objected to the manhandling?" she suggested.

His glare said he didn't find her funny.

Taryn laughed anyway.

"Send out a feeler, and we can teleport to the music room," she said.

With a brisk nod, he closed his eyes, concentrated, and held out his hand. Mere seconds later, they were downstairs, with Creed charging for the door as he bellowed Narissa's name.

Brenna and Eoin came around the corner but quickly scrambled out of Creed's way when they saw his thundercloud expression.

"We felt the ground rumble," Taryn said. "Do you know what caused it? Was it your wards?"

"I don't think so. This felt different somehow," Brenna admitted. "Where's Fintan and Narissa?"

"I'm not sure. A man named Noah arrived earlier, but I got the feeling he's a friend of Fintan's. Narissa disappeared from her bedroom less than a minute ago. Hence Creed's rage."

"Noah's not a stranger to the place," Eoin stated, easing Taryn's concern. "He comes around for dinner when he needs to rabbit on about his brother tryin' to control his life."

"Brother?" It clicked, and Taryn gasped. "Oh, God, I'm an idiot. He practically said as much upstairs, but I don't know why I never made the connection. *He's* Noah Riley, Damian's brother."

Although Viv and Sabrina had mentioned him, Taryn had yet to meet the man at a family function. About six months ago, Noah had shown up at the Black Cat Inn—Eoin's family's establishment—looking for his on-again-off-again girlfriend, and the truth of his parentage came to light. Taryn couldn't believe the resemblance didn't register immediately. The guy was a rougher, taller version of Damian. Hotter, in her opinion, but her tastes ran to less polished, more earthy.

"Where would they have gone?" Taryn asked. An image of a dungeon-like room floated across her vision. "Never mind. Where is the place with the stone walls and pillar candles? It looks ancient, like it might be below the house."

"The ceremony room?" Brenna asked Eoin.

"Aye, that's the only one I can think of."

Taryn shook her head. "This house is a damned maze. How do we get there?"

"It's down the corridor. Come on." Brenna led the charge, and they found Creed along the way, opening and closing doors with a litany of curses punctuating every slam.

"Follow us, fella." Taryn tugged him along. "Brenna's our Pied Piper."

"I'm going to wring her neck," he muttered.

Eoin took exception. "The feck you are!"

"He means Narissa," Taryn soothed. "He's mad because she didn't do as he ordered and teleported away."

Creed glared. "Whose side are you on, traitor?"

She squeezed his arm. "I'm on the side of truth. Now, hush."

Two minutes later, they were inside a study that looked like it belonged in the Beast's castle. Taryn half expected Mrs. Potts and her son, Chip, to cruise in and sing Tale As Old As Time.

"Wow! I'm in love," she gushed, forgetting everything to stroke the gold velvet sofa and take in the majestic room with its dome ceiling and sparkling chandeliers. "Now I know why you never showed me this place, Brenna. Sorry, but I'm never leaving here again."

She felt Fintan mere seconds before his arm wrapped around her waist.

"Aye, and I'd love nothin' better, *aoibhneas mo croí*," he murmured in her ear.

"This has nothing to do with you and everything to do with this room," she said pertly, peeling his arm away and facing him. "But if I have to sleep with you to get it, I will."

His grin flashed. "It will require a daily shag."

"It would definitely be worth it," she breathed with another longing look around.

"I don't mind if ya only want me for these books."

Meeting his dancing eyes, she grinned. "Just so you're okay with the knowledge."

"Now that's out of the way, can I snog ya, then?"

Mesmerized by his teasing light, she leaned into him.

Creed shoved the flat of his hand between them.

"Where the hell did Narissa go?" he snapped.

Taryn couldn't say she wasn't grateful for the interruption. All her objections and indignation about Fintan ghosting her had flown out the window. It was difficult to say which seduced her more: the library or his roguish charm.

She suspected the latter.

What the hell was wrong with her? Where was her spine?

Fintan opened his mouth, but Narissa stepped from a private room off to their left. Behind her was the "dungeon" Taryn had envisioned in her head.

"Calm yourself, sugar. There's no need to get your boxers twisted up," Narissa said, giving Creed an admonishing look.

"I don't wear boxers, as you well know," he growled.

The jaws of everyone present dropped, except the two bickering.

Brenna rushed over and tugged Taryn's arm. "Did he just admit they were once lovers?"

"He did," she replied in a low voice. "I've been waiting for this explosion." She glanced up at Fintan. "Speaking of, what shook the house?"

"A spell gone awry." He gave her a considering look. "I've an idea, and I'm hopin' you'll help me."

"What do you need?"

"An introduction."

***

AFTER THE MIRROR WAS REPAIRED TO FINTAN'S SATISFACTION, HE joined his family for dinner. Creed remained at the estate, grudgingly, to watch over Narissa, and a crowbar wouldn't remove him. If one were inclined to believe he still cared for her, they might suspect it's why he took the seat next to her, cock-blocking flirty Noah.

Like Fintan, Creed remained quiet throughout their meal,

speaking only when spoken to. Perhaps, like him, his friend was considering what had happened in the ceremony room earlier. Or maybe they were two sorry sods pining over women who didn't want them.

Taryn sipped her wine, then placed the glass on the table before addressing him. "You said you wanted an introduction. To who?"

"Micha Forsyth."

Her brows shot up as she picked up her silverware. "Why?"

"I'm after askin' him some questions."

Her inner dialogue said she wasn't buying it, and Fintan hid a grin behind the rim of his pint glass.

"I can sense your amusement, you know," she said dryly.

"Aye."

"So, how about being more forthcoming?"

He grinned openly. "If you've a need to be forthcomin', I'll listen."

The kick to his shin was unexpected, but he winked when he really wanted to rub his abused limb.

"Remind me to take away all your pointy-toed shoes, yeah?"

Taryn snorted and raised her glass for another sip.

Fintan laughed, appreciating the feck out of her temper. The feistier she became, the more she appealed to his inner beast. The thought sobered him. He had no wish to feed his monster's desires. Protecting Taryn from his Siren, and eventually the Incubus he would become if left unchecked, was paramount.

Her hand closed around his, and she shook it to get his attention.

"Don't. I don't need you to save me from anything, Fintan. I've spent forty-something years doing that all on my own."

"Sure, and how well did that work for you with Morcant?" he snapped.

Hurt flashed across her face, and she withdrew. Regret swamped him, and before she could pull away completely, he caught her hand. She hadn't known the man was worse than the devil and ten times as deadly until it was too late. Fintan had no right to hold it against her.

"I'm sorry, Taryn-Taryn. I'm a proper arse, yeah?"

"You are," she agreed coolly, tugging her hand.

He refused to relinquish it and kissed her knuckles instead. "Forgive me, *aoibhneas mo croí*. Insecurities and frustrations got the best of me, to be sure."

She remained unmoved by his apology.

With a resigned sigh, he released her.

"I've been mad with jealousy, wantin' to kill every man you've met since the moment I knew it wasn't me you were meant to love," he confessed. "My greatest fear was that you'd love someone else."

Expression tight, she nodded and swallowed hard. "I get it, but you don't need to be a dick about it. The past can't be changed, Fintan."

"Aye, and that's the ugly truth of it, love, but I want to. I've a powerful need to go back and never let you out of my sight. To cling to ya from the time we met and remain holdin' ya to me dyin' day."

Closing her eyes, she shook her head.

He didn't know what she meant by the gesture. In her mind, she'd constructed a wall, blocking her thoughts, and on the outside, she masked her emotions with a tight smile. She was getting too bleeding good at shutting him out.

"Let's get back to the subject we started before dinner. Why do you want me to introduce you to Micha Forsyth?"

Fintan hesitated as he considered how much he wanted to reveal. Directness could only help his situation, which Taryn required from friends and family. Still, tangling her up in his mess didn't sit well.

"Just say it, Fintan. For fuck's sake already," she said, thoroughly exasperated.

Grinning, he picked up his utensils and cut into his steak.

"You're not going to tell me?" she asked incredulously.

"Look, and I'll be tellin' ya, but when we are in private, yeah?"

Leaning forward, she glared. "I've changed my mind. I'm not sleeping with you for your magnificent library."

"Sure, that would be a feckin' shame, and it's understandable, it is." He nodded sagely. "I've a mind to gift it to ya anyway, but I won't."

She snorted, and her mouth curled before remembering that she was supposed to be vexed with him. "Keep your stupid B&B library."

"B&B?"

"Beauty and the Beast."

He waited. Once Taryn warmed to a subject, she would spill the beans. It didn't take long.

"I've always thought it was the perfect story," she said with a wry smile. "And I've had library envy my entire life."

"And if I said I'm not familiar with the tale, what would you be tellin' me?"

Her luscious lips curled into a genuine grin, and a sparkle entered her eyes. "Are you saying you've never heard of it or seen the movies? I'll call you a damned liar."

Fintan laughed. "I want to see it from your eyes."

"Hm, okay. It's about a woman who's sick of her life in a small village. She trades herself to the wicked beast to save her father, only to discover Beast, that's his name, isn't as fearsome as he pretends. In fact, he's a cursed prince and the biggest softie who ever lived. He cares for everyone around him." She gave him a pointed look before resuming. "Anyway, Belle and Beast fall in love, but the horrid man who covets her decides to kill Beast. A battle ensues."

"And?"

"Beast is gravely wounded, banging on death's door. Belle, realizing too late that he's the one, sobs over his lifeless body, declaring her love. Her tears break the curse on the castle's occupants, Beast included, and he returns to his handsome-prince form."

Her dramatic retelling amused Fintan. It was the small things. The way she leaned into him as she warmed to her story. How her hand flitted, and she touched his arm when she spoke of love. Her enchantment with the tale was relayed in the cadence of her speech, as was her enthusiasm to convey it.

"And the horrid man?" he asked.

Taryn's eyes flared wide as if ready to impart a secret. "Well, Gaston, the clueless hunter, is vanquished."

"As every evil scoundrel should be," he agreed. "So you were in love with Beast as much as puir Belle?"

"What wasn't to love? I mean, sure, he was grumbly initially, but his kindness came through in small ways, and he provided her with everything she could ever desire. They started as enemies but soon fell in love with each other's inner beauty."

"Like us?" he asked softly.

She hesitated, and he held his breath.

"I've never been your enemy, Fintan," she replied, equally as soft. "Not once, even after you hurt me."

"I'd take it back if I could."

"But you can't." She picked up the fork she had abandoned. "And we're not in love. We never were. Whatever feelings we experienced a half a lifetime ago were lust-related urges by kids just out of their teens. So let's leave it in the past, okay?"

"You don't believe that any more than I do, Taryn-Taryn," he said, praying to the Goddess he was right. Since deciding to tell the ancestors to go bugger themselves, he was all in and intended to spend the rest of his life making up for past mistakes if she'd let him.

"Micha Forsyth," she said, changing the subject. "Who is he to you?"

"I can't say for certain, but I'm thinkin' he's related to my da."

"But your last name is Sullivan, I assumed…" Taryn waved a hand. "Never mind. Tell me."

"My parents were never married. I'm a bastard by birth."

"So your father's surname is?"

"Forsyth."

"Of course, it is," she said darkly.

CHAPTER 16

Taryn's breath whooshed out, and she felt deflated. Leave it to her to get cozy with the one person who might not be who they seemed and was obsessed with an important artifact belonging to Fintan.

"Ya didn't know, *aoibhneas mo croí*," he said, entwining their fingers.

"It still doesn't mean I'm not a terrible judge of character. Christ! Anyone can look at a man I've dated, or plan to date, and they'll see he's a sleezy snake-oil salesman long before I do."

She didn't apologize when he winced and released her hand. Letting him off lightly for his past actions would teach him nothing. Forgiveness, for forgiveness's sake, just to make oneself feel better, was ridiculous and not something she subscribed to.

Fintan was regretful—she didn't doubt that—and his remorse put him miles ahead of any other man in her life with the exception of Damian and Trevor. Still, she refused to be a pushover.

"The only reason I'm not at home right now is because you asked me for an introduction, and I was curious."

"Sure, and let's back up here. Who is it you're after datin' that isn't me?" His expression darkened, and he folded his arms across his chest.

Going into full avoidance mode, she sipped her wine and glanced down the table at those present. No one seemed to be paying attention to their conversation.

The weight of Fintan's disapproval and hurt would drag Taryn under if she didn't address it. She cleared her throat and put the glass down.

"Micha. We clicked on the video call, and when he asked me out, I accepted."

He watched her like a wolf does a rabbit. His gaze felt predatory, with an underlying hunger. She also sensed his disappointment in her, but she didn't want to be party to the expectation his love declaration brought. However, she wasn't about tormenting a person when they were feeling down.

"The date was set up before you expressed your love, Fintan. I wasn't doing anything to get back at you. It was me trying to get on with life."

His response was forever coming. Or so it seemed. In reality, less than a minute had passed.

"I'm not expectin' you to claim you love me when that's not what you feel. But have a care with this Micha, yeah? While you're beautiful and a worthy prize, it may not be the one he's after, all the same."

She locked eyes with him. "I haven't dated since Morcant, but Damian has promised to investigate everyone I may be interested in."

Shoving back his chair, he rose. "Grand. I'll wish ya a good night, then."

"I'll call you when I can plan the introduction."

"It's best if you don't. I'll see to it meself."

Her chest tightened as he strode away, and Taryn wanted nothing more than to run after him. To beg his forgiveness. But she wasn't a young girl chasing a rising rockstar, so she let him go.

With a sigh, she tore her attention from his rigid back and met Creed's understanding gaze.

"It's okay to have boundaries, Taryn," he assured her. "Smarter for your sanity."

"Yeah? So why does it hurt so bad to reject what he's offering?"

"Because you still care, even if you don't want to."

She cocked her head. "Is this a takes-one-to-know-one situation, Creed?"

"No. This is an observant man telling a friend she can never be too cautious."

"I thought Fintan was your friend."

An amused half-smile curled his lips. "He is. Probably one of the best I have. Certainly the longest. But I'm not blind to his faults or his problems."

"So I shouldn't apologize for wanting to date someone else?"

"Not if you truly want to date them. If it's to rub it in his face, then yes. You definitely should apologize." With that sage piece of advice, he stood and held a hand out to Narissa. "Time for bed."

Her brows shot up, and a sly smile curled her full lips. "Why, Creed Caldwell! I declare, I didn't believe you cared enough to ever sleep with me again."

"I don't, and I'm not. You're exhausted and haven't fully recovered from today. Stop with your games and get your ass upstairs."

Narissa's chin shot up, and the light of battle entered her eyes. "You're not my caregiver. I'm capable of lookin' after myself, sugar."

With a frustrated huff, he drew back her chair and scooped her up.

"You'd cut off your perfect nose to spite your face, Narissa Sullivan."

"It's Wells. Narissa Wells."

His mouth twisted as if he suppressed a laugh. "Oh, drop it already. Everyone knows your real name by now. You're not hiding from Odessa and your mother anymore."

"It's my legal name."

"This is probably the dumbest argument we've had," he muttered.

"No, sugar. That would be the one where you wouldn't believe I didn't betray you."

Creed's features transformed into an icy mask.

"Time for bed," he snapped.

After they left, Taryn rose and gathered the dishes. After witnessing the sad state of affairs between Creed and Narissa, she easily convinced herself to seek out Fintan and apologize. She didn't want bad blood between them or for him to continue to avoid her whenever she visited Brenna.

"We've got this, love." Eoin took the plates from her hands. "You're our guest, yeah?"

"I can help."

Brenna kissed her cheek. "Shoo. Go find Fintan."

"How did you—"

"Oh, maybe it's the fact that everyone at the table tried to talk to the two of you at one point or another and were ignored?" she teased. "Seriously, though. It's the first time I've seen him not actively hide from you, and he's wearing his heart on his sleeve. That's promising on many levels."

"I don't know what to do," Taryn confessed. "I don't want my heart broken by him again."

"Again?"

Brenna and Eoin shared a confused look. "When was the first time?" she asked.

"When he was in a boy band."

"It wasn't a feckin' boy band!" Fintan growled behind her. "And ya bleedin' well know it, ya do!"

She grinned at her gobsmacked friends. "It totally was!"

"For feck's sake!"

One second she was laughing, and the next, she was balanced over his shoulder, face to face with his perfectly muscled ass. Squealing in surprise, she clutched his hips for support.

"Fintan Sullivan, you put me down this instant!" she demanded.

"No. I've things to say, and you're goin' to listen, woman."

"I've always listened. Manhandling me won't endear you to me, by the way."

He continued until they were in the ceremony room. Once there, he set her on her feet, held up a finger to indicate she should wait, and went back to slam the bookcase door closed. When he returned, he wove his fingers into her hair and drew her close. For the longest moment, he studied her mouth before meeting her wary gaze.

Inside, she was wild with anticipation. Outside, she tried to maintain a calm.

"You're a feckin' liar," he murmured against her lips.

"Oh?"

"Aye. Manhandling turns you on and endears me to ya." He captured her mouth in a bone-melting kiss. When he drew back, he was grinning. "There are stars in your eyes, Taryn-Taryn."

"I'll be the judge of that whole endearing thing," she growled, dragging his head down to hers. "Now, shut up and get to snogging."

Fintan laughed instead. Wrapping his arms around her waist, he lifted her against him and met her death stare. Earlier, when she was conversing with Creed, she'd forgotten to block him, giving full access to her thoughts and emotions. He'd felt her longing to be with him, and he was damned tired of the dance.

"We need to get this mess between us sorted," he said.

"Why are we here, in the dungeon?"

He found himself laughing a second time and realized, despite the direness of the Bloodstone situation, whenever he was with her, he felt freer than he had in years.

"This room quiets the voices in my head," he confessed. "There are two places I can go to escape the ancestors. Here, and the sitting room attached to my bedroom."

"Really? You get a break from them?"

"Aye."

She was stroking a finger along his brow in an absent-minded way. "Good. So the next time they hijack your mind, I'll remember to drag you in here."

"Sure, and a response like yours makes me believe you'll be stickin' around."

"I'd like to, but I don't want a repeat of the last time."

When he would've set her down, she wrapped her legs around his hips. Eye-level, she captured his face between her palms.

"Don't start something if you don't intend to finish it, Fintan. If you don't want a lifetime together, tell me. Because I can handle the truth, and I'm up for a few weeks of love making if that's all you intend. But what I can't and won't tolerate are false promises."

"I'd keep ya forever, and that's the Goddess's honest truth, *aoibhneas mo croí.* But know I'll be fighting my ancestors every step of the way."

"So what makes this time different from the last? How will you defeat them?"

"Bloodstone's necklace."

"But you gave it to Odessa."

He nodded. "Aye. And I've a mind to get it back."

"If you're not going to kiss me, put me down and fill me in on the plan."

"Who said I wasn't going to?" he teased.

"You make me crazy on a good day, Fintan Sullivan," Taryn muttered, gnashing her teeth together.

Again, he laughed. "You make me mad as a March hare, too, love, but I'm thinkin' it isn't for the same reason."

"Put me down, you oaf. "

"When did ya resort to name-callin'?"

"When you left me on that platform."

His blood cooled in the face of her continued hurt, and he released her.

"Then let's get this sorted, yeah?" Stepping over to the chest, he removed a blanket and pillows. After laying them out on the floor in a circle, carefully skirting the casting area, he gestured toward the nest. "Make yourself comfortable, Taryn-Taryn. I think we're in for a bit of a discussion."

Though he wanted to cuddle her close, he sat opposite her. She should make the first move if she were willing. Her dark frown and the buzzing in his mind told him that she wasn't happy about the distance. Smothering a grin, he lifted a brow and patted the spot next to him. With an arch look, she shifted closer, and he dragged her against him as he reclined back.

"Ya look knackered. Are ya wantin' to sleep first?" He hated to wait, wanting to erase the misunderstanding of years past, but he'd follow her lead and allow her to rest if she preferred. The day had been a particularly long one.

"No. You told me earlier you loved me and always had." Two heartbeats passed. "Is it another line?"

"I didn't lie to ya then, and I'll not lie to you now."

"But you did." She rose up, resting on one elbow to look him in the face. "You swore you'd be back."

"It wasn't an intentional lie, and you know it. I told you the why of it."

She studied him, and during the pause, Fintan kept their mental connection open so she could see what was in his heart. "Feel through our bond, *aoibhneas mo croí.* Know that I speak the truth."

Acceptance.

Not only was it reflected on her face, but it embraced him the moment she thawed. She tucked under his arm and snuggled down. "Okay," she whispered.

Fintan closed his eyes and thanked the goddess Anu for small favors.

"What we shared in those first weeks was like nothin' I'd ever experienced before, Taryn-Taryn. I was gobsmacked from the moment I saw ya. Sure, and I won't say love at first sight, but I was infatuated all the same." He kissed her temple, smiling when she released a happy sigh. "I was chuffed when you decided to stay in Ireland, then when you agreed to follow me around Scotland and England."

"But after the Edinburgh concert, Peter died," she concluded.

"Aye. And I told ya as much at the time. When I said I'd meet ya in a week in Liverpool, I fully intended to. But the instant I crossed the border to this estate, I was bound to it."

She wiggled to rest atop him, and her frown was one of confusion. "Bound? As in, a slave to the property?"

"Aye. Close enough." He swallowed in remembered torment. "The ancestors wouldn't let me leave or use a phone to call you. Whenever I tried to sneak away, I experienced one of those grand three-hour naps like ya witnessed."

"And you've already said they wouldn't allow you to text me without retribution."

"Aye, though I tried that, too," he said. "It earned me electric shock therapy."

"Ohmygod!" Her horror was justified.

"I was in love with you by then, but I couldn't find a way

around it. I was more tortured by the idea that you hated me than by what they unleashed on me brain."

"Oh, Fintan." Tears shimmered in her sad eyes, and his heart broke all over again.

"I've thought about you every day since. Wonderin' what your life was like. Only when I agreed to avoid you did the ancestors give me a respite from their games."

"But then I started coming here to see Brenna, so how did you manage to remain unharmed?" she asked.

"They were a bit more lax after all this time. Likely knowin' ya wouldn't have me after no contact for over twenty years, but I can't say with all certainty." He stroked her hair, her jaw, her neck, anything he could touch, trying to convince himself she was really here, in his arms. "I tried to keep the feelin's buried, hidin' them even from meself. Any other way was misery."

"But you said you thought about me every day. How did they miss that?"

"When you came to visit, I'd duck into this room or the changin' room upstairs, where they couldn't access my thoughts." He gave a half smile. "I allowed meself forty minutes, no more, no less."

"You really do love me," she whispered with wonder, almost as if she could hardly believe it.

"Aye."

Her smile was the summer sun in winter. "Good. Now tell me about this plan to retrieve Bloodstone's necklace."

"You aren't going to say it in return?" he asked, experiencing a small amount of outrage that she hadn't told him she loved him yet.

"No," she said archly. "I said I forgive you for leaving me waiting, not that I'm ready to lay my heart at your feet to be trampled again."

"Ouch." Fisting her hair, he rolled on top of her. When his nose was less than an inch from hers and his body was cradled by her thighs, he said, "At least promise you're bammin' me about dating that bastard?"

She giggled.

He growled.

"I'm not above chainin' ya to me bed, Taryn-Taryn."

"I'm not above letting you, Fintan Sullivan." A sly smile curled her lips. "Now, maybe you should prove that five-note orgasm claim."

With a bark of laughter, he pulled away. "Not until you tell me you love me. I'm holdin' that one in check."

"Rude."

CHAPTER 17

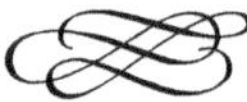

Taryn was reticent to tell Fintan she loved him, and she
didn't need to examine why. Too many times in the
past, she'd freely given her affection, only to have her soul
battered and abused. Trusting someone to keep her heart safe no
longer came as easily for a woman in her forties as it did for her
younger self.

At nineteen, she'd viewed everything through romance-
tinted glasses. A look, a touch, a sigh—they all sparked dreams.
But later in life, longing looks were met with skepticism. She
tended to overanalyze or dismiss overtures for fear of being
wrong and appearing a fool.

"Men aren't much different, *aoibhneas mo croí*. We fear rejection, too. Maybe more. Women are emotionally stronger because
they've had to be, yeah?" Fintan said.

She silently cursed their damned link. It would be better to
keep her worries to herself, but she was failing spectacularly
at it.

"You'll be better with practice," he assured her, extending a
hand to help her stand. Tugging her close, he touched his fore-

head to hers. "Sure, and it's maddening now, but we'll work on it. And if you're absolutely opposed to Fate's gift, we'll find a way to sever it."

He'd made it sound like rejecting Fate's gift was akin to rejecting him, though his words were meant to be supportive. Why did she suddenly feel like the worst sort of bitch?

"I'm not one-hundred percent opposed, but I don't necessarily love that you can hear my every thought either."

"Do you want me to pretend I don't hear ya, then?"

His compassion and understanding ran deep, and Taryn appreciated his unexpected kindness.

"No," she said, resigned. "That would be worse and feel too much like a lie."

"Let's call Damian and ask for a spell to filter such things," he replied. His lopsided smile zinged through her, but she ignored the pesky attraction because it came with commitment she wasn't ready for.

"Do you think that's possible, Fintan? That perhaps I can prevent your access to my deeper emotions?"

He frowned, and Taryn reevaluated her comment.

"Oh! I didn't mean you and I shouldn't share a loving connection. Only to save you from all my self-doubt and recriminations."

"And I'd save you from me own, too. But I also want you to know I'm being honest with ya and holdin' nothin' back."

Honesty shone from his troubled eyes, and her shame expanded to overwhelming proportions. She'd been busy trying to protect herself and keep any doubts hidden when she should've been voicing them and resolving their issues.

"Thank you for trusting me with your truth, Fintan. And if it's any consolation, I don't want to date Micha or anyone else." She smiled as she stroked his jaw, absently noting his stubble. "I've always cared about you. Even when I desperately wanted to hate you for disappearing like you did." Holding up a hand to prevent his protest, she said, "We don't need to readdress it. I believe you. It's just a matter of convincing my head and heart to take another chance. It's like baseball. Three strikes and you're out."

"And I have two against me?"

"No, not you. I meant me, striking out at love twice. Here I am, standing at the plate, staring down the pitcher, and knowing he intends to throw a curveball. How do I prepare for it?"

"Just keep your eye on the ball, *aoibhneas mo croí*. Free your mind and do what comes naturally. I promise you'll hit the bleedin' thing out of the park."

"You make it sound so easy when we both know it isn't," she said forlornly.

"It's not my intent. I only want to ease your fears."

Feeling as if she'd talked the issue to death, she nodded. She stretched on her tiptoes and kissed him lightly. "Thank you. Let's discuss your plan."

"It's only half-baked, as you Americans say."

Grinning, she shook her head. "Maybe we should get half-baked and hash the rest out."

"Are ya always goin' to be a bad influence?"

"Whenever I can."

He chuckled. The pitch was low, bordering on wicked, and it shot throughout her body, distributing delicious shivers. It gave her the smallest taste of his power.

His expression hardened. "I didn't mean—"

Taryn placed a finger over his lips. "I'm not objecting, and you didn't steal anything, Fintan. Please don't freak out."

The tightness around his eyes and mouth eased. With a kiss of her fingertip, he drew her hand down and placed it over his heart.

"Thank you, Taryn-Taryn."

"Let's take things one problem at a time. When we've dealt with Odessa and Bloodstone's necklace, we'll work on us, okay?"

"Aye."

"I'm sensing you want to know about Micha." His silence was answer enough. "Okay, so it's my understanding that he began working for the Witches' Council about four months ago. I met him about six weeks ago when I turned over an artifact I discovered at an estate sale in Salem."

"Just how often do you find those bleedin' artifacts?"

She laughed. "Quite a bit. Most people can't sense the magic they hold and want to get rid of garbage. Others believe they are being sentimental for hanging on to grandma's trinkets."

"Why start huntin' them in the first place?"

His interest seemed genuine, and it was easier to reveal her reasons.

"It began after Morcant."

"Ah. It's a recent thing?"

"Yes. I couldn't escape into my books anymore, and whenever I was at the shop—Soleil and I have one downtown—I'd get restless. The driving need to search out objects was strong. Weirdly, I haven't experienced it since finding the amulet."

"Have you never spoken to anyone about your trauma?" he asked quietly.

"Not really. Damian once or twice, and only because he sensed my turmoil." She shrugged and looked away. Everyone meant well, but how could they understand the self-contempt attached to bringing a killer into their home?

"Taryn."

"I'm okay." She brushed off his compassion. "To answer your question, Damian offered to take away the worst of it. But what if it resurfaces when I least expect?"

"What did that bastard do to you, love?"

"Nothing as horrible as what he did to Josie," she replied quickly. But Morcant had undermined her confidence and taught her to distrust herself. He almost killed her niece, for fuck's sake! And he had murdered Viv. Thankfully, Damian had a

Death Dealer in his back pocket. Yet coming back from that was the hardest for Taryn. Her stupid decisions had caused trauma for those she loved.

Fintan embraced her from behind, resting his chin on her head.

"I'm sorry, Taryn-Taryn," he said through their connection. *"If I'd have been stronger, maybe he wouldn't have gotten close to ya."*

"If not me, he would've targeted Soleil. I'm glad it's my burden to bear and not hers."

"Josie shares in your burden." Fintan hugged her tighter, and Taryn allowed his soothing energy to permeate her fragile shell. "You should talk to her, and soon," he advised.

"I will. I owe her a sit-down and a massive apology."

"Grand. Oh, and Soleil is stronger than ya give her credit for." He shifted her to face him. "I've seen her give Trevor shite, and it's a feckin' joy to watch."

Taryn laughed, feeling oddly lighter, before sobering again. "I hate that the Authority allowed Buttagier to use us as pawns. If they're willing to—what is it?"

His face contorted as if he were in pain, and her panic spiked.

"Fintan?"

Falling to his knees, he clutched his head. "Run!"

"What?"

"Run!" he commanded. His voice deepened, wrapping around her and compelling her with the single word. All will left, and she headed for the exit.

"No, child!" a man shouted inside her mind. Halting, she spun back and searched for the source.

The blue-green light emanating from Fintan stole her breath with its brightness, but it was the fear etched on his face that froze her to the spot.

"Go!" he shouted. "I can't hold it back."

"It?" she squeaked. Did he mean his Siren?

Understanding came with the barrage of his frantic thoughts and those of another.

It will consume her.

Freedom.

Power.

Fuck her.

The last three weren't Fintan. Or not the him she'd come to know.

His eyes glazed as his body transformed, growing a foot in size. The creature's shoulders were one and a half times that of Fintan's, and the bulging muscles tore through his clothing like paper. Muscled thighs befitting Mr. Universe played peek-a-book with the shredded chinos, and ultra-thin iridescent scales formed over his exposed skin. If she hadn't stood within a few feet of him, she'd have assumed his skin had taken on a sweaty sheen.

Then, Taryn caught a glimpse of the forming erection. Heart beating like a wild bird's wings in a cage, she met the creature's burning gaze.

Desire was reflected back. There was also a predatory gleam, as if the creature felt the need for dominance. To possess.

It grinned.

"Holy fuck!" she screeched.

"Holy fuck is right," Creed said from the doorway. "Is that Fin? For the love of all things Hulk! Who knew he was sporting an anaconda? Has he—oh, shit. He doesn't look as thrilled to see me as he does you."

A horrified laugh escaped her, and she slapped her hand over her mouth.

The Siren frowned at her, and his head pivoted toward the door. All at once, the predatory expression disappeared, replaced by outrage.

Intruder.

Rival.

Destroy.

The creature had cataloged Creed as competition for Taryn's affections, and she feared for him. Fintan's musician's fingers elongated, and shiny black nails replaced the tips. The claws were easily five inches long and another two in width, resembling a grizzly bear's paws. And like a bear, they probably weren't razor sharp, but they'd do substantial damage.

"No!" Forgetting any threat to self, she jumped between them.

"Mine," the Siren hummed, and a shiver of awareness rolled over her.

All will abandoned her for the second time, and she stepped forward to within touching distance.

"Taryn, we need to teleport out of here right now," Creed warned. "That thing isn't the Fintan you know."

"What's happening?" Noah's voice drifted to her. The creature's reaction was immediate.

He grew another half foot and flexed threateningly.

"I guess now's not the time to discuss Damian's thoughts on Bloodstone's necklace," Noah said dryly.

"How the hell can you joke when that thing's one-eyed monster is staring you down?" Creed demanded.

Horrified amusement bubbled inside her, and she giggled. Her humor was on the darker side, and uncontrollable laughter was an embarrassing side effect.

Other than an irritated shake of his head, the Siren ignored them, hyperfocusing on her. His claws retracted as he wrapped a hand around her neck and dragged her closer.

"Mine," he hummed.

"Fintan's," she found the courage to whisper, breaking his hold on her.

It grinned, displaying gleaming-white, vampire-like teeth. The rest of his shirt fell from his torso as ebony bones sprouted from his shoulder blades, unfurling into the shape of dragon wings. At the topmost joint, a claw, about twice the size of those on his hands, formed. The flexible outer membrane of the wing was similar to a bat in texture, but the color was a rich oceanic blue.

"Taryn—" Creed clamped his jaw shut when Fintan bared his teeth.

"You should go, Creed," she urged. "You both should."

"We can't, in good conscience, leave you alone with that thing, love." Noah cultivated a tone that was soft and unthreatening, and the creature dismissed him, keeping his focus on Taryn.

"He's little more than an animal right now," Creed argued.

The Siren's aquamarine eyes locked with hers, as if challenging her to run. Deep in her soul, she knew if she did, it would give chase. But just as assuredly, it wouldn't hurt her if she stayed.

"Go, guys. I'm not leaving Fintan."

His creature purred its satisfaction, and panic filled her as she realized the harmonious sound tickled all her private parts.

"Five notes," it murmured.

As another wave of pleasure swept her, Taryn's eyes flew wide.

The amused half-grin was pure Fintan.

Other than a savage curse, Creed said nothing, but Taryn had the sense they'd departed.

"Fintan, if you're in there, I need you to return now," she urged.

It wasn't that she didn't appreciate a panty-incinerating experience, but his warning rang in her mind. He'd feared the Incubus. And though she doubted that's what the creature in front of her was, she knew if it absorbed her magic when she crested—three more notes, but who was counting?—Fintan would become his greatest fear.

"No," it hummed, causing another tsunami of pleasure.

"Stop this!" she ordered. "I love Fintan, and—"

The Siren's arms hauled her against him, lifting her off her feet.

With a squeal, she clutched his shoulders. The texture of his scales wasn't as expected, and her fingertips encountered warm skin. Wherever she touched him, he lit from within, giving off a jellyfish-like bioluminescence.

"That's incredible," she breathed.

His wings encircled them, plunging her world into darkness except for the shimmer of light off his body. The bottom bones supporting the lower sail's membrane provided a place for her to stand, putting them face to face.

"You," he said.

Incredible.

Mine.

Fuck.

"Nope!" She applied the brakes on the Siren's runaway train, especially when his anaconda tried caressing places only Fintan's snake was allowed entrance. "No fucking! That thing you're packing will rearrange my internal organs."

"Will fit," he purred, causing her another pleasurable shudder.

Moisture gathered at the apex of her thighs. If it wasn't for the small matter that she loved Fintan and if she were into sex with anything but humans, she might've been persuaded to give the Siren a go.

Was that four notes? She'd always been bad at math.

A gleam entered his eyes, and it looked remarkably like a challenge.

She frowned. "How many people have you had sex with in this state?" she demanded. "Because I don't think you're an ordinary Siren."

His grin flashed, and he buried his nose against her throat, inhaling deeply right before swiping his tongue from the base of her neck to her ear lobe. Though a bit longer and thicker, the texture of his tongue was no different than a human's, and it put naughty ideas into her head.

"Ye—," he began.

She clapped her hand over his mouth. "Not another sound, mister!"

Humor lurked in his twinkling eyes, and she had the stray thought that Fintan might be pranking her. Would he risk such a thing?

"Please send Fintan back to me," she begged.

"Five," he hummed.

Her body was an earthquake unto itself, and she blacked out.

CHAPTER 18

*T*aryn woke in slow increments. Languid and happy, she snuggled closer to the body heat wrapped around her. Beneath her shirt, warm, tantalizing fingers traced a lazy pattern across her abdomen, and she smiled at the deliciousness of the touch.

"Mmm," she murmured, covering the hand with hers and lowering it to the waistband of her panties. "Magic-finger exploration should start much lower."

Fintan's deep chuckle made her smile. "Sure, and I was waiting for your permission, *aoibhneas mo croí*." He shifted to see her expression.

"I—"

The events in the ceremony room came crashing back, and she jackknifed into a sitting position. Or as much as a sitting position as her forehead connecting with his face would allow.

"Fuck!" He fell back on the mattress beside her, cupping his nose.

"Fintan!" Taryn attempted to roll but got tangled in the sheets and flailed her arms. Her fist cracked him in the jaw. "Ohmygod! Fintan, I'm so sorry," she cried, when he swore again.

She scrambled to her knees, but stopped short of helping him. Shock held her still.

"Um, where are my pants?"

He sat up, and the sheet fell below his waist.

"And where are *yours*?" she asked with a horrified gasp. "Did we… Did you… Are you an Incubus?"

He scowled.

"I'm going to take that as a no. If we'd had sex, you'd be in a better mood," she concluded.

"Ya hit me in the feckin' face, Taryn-Taryn. Twice. How grand a mood do you expect me to be in?"

"Fair point. So did we?"

"No." His reply was nothing short of surly. "You're right. I'd be in a better mood."

She giggled.

A lopsided smile curled his mouth. "The pants you're seekin' are on the chair behind ya. I assumed you'd be more comfortable sleepin' without your jeans."

"You're a prince among men, Fintan Sullivan." Only inches away, it seemed natural to kiss him for his thoughtfulness. Leaning in, she brushed his nose with hers, then lightly bussed his lips.

"Don't be spreadin' vicious rumors," he murmured against her mouth before nipping her lip.

"Oh, I intend to tell the entire world. Boy-band alumni, Fintan Sullivan, appears like a grumpy shit, but he's actually the sweetest man you'll ever meet—"

Taryn ended on a scream as he tackled her.

"It wasn't a feckin' boy band!"

Suddenly, she didn't feel like teasing anymore. There were questions she needed answered.

"Seriously, about your Siren, what happened downstairs?" she asked.

His face darkened, and he delayed answering to brush her hair from her cheek. His hesitancy made her take stock of her body. Other than relaxed, she wasn't sore where it counted, meaning the thing had left her unmolested after she passed out.

"Fintan?"

"Aye, it didn't hurt you, love."

"That's a good thing. So why are you so serious?"

"I've felt it struggling to get free since I visited your home, but I thought I had control. It snapped the chain before I could stop it," he said.

"And that bothers you."

"Aye. I've told you. It wants you for its own." Solemn, he met her eyes. "The vision of your grave haunts me, every feckin' minute of the day. What if my monster is the one to cause your death?"

"I didn't truly fear him, and I don't think he's as bad as you believe. The Incubus, if he ever is born, maybe, but not your Siren." She wrapped her legs around his hips and pressed her pelvis to his, smiling when she felt his arousal. Despite his worry, his desire for her hadn't diminished. "He didn't want to hurt me, Fintan. Don't ask me how I know, I just do."

"Ya can't."

"I can." Taryn traced his furrowed brow. "He was teasing me with the humming. The laughter in his eyes and his playful grin said as much." When he still didn't seem convinced, she asked, "How long was I unconscious? When did you return to your body?"

"It took a long minute, to be sure. He was guardin' you like a feckin' mastiff."

"See? If he wanted to hurt me or steal my magic, he could've. But he is a version of you, Fintan. He knows right from wrong."

"No, and never mistake that he does, Taryn-Taryn. If the craving were strong enough, he'd have been on ya."

"Well, now I feel unwanted and totally rejected."

Fintan arched his back, pressing his erection against her, and arched a brow. "Then ya clearly have no feeling below your waist."

She compressed her lips to keep from laughing.

"You confessed to lovin' me," he said, with a satisfied air.

"When?" Taryn tried to recall their conversation since waking. "I didn't—"

"You told me Siren."

Had she? When?

"Stop this!" she ordered. "I love Fintan, and—"

The scene popped into her mind, but the view was of her upset visage, with pleading eyes.

Fintan's memory, not hers!

"You were there?" she asked.

"Aye, below the surface. I could hear and see everything."

"You weren't egging him on?"

"I don't know what that means," he admitted.

"Encouraging him."

"Ach, no! I wasn't eggin' him on, love. He wanted your confession for himself."

His sincerity was annoying. If she had the slightest inclination he was messing with her, she'd read him the riot act and be on her way. But his energy was genuine, and she was left confused about what she should do. Admitting she loved him wasn't something she was prepared for at this juncture.

"It's all right, *aoibhneas mo croí*. I'll not push it."

Fintan shifted, intending to pull away.

Taryn tightened her legs, locking him against her. "I do love you, but I'm afraid of getting hurt."

"Aye. And I'm afraid of hurtin' ya, but it won't be because I don't love you back. And it won't be because I'm not going to try me feckin' best to make you happy."

"Like I said, I'm not scared of your Siren."

The truth was laid bare between them.

Their mental link pulsed, humming, as if energy flowed through, making it stronger.

"He loves you, too, Taryn-Taryn."

"Maybe don't tell him, but I might have a soft spot for him also."

Fintan's grin held no sign of the vampire-like fangs of the creature, but the humor behind the gesture was the same.

"So, I'll be hearin' it from you again."

She pretended ignorance. "What's that?"

He sat back on his heels and rested his hands on her knees.

"I think ya know." Running his fingers along her outer thigh, he hooked them around the waistband of her bikini briefs and inched them downward. He paused before uncovering her mound. "You'll need to say it if you want another five-note orgasm, love."

"I don't know if I can handle another one. It took me"—she frowned—"How long was I out? You never said."

"About two hours after I broke free. I don't know how long that actually took."

"Two hours? Huh. I guess that means I'm rested enough."

He chuckled, low, sexy, and full of promise, causing her stomach to clench. "Two hours is a mighty long time for me to resist your charms, love. I should be receivin' a feckin' medal for heroism in the face of all that temptation lyin' half naked in me bed."

"Should I conjure one for you?"

"Sure, and I wouldn't reject it." He dipped his head, his lips brushing the sensitive skin of her lower abdomen. "A reward's a reward."

Taryn huffed a laugh. "So you're saying we have two hours to make up for?"

"Aye. Two hours of lovemakin' is long enough to be rewardin' me for not takin' full advantage. But if we run over, I won't be complainin'."

She bucked against him, enjoying the heat of his mouth and the soft scratch of his stubble against her skin. "Stop stalling."

He lifted his head, and wicked intent glinted in his eyes.

But he didn't rush.

Hell no! He crawled up her body and kissed her like he had nowhere else to be. Slow, deep, exploratory. His mouth teased hers open, tongue sliding in with unhurried confidence, coaxing a moan from her throat. She sank her hands into his hair, anchoring him there. The connection was electric, and their bond hummed like a tuning fork struck too hard.

Her skin felt tight and too small to contain the building pressure.

"You say stallin'. I say takin' me time and doin' it right."

"Mm. From what I remember, you always managed to get it right." She pressed the back of her hand to her brow and affected a thoughtful pose. "But my memory is foggy because it was so, *so* long ago."

He nibbled a path along her jaw, nipping gently at her chin, then down her throat to where her pulse thundered and gave her away.

"So it's a reminder, you're needin'?" he asked. His gravelly growl tickled low in her belly.

"Yes, that might be nice." Taryn traced the curve of his naked back, a muscled marvel.

Fintan bent and pressed his lips to her inner thigh, warm breath fanning over sensitive skin as he worked her underwear down her legs.

"Tell me. Do you remember this, *aoibhneas mo croí* ?" His hot mouth closed over her.

"Goddess, yes!" A thread of need wrapped around her. "I remember everything about you, Fintan. About us."

His gaze locked on hers as he kissed his way across her stomach, the curve of her ribs, the center of her chest, and upward. When he reached her mouth, he hovered there, his lips a breath away.

"Should we start a timer?" he teased.

Comprehension escaped her. "For what?"

"Two hours from now."

"Shut up and get to snogging," she growled.

Their mouths met, and this time, it wasn't teasing or tentative. It was hungry but reverent, and laced with everything they hadn't dared say out loud.

His weight settled over her as her thighs parted, welcoming him closer, and she felt the hard press of him between them. Her breath caught as he stroked her, fingertips lightly dragging over her bare skin as if he intended to memorize the shape of her. When he finally slid his fingers lower, finding her slick and ready, she rocked into him with a soft curse.

"Fintan..."

He worked her with slow, deliberate precision. Circling, teasing, dipping. Never too much, never too little. Just enough to keep her on edge. She writhed beneath him, her hips lifting of their own accord, chasing the pressure, and her world narrowed to sensation.

She mapped the grooves of his spine and dug in as he rolled his hips to find the right alignment. When he finally entered her, it was a slow slide that stole her breath and made her toes curl.

Neither of them spoke for a long moment.

"This..." He braced himself above her, forehead to forehead, his breath ragged. "This feels like comin' home, *aoibhneas mo croí.*"

"Yes." Taryn pulled him in for another kiss. *"And I never want to leave."*

"I never want ya to, either."

He moved in a deep, deliberate rhythm that made her body

rise to meet his without conscious thought. Their magic pulsed with each stroke, heat building between them like a live current. Her nails raked lightly over his shoulders, anchoring her against the storm building inside her.

But he didn't give her what she expected. Not yet.

FINTAN'S MOUTH FOUND HER NECK, HER SHOULDER, HER collarbone, anywhere he could reach and still stay sheathed within her warmth.

"I know this is new for you."

She snorted a laugh. "Not hardly."

"Shhh, woman. I'm tryin' to have an honest moment here, yeah?"

Taryn mimed zipping her lip, then ruined it with a grin and a grab.

He stilled her hand.

"It's not the sex that's new, Taryn-Taryn. It's the trust." He brushed a kiss on her cheekbone, his voice quieter now. "And I aim to prove it's worth it. That we're worth a second chance."

Her love—bold, bright, and more magical than anything he'd ever experienced—blasted through their link, embracing him but ruining him at the same time.

Fated mates were gifted with bonds like theirs, and he expected, no matter how long he lived, he'd never feel this close to another. Never desire another woman with the intensity he felt for Taryn.

"I feel exactly the same," she whispered, staring at him with something akin to awe.

He nodded slowly, forehead resting against hers. "Aye, and I'll earn every second you share with me. I'll never stop strivin' to make ya happy, Taryn-Taryn. I promise."

There was no more talking after that.

Fintan kissed her again—deeper this time, hungrier. Positioned between her thighs, one of his hands cradled her hip, and he slid the other up her side to cup her breast. His thumb brushed her nipple, and he sent a magical pulse across the delicate flesh.

She gasped into his mouth, causing his grin.

"Beautiful," he murmured. "Every fuckin' inch of you."

Taryn moaned, her back arching toward him as his mouth closed over the tight bud.

"Fintan," she breathed.

Pulling out, he shifted lower to taste her. He flicked his tongue, stroked, circled, and suckled with maddening control. His hands pinned her writhing hips as he tasted his fill. Relentless and focused, like worship was a sacred act and her body his altar. When her fingers clawed the sheets and her legs trembled, he spread her wider, accessing more. There wasn't a part of her he left untouched.

Taryn's sexy, ragged little pants were raw and desperate. Music to his ears. And when her orgasm hit, it tore through them both, hotter and faster than lightning. Her body clamped down, shaking beneath him, but Fintan didn't stop. He licked and soothed her until she was gasping, trembling, claiming she was too sensitive to bear another touch.

He chuckled against her inner thigh and trailed the lightest of kisses up her smooth belly.

"Dude." Her fingers wound in his hair, and she forcefully urged him upward. "Holy hell, Sullivan."

"Don't be thinkin' we're done, love."

"I'd cut a bitch if we were."

With a chuckle, Fintan sucked her lower lip. "When did ya become so aggressive?"

"You don't want to know." She caressed down his neck and the line of his shoulders as she trailed the movement with her gaze. "You've filled out more than I would've expected."

Fintan nodded. "No longer a boy."

"Mm."

"Ya sound sad."

"I am. I missed seeing you mature. In a way, it feels like I'm meeting you again for the first time."

He smiled lazily against her mouth as he thumbed the hardened tip of her nipple. "I feckin' love how you've matured, too, Taryn-Taryn.."

She laughed, breathless, and he felt it to the base of his cock.

Eyes locked on his, she said, "If you don't move, I'm going to flip us over and do it myself."

Fintan growled in approval and slid inside, slow and measured. And she took every inch.

Taryn gasped, clinging to his shoulders as her body adjusted around him. She was hot and perfect, and he filled her in a way that left no space for thought. Once fully seated, he paused to enjoy her pleasure through their connection, allowing her to feel his.

Then he began to move in a steady, rolling rhythm that drove them both crazy with the buildup. Every time he pulled out and thrust back in, it was like striking a match. With each stroke, they burned hotter than before. Moving together, their bodies were two halves of a whole reuniting. Every moan, every gasp, every whispered word fed through the link between them and carried them closer to their goal.

Fintan shifted, angling deeper, and Taryn cried out. Her arms and legs wrapped around him, locking her sweat-slicked body with his. Their rhythm turned frantic, desperate.

Her second climax was deeper, full-bodied. When it hit, she shattered with a sob, tightened her legs around his hips, and rocked her pelvis hard against his, as if determined he should feel what she did.

And he did. Seconds later, he followed her over the edge, and her name was torn from his lips as he pulsed inside her, hips grinding to prolong the moment.

After, they collapsed in a tangle of limbs and breath, the room spinning around them.

When he was able to catch his breath, he pulled her into his arms, burying his face in her neck. "If you ever go, you'll break me, *aoibhneas mo croí.*"

CHAPTER 19

Sleep was elusive, and Fintan spent the remainder of the night watching Taryn. He couldn't quite believe she was really in his bed or that his mind hadn't snapped, thrusting him into a fantasy world he never wanted to wake from. Every breath she took solidified the truth and tied him to the present.

For so long, his nights had been haunted by what-ifs. When he'd told her he fell for her from the moment he saw her, he wasn't lying. Had his ancestors not intervened and held him hostage, he'd have returned to her and never left her side again.

Her trials in the interim had put an ache in his heart, and that pain would remain firmly lodged there forever. If she hurt, he hurt.

He thanked the Goddess daily for Josie's sacrifice regarding Morcant. Although Taryn was tough, her sister was tougher. It's not that Josie lacked a softer side; hell, he'd seen glimpses of her future along the way and knew she cared deeply. But she compartmentalized with an ease Taryn would never possess.

Fintan had no idea where they went from here, or why the ancestors weren't making his life a misery for defying them.

Was it too late? Had they resigned themselves to his downfall? Had he crossed that line never to go back?

If this were what it felt like, heaven at home, he'd gladly stay sequestered away forever with her.

A smile curled Taryn's lips, and Fintan wanted to taste her again. Holding himself in check wasn't easy after so many years of denying himself the pleasures of the flesh. Yet he didn't dare move in case he broke the fragile spell holding this moment together. For decades, he'd told himself solitude was safer, and the monster inside didn't get a future. But he wanted this. So badly. And not the sex. The sense of belonging to her.

Giving in to temptation, he brushed his fingers along the curve of her tantalizing hip.

Taryn frowned and peeked one eye open.

He froze.

"You're awake," he stated inanely.

"How many years did you deny yourself sex?"

"How long have ya been listenin' to my thoughts?" he countered.

"A few minutes only. You're right about Josie, I think." Reaching up, she lightly raked her nails along his jaw. "How many years have you denied yourself, Fintan?"

"From the day I left you."

Her hand dropped, and her face froze in shock.

"Sure, and maybe part of it was self-punishment for not being stronger and returnin' to ya. But from the moment the ancestors entered my head, my magic grew, and I feared my monster."

She rolled to a sitting position and grasped his hands. "I'm so sorry you felt you had to live in seclusion." Her voice was low and carried a gravity that wrapped around his ribs and squeezed.

He opened his mouth to deflect—to joke or say it didn't matter, but her sadness did him in. Loneliness had made him half mad, but he couldn't admit it aloud. Couldn't tell her the reason he was a grumpy bastard was because he was miserable without her.

Moisture welled in her eyes, and Fintan felt those building tears in his soul.

"Don't cry for me, *aoibhneas mo croí*. I'm not worth it."

"Shut up, you idiot! Of course you are." She lunged for him, wrapping her arms around his neck and squeezing tightly. "You're worth everything," she whispered fiercely.

"I'm not, Taryn-Taryn. I made your life a misery when you visited."

"But we both know why, and I can't say I wouldn't have done exactly the same." She drew back and smiled through her tears. "I might've slipped you a boxful of laxatives to keep you from coming back."

"I'd have returned," he assured her. "I wouldn't have eaten another thing ya gave me, but I'd have returned, to be sure."

"Do you think they will leave you alone now?"

"You're here, and that bleedin' necklace they hate so much is gone." He shrugged and drew her down to lie beside him. "We can only hope it's enough to appease their selfish nature."

Taryn rolled onto her stomach and rested on her elbows. Her face was still damp, and Fintan gently brushed away the evidence of her sadness and sympathy.

"I wasn't faithful to you," she said softly.

His heart stopped. "You mean the weeks we were together?"

"What? No! What do you take me for?" she demanded

Fintan's relief was profound, and he did his damnedest not to laugh in the face of her outrage.

"Then what are ya on about, love?"

"You were faithful to me all these years, but I wasn't faithful to you."

"Why would ya be? I hurt you when I didn't return. How could I ever expect you wouldn't move on?" He was being more reasonable than he'd normally be. Yes, jealousy was eating him up, but the blame lay solely at his door, not hers. "You'd have been mad to wait over twenty years for me to come knockin', Taryn-Taryn."

"I know." Still, she sounded sad, and he could feel her brain buzzing.

As an idea formed in his mind, he rushed to block her from his thoughts.

"I've a grand plan. Don't move."

He jumped up and ran for the wardrobe. A quick search of the top shelf provided what he was looking for, and he pulled the old t-shirt over his head, then slipped into his favorite jeans, but left them unbuttoned. Fintan pulled another shirt from the shelf, and as it passed by his nose, he smiled. Her long-ago scent still lingered on the material from his spell to preserve it. Once a year, on the anniversary of their first meeting, he allowed himself to hold it close and wallow in the memories of their aborted romance. Yes, he was a sentimental fool, but no one ever measured up to Taryn-Taryn Stephens by his ruler.

"Put it on." Fintan handed her the shirt.

Eyes wide and jaw slack, she stared at the material. "You kept the shirt from our first meeting?"

"Well, you turned out to be easier than ya led me to believe, but I still had to work for it that night, yeah?"

She laughed as she slipped into the t-shirt. "It's not my fault. I was charmed by an Irish singer in a boy ba—"

"If ya feckin' say it, I'll not be responsible for me actions," he warned.

The flash of her straight white teeth hit him low in the gut.

"Now what?" she asked. Her eyes shone brighter than diamonds under LED lights, and he basked in her eagerness, felt through their connection.

"We start over." Fintan lifted his hand, pausing a hairsbreadth from her face. Removing the block, he let her access their link. "May I?"

It took but a moment for her to understand, and a small smile played on her mouth as she nodded. With trembling fingers, he stroked her silky smooth cheek, tracing her jawline, then cupping her neck.

"What's your name?" he asked huskily.

"Taryn. Taryn Stephens." And in an exact recreation of that night, her voice held the same sexy breathiness he fucking adored.

"Well, it's nice to meet ya, Taryn-Taryn Stephens. I'm Fintan Sullivan."

She giggled, like the first time, and he grinned, relieved she understood him as well as she did.

"That was made obvious at the beginning of your set," she said pertly.

Recalling his boggled mind and careless reaction to the fact, he shrugged. "And now the introductions are out of the way, can I snog ya, then?"

"Snog?"

"Kiss. I've a powerful need to kiss ya, love."

She nodded, not as bashful after all these years, but her radiance hadn't dimmed. Similar to the first time, her agreement created a starburst of happiness in his chest, and his stomach tightened. He wasted no time leaning in.

Taryn was the sweet nectar to his buzzing bee, and the sense of rightness was still there, making him deliriously happy. They didn't need flowery words or any of the ridiculous gestures standard in a new courtship, and for that, Fintan was exceedingly grateful.

Putting the slightest of distances between them, he pressed light kisses across her closed lids, along her nose, trailing to her ear. He drew the lobe between his teeth, gently biting down before sucking.

Taryn gasped and clutched his shoulders tighter.

"It's a good thing Donal's not here and we already have a

room." Tipping her head, she gave him full access to her throat, and he obliged her with love nips from her jaw to her collarbone.

She moaned, and his Siren took note.

"Down, boy," she told it.

Her response threw him off his game, and he drew back in surprise.

"Ya heard it?"

"Am I not supposed to? He comes through loud and clear." Frowning, she sat back on her heels.

"So you're linked to it, too," he replied, stunned by this new turn of events. Fintan's ardor died as he considered what it meant.

Inside, the Siren grumbled in protest.

"He's not happy with you," she said with a light laugh. "And to be honest, I feel let down that we aren't recreating the rest of the night."

"Ya want I should get on stage and sing to you?" he teased, attempting to dispel the heaviness associated with his discovery.

"Yes, but probably not a good idea with him close to the surface."

He grimaced. Fuck if he shouldn't have been the one to consider it.

Taryn glanced out the window at the rising sun and held out her hand. "Let's go dig up something to eat."

"I can conjure whatever ya want."

"I know, but we need to keep our hands busy until you come to terms with your inner Keyhole Casanova."

Ignoring her hand, he swept her up in his arms and visualized the kitchen. After sending out a feeler and learning the room was empty, he teleported them. As soon as they arrived, he set her on the long metal table, but she squealed, jumping back into his arms.

"Ohmygod, it's freezing on my bare skin."

"Feck! I wasn't thinkin', love. I'm sorry."

"Hm, well, since you're holding me and it's the place I love best, I won't complain."

Fintan grinned. It amazed him to realize he'd laughed and smiled more with her in the last day and a half than he had in twenty-something years.

"Goddess, I love you, Taryn-Taryn. They'll never be another day gone by that I won't be showin' and tellin' ya it," he promised.

Happiness radiated off her, but he felt her briefest of doubts through their bond, and it pained him.

"Please don't give in to your fear, love," he begged silently.

"I'm doing my best not to," she said, stroking his lower lip with her thumb. "Your sincerity helps."

Fintan closed his burning eyes, blinking back grateful tears. "Thank you."

"I don't ever want you to feel the love is one-sided, because it's not. I love you, Fintan, and that's why I'm so fucking afraid. If this goes south, if it turns out that we don't make it, I'm going to be so damned broken."

"We'll make it." He pressed his forehead to hers. "We're fated and share a bond. And it's unbreakable, *aoibhneas mo croí.*"

"God, I hope so." She kissed him with enough passion to make him forget his fucking name.

He was still trying to gather his scattered wits when she slid down his aroused body and patted his ass.

"Now, make me an omelet while I brew the coffee," she ordered.

"Tea. We drink tea in this country," he said absently, watching her tight little ass swish as she crossed the kitchen.

Mine.

"No, boyo," he told his Siren. "Mine!"

CHAPTER 20

"Fintan?"

Taryn poked his shoulder, waking him from sleep.

"I'm a wee worn out, *aoibhneas mo croí*. But if you give me another hour or two, I'll pleasure ya like—"

"Fintan!"

The urgency in her tone penetrated his sleep-fogged brain, and he sat up. "What—oh, shite! Am I dreamin' then?"

"If you are, I am," she croaked.

At the foot of their bed, Uncle Peter impatiently tapped his foot. He uncrossed his arms as soon as he realized Fintan was awake and focused on him.

"Grand. Now, we've a need to hurry, boyo. Follow me." So saying, his uncle drifted through the closed door.

"Jaysus! What a fuckin' nightmare to wake to!"

Taryn nodded mutely, her attention locked on the door. She was white as the sheet she clutched to her naked breasts. "He was really here, wasn't he?"

"Aye, and he'll be back." Fintan nudged her, hoping to

prompt her into action. "You should dress, Taryn-Taryn. He'll be salty as a sailor when he discovers we haven't hightailed it after him."

"Oh! Right."

With a wary eye on the door, she scrambled up. It took a simple snap of her fingers to clothe herself, and Fintan was sad for it. Naked Taryn was a sight to behold, and he mourned whenever she covered up. Of a certain, he was a horny bastard, but they had years of separation to make up for.

He rose, smiling when he caught her hot gaze eating up his body. "Should I tell Uncle Peter to feck off?"

"I wish, but no. I'll be unable to get off while worrying about him watching us."

"I'm not a feckin' pervert, girl," Peter snapped from behind Fintan, scaring the shite out of him.

"What the fuck, man!" He pointed toward the door. "Are ya after givin' me heart failure?"

A grin transformed his uncle's face from craggy to jovial elf, and his mischievous twinkle said he'd done it on purpose.

"If you ever enter when Taryn's naked again, I'll exorcise your feckin' spirit from the house, yeah?"

"She's always in a naked state, same as you, boyo. You've been at it for two bleedin' days. I've not wanted to disturb ya, knowin' the two of you needed to reestablish your love, but time is of the essence, it is. So get hoppin'."

Taryn's chirp of laughter drew Fintan's gaze.

"Sure, and it's the craic now that you're dressed, but I'm still bare assed with me flute out."

"In my experience, men enjoy their 'flute' hanging in the breeze and don't care if others see it. Probably hoping someone will jump on it and play a few notes."

"Keep your sexy thoughts to a minimum, love, or I'll have a cock-stand before ya know it," Fintan warned within the confines of their bond.

She smirked, damn her, but honored his request. "Women are more modest in nature."

"I've never understood modesty, meself," Peter said. "Nothin' is as grand as a woman's body."

"I'm not so self-critical that I don't believe I'm attractive, but having it all hang out is uncomfortable and dangerous in the wrong company. Thank goodness you're one of the sweet ones." She smiled warmly at Peter and won his uncle's heart in an instant. "I prefer to keep my wares under wraps until I'm in private with my man."

Her eyes shone when she turned them to Fintan, and damned if he didn't want to puff up his chest like Uncle Peter. Shaking off her enchantment, he pulled on his discarded clothes and shoved his feet into trainers. He had a strong suspicion they were in for a hike through the house, although why ghosts weren't inclined to teleport was beyond his comprehension. Someday soon, he'd ask his uncle.

"What's so all-fired important, Peter?" Taryn asked as they hurried to follow him.

"What she means is why the feck couldn't this wait until mornin'?" Fintan clasped her hand, drawing her closer to avoid a table in the darkened hallway.

Her breathy "thank you" almost made him turn back. Every look, touch, sigh, or word she spoke aroused him.

Taryn squeezed his hand, reminding him she'd heard his internal thoughts. *"It's the same for me, Fintan."*

Without slowing, he raised her hand and kissed her knuckles.

Peter halted before a paneled wall on the second-floor landing, shot a covert glance upstairs, then gestured to him to tug a sconce. The exposed passageway was new to Fintan.

"Sure, and I thought I'd found them all," he muttered.

"This old estate still has a few surprises for ya, boyo." Peter ushered them inside the narrow tunnel, peeked his head out to check for goddess knew what once more, then told him to shut the door.

The instant the panel clicked back into place, the cramped space illuminated, revealing a larger room beyond the small entry.

"This is exciting, but why the covert skulking?" Taryn asked.

"Spies, girl. Spies everywhere."

Fintan shared a concerned look with Taryn.

"Is it possible for a spirit to turn insane in the afterlife?" she telegraphed.

"Aye," Peter said. "But I'm not mad."

She gasped, and Fintan's jaw dropped right along with hers.

"You heard her?" he asked hoarsely.

"We're Sullivan's. Sullivans are the original Sirens from the sea gods, my boy. How do you think they communicated underwater? Sign language?" Peter scoffed. "No. They read the minds of others."

"Yeah, I knew we could with family, but not with anyone not sharing our blood."

Peter paused in leading them through the vast chamber and faced them. "You and Taryn can share one mind because of what you are, Fin. You're not destined to be mates for the duration of your lives, and so ya weren't gifted with the bond ya think you have."

The breath left his lungs, and Fintan swayed on his feet. Taryn appeared equally as devastated. Rage followed on the heels of his shock, and he shook his head like a wounded bear.

"Fuck all the way off with ya!" he growled. "What fuckin' game are you and the ancestors playin' this time, Uncle? Because we'll not be part of it. Taryn is the love of me life."

Mine.

"Fintan," she warned, sliding her arm through his and hugging it. "Don't lose your shit, sweetheart. You'll open yourself up to your Siren. I can feel his rage building, too."

.   .   .

FINTAN'S MUSCLES TWITCHED, AND THE SKIN ALONG HIS ARMS rippled. Having heard the Siren's possessive growl, Taryn feared he was in the throes of a transformation. Her heart jumped into her throat.

It was hard to shove aside Peter's claim that they weren't fated mates, like Viv and Damian or Soleil and Trev. Was it true? If not, why would Fintan's uncle push his buttons? Was it to trigger the Siren? If so, why?

She met his considering gaze, and the sick feeling of having her privacy invaded twice in one night sparked her anger. "Stay out of my head. Siren blood-gift or not, I don't like anyone else poking around."

"But not our boyo, yeah?"

"What are you trying to pull, Peter? Because whatever it is, I want you to knock it off. Triggering Fintan's creature is dangerous in the extreme."

"You think you know what he's capable of, but you don't," Peter warned. "In here, he can't hurt me, but he can certainly hurt you."

A shiver of apprehension traveled through her, but she lifted her chin. "He won't."

His crafty expression indicated he knew her bravado was false, and he glanced sharply at Fintan. "She fears ya, boyo."

"I don't!" she denied hotly. "Stop this right now!" Taryn stepped forward, prepared for battle. "I don't know how to beat the hell out of a ghost, but I'm not above trying."

"Me thinks the girl protests too much," he taunted. "That you're afraid of him but don't want him to know."

"I swear to God, I'll—"

The Siren's granite-hard arm encircled her and tugged her back against him. She barely suppressed a scream as his claws swiped the air before her. But it wasn't her the creature wanted to harm.

It was Peter.

Protect.

Mine.

"Good. He's here," he said. "Now, leash your admirer, girl, and follow me."

"What?"

"Fintan wouldn't have released it, and I needed the Siren for this next bit," Peter told her matter-of-factly, showing zero remorse for provoking a dangerous beast. "I knew if they were both angry enough, he'd transform."

A small amount of the Siren's tension eased, and Taryn felt it huff in irritation. Fintan was going to be equally annoyed when he returned.

She pushed at the steel bands encircling her, not budging those solid arms an inch. In fact, he tightened his hold, hunching over her like a bodyguard protecting their charge, and she feared he'd never release her.

Then another scary thing registered—the erection forming against her backside. Like his arms, it was iron hard and growing by the second.

"That thing is going to snap my spine, buddy. Can you rein it in?"

He huffed a laugh, and though gruff, the magical sound relaxed her, causing her to lean back against him.

"Oh, shit," she muttered. Was the power of his voice able to steal her will, or did he put off some type of pheromone able to lull her into submission?

"Mine," he purred.

"Fintan's," she retorted.

Burying his nose in her hair, he inhaled and then rubbed his cheek against hers, ending with a kiss on her temple.

"Love."

Her heart hiccuped.

Were he and Fintan the same? Or were they two different souls crammed together in one body? If the latter, how lonely must it have been all these years, trapped without human contact!

His claws retracted, and his arms loosened. But he didn't free her completely. Instead, he shifted Taryn, lifting her to make her face level with his.

Her jaw gaped. Gone was the mythical-looking creature she'd met the first time, and in his place was a tall, well-built man who bore an astonishing resemblance to Fintan. There were subtle differences in his eye color, hair, and body composition, but he was a handsome fucker.

"Love," he said again.

"Uh, thank you?" What was she supposed to say to a magical monster able to detach her head with a swipe of his wrist?

His overbright eyes crinkled with amusement, and he cocked his head. "Five notes?"

"No! Absolutely not. No way, no how."

Peter's rusty chuckle rang out, attracting the Siren's warning glare.

"You can't kill our audience, buddy. He's already dead." She pitched her voice low. "Also, Fintan might not be so happy I'm receiving orgasms from other guys. Not that the last one wasn't lovely and all."

His gleaming teeth flashed in one of his rare grins, and there was no vampire-ish quality to them like before. "You like?"

"Who wouldn't? But still, not cool to hum a woman into a coma against her will."

With a thoughtful frown, he set her on her feet.

"'Kay."

Her brows shot up. "Wow. You caved pretty fast."

Laughing, he palmed the back of her head and drew her against him. There was no denying the adoration on his face, and a huge part of her felt bad for him. Wrapping her arms around as much of his washboard waist as she could encircle, she hugged him.

"Thank you."

His fingers were tender as they stroked her back, and unexpected tears filled her eyes. She was familiar with loneliness, just like him. Blinking away the evidence of her sorrow, she gazed up at him.

"I can't keep calling you 'buddy.' Do you have a name?"

"Ardghal."

Her heart stopped. Surely she'd heard wrong?

"Pardon?" she croaked.

"Ardghal."

"Bloodstone?" she screeched, making him wince. The blood drained from her head, and she swayed on her feet. "How is it possible? Oh, God! Oh, God!"

CHAPTER 21

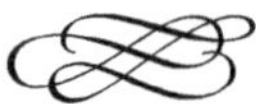

*D*ots appeared before Taryn's eyes, and her vision went dark. Why the hell was she always blacking out in his presence?

Bending his knees, he cupped her face and gave her a gentle shake.

"Stay with me," he urged through their link.

"But you're Bloodstone? Like *the* Bloodstone? How can that be?"

A troubled frown drew his brows down as he stroked her hair. Taryn couldn't say how or why, but she sensed his struggle: a desire to explain and the frustration accompanying it because he couldn't voice it.

"Fintan is going to be *so* pissed," she said, still reeling in shock.

"It's a feckin' freak incident," Peter said beside her.

Taryn patted Ardghal's hands, indicating he should release her, which he appeared reluctant to do.

She raised a brow, challenging his continued claim.

His mouth curled, straightened, then swept upward again, as

if he were fighting his amusement and losing. Finally, he held up his arms and stepped back.

"Thank you." With a stern look at Peter, she said, "I think it's time you explained what you know."

"No need to get your knickers twisted, girl," he grumbled, but he hadn't lost his mischievous sparkle.

"You're a devil. I'd be surprised if you aren't half leprechaun with your devious acts and half-truths," she retorted without heat.

He chuckled along with Ardghal.

Taryn rolled her eyes. "So you needed the original Siren. Why?"

"To access treasures. An enchantment binds them, and since he's the one to cast the spell, he'll be the one to break it."

"Are you sure it was him? Could it have been someone else a century or two later?"

Peter scowled as if she blasphemed. "Don't be soft in the head! Of course he did it."

The Siren huffed a laugh and swatted her on the ass, pitching her forward. Luckily for her, he caught her before she stumbled into a stone wall.

"Not cool, dude."

Proving remorse was beyond his capability, he chuffed.

"This is why women today might find you obnoxious. We don't like men who push us around, especially physically."

He compressed his lips, and she was startled by how human he seemed in this form. Warming up to him was a terrible idea, and she pasted on her I-mean-business expression. "Take us to the treasures, Pete. The sooner we can find them, the sooner Fintan can return."

Mine.

"Fintan's."

They walked for what seemed like hours through twisting tunnels. The torch she'd conjured only lit up five feet in front of her at best, casting eerie shadows on the cave walls. Periodically, Ardghal would reach out and redirect her around a potential hazard. How the hell did he see in the dark? A Siren side effect?

If he weren't so damned protective, she might fear the two of them working in conjunction to get rid of her.

Ardghal chuckled the second she'd considered it.

She'd forgotten he had free access to every blasted thought she had.

"I'm getting tired. How far have we gone? England?"

"Jaysus! Do ya do nothin' but complain, girl?"

"This damned club is heavy, and I'd use it over your thick skull if you were corporeal, you ass."

Ardghal swept her up, scaring a scream and maybe a little pee from her. The torch tumbled from her hand, coming to rest against a stone boulder, and snuffed itself out. Plunged into blackness, she clung to him.

"I never thought I was scared of the dark or claustrophobic, but I might be a little of both," Taryn admitted aloud.

"Carry."

"Well, I guess cavemen are good for some things," she muttered.

His chest shook with his laughter, and she wondered—not for the first time—if all his grunting and posturing was an act.

"Maybe a little," he said.

A rush of desire settled low in her belly.

"And there's your reason why, love."

She closed her eyes against the sensual assault.

"Fucking A! How did the women survive around you? Were they burning their undergarments and fighting over who bedded you if you happened to speak?" She held up a hand. "Don't answer that. I agree. The less talking you do, the better."

"Are you sure?" he asked, pitching his voice low and intimate.

Taryn whimpered. "You're a cruel man."

"Most women loved it when I spoke intimately to them." He sent it

through their mental link, and Taryn was positive his amusement rode the current along with it.

At least he wasn't throwing her into an orgasmic apocalypse —wait a minute! Why the hell was she complaining anyway? What woman—

"Have you forgotten your beloved Fintan already?"

Shit. He was going to kill her.

"The boy's in love. He'll not harm a single hair on your head."

"Boy?" she asked aloud with a scoff. "He's going to kick puppies. He hates being called a boy."

Ardghal grinned.

"Is it getting lighter in here? How am I able to see your face?" she asked.

With a tilt of his chin, he gestured in front of them. Taryn had been so focused inward on their conversation, she'd missed the underground pool.

Tucked beneath a blanket of moss, the grotto shimmered like something stolen straight out of a dream, or a really bougie spa commercial with better lighting. The air was cooler, holding onto the dampness caused by the pool. And the water was a sight to behold. It wasn't just clear, it *glowed*. Not in an aggressive, neon nightclub kind of way, but soft and ethereal, as if the moonlight had decided to take a dip.

The bottom was smooth and likely made the pool deceptively deep. Boulders lounged like ancient sentinels, and their edges were kissed by a silvery luminescence that pulsed, as if the grotto itself was breathing. If magic had a favorite hideout, this would be it—private, pretty, and dangerous enough to make a person's pulse skip. It's the sort of place where visions blur with memories, and the water hums in a minor key when Sirens get too close. Instant atmosphere. Just what a musical muse might order.

And although her elemental magic felt heightened, Tayrn had a strange sense she shouldn't be there. Like this place was too magical for a mere witch, and it might tempt her to do terrible things.

Peter stopped by the pool's lip, his back to them, and he appeared as mesmerised as she was.

Part of her wanted Ardghal to put her down so she could dive beneath the surface and explore every last rock. And speaking of those rocks, they lit up brighter than bottled starlight. With every step closer, another sigil appeared, signaling Taryn's pulse to accelerate. The water pulsed with a rhythm too close to her racing heartbeat, as if the grotto had been waiting for its Siren all along.

Still holding her against his too broad chest, Ardghal hovered at the edge, and the glow from the pool painted silver-blue on the undersides of his throat and the sharp line of his jaw. He was otherworldly.

"I shouldn't be here," she whispered through a suddenly parched throat. "This is all kinds of wrong."

His gaze snapped to hers, as if he'd forgotten she was present and was startled to see her. With the slightest shake of his head, he turned his attention back to the water.

"Ya have to be here, girl. Ardghal needs your magic."

Taryn's heart stalled right along with her lungs, and her bowels were close to becoming liquid, too. She struggled against the Siren's hold. Fighting his granite chest and arms was all but useless, but she wasn't going down like a helpless heroine in a forties movie.

"Be still, woman!"

She froze. Whether compelled or in fear, she couldn't say, but she wasn't taking chances with an irritated seven-foot creature able to drop razor-sharp incisors and sprout claws in a blink. When she could regain use of her limbs and manage somehow not to scream her terror, she touched his jaw.

"Please don't do this, Ardghal. You said you loved me. That's not stealing my magic and leaving me for dead."

He quirked a brow.

She dropped her arm.

"Yeah, I can see how that might work for psychos, but you don't strike me as the lunatic type." Taryn gave him a sickly smile. "I mean, sure, I haven't known you long, but you seem like a good guy. Kind. Generous with orgasms."

The corners of his eyes crinkled, and those hypnotic orbs glowed with laughter.

Feeling foolish, she glanced at Peter, who was staring at her like she'd just escaped the loony bin and was still bound in a straitjacket.

"What are ya on about, girl?" He shook his head. "Today's youth," he said in disgust.

Maybe she'd streamed one too many episodes of the popular stalker show. The guy's love interests tended to end up in a clear box in the basement or dead. And after Morcant, perhaps Taryn was leery of men claiming to love her.

"I should've killed him," Ardghal growled.

Would it have been an easy feat for him to kill an Arcane Devourer? The fantasy was nice. A shiver took her, but it wasn't sexual. It was one of appreciation for a protector, which was odd since she'd painted him with a potential-serial-killer brush.

With a sardonic smile, he set her on her feet. "This grotto neutralizes my voice's ability to control others when I wish. We can speak freely without you worrying about death. *La petite mort* or otherwise."

"I wasn't worried," she muttered, avoiding direct eye contact.

He chuckled.

"Oh-kaaay. So!" She clapped her hands together, wincing when the over-loud noise resounded. "Sorry. Um, can someone tell me why an uber-powerful Siren needs my magic in a dark cave in the middle of the night?"

"It's quarter seven in the mornin', and it takes two of ya to light the sigils," Peter said.

A glance showed they were already lit. "Uh, Peter…"

"They won't stay illuminated if you leave, love." Ardghal tipped up her chin and smiled in the face of her confusion. "Long ago, I brought you here to bury important artifacts. Together, we locked them beneath the earth's surface, hiding them from others who would use them for nefarious reasons."

Annndddd she was back to believing him insane. Great.

"I hate to break it to you, Ari, but I've never met you before yesterday. And I certainly haven't—"

He silenced her with a finger on her lips. "You were born again. What you would call re-in-car—"

She shoved his hand away. "Reincarnation, and I know what it means. But you're a few Froot Loops shy of a full bowl, buddy."

Tilting his head, as if studying her for a way to get his point across, Ardghal watched her.

"You might not know what that means. How about a few threads short of a sweater? No? Don't have all your dogs on one leash?"

He raised his brows.

"Older saying might be better. Let's try no grain in the silo." She tapped her temple and gave him a commiserating look.

His lips twitched, but he remained silent.

"Okay, I'll bite. Who do you believe I was?"

"Your name was Elizabeth, and you were my wife."

Wife? Did Sirens take brides? Was that something else she needed to worry about in addition to his "mine" bullshit? Nope, nope. All the nopes. She was going to need an adultier adult than either of them. Preferrably one that didn't reside at Batshit Manor.

His expression darkened, and Taryn had an oh-fuck moment, having momentarily forgotten he could hear ever damned thought in her head—mental brick wall or no.

"You *are* mine. Were. First."

"And what about Fintan?" she snapped. "You keep conveniently forgetting about him."

"I could kill him if that would make you feel better," he replied silkily, with menace in his narrowed eyes.

Her knees went weak.

Sensing her distress, Ardghal sighed and guided her to a nearby boulder, then eased her down with a hand on her shoulder. "Apologies, love."

He squatted in front of her and wiped away a rogue tear. His fingertips on her skin shouldn't have felt so soft, so tender, and yet, they matched the sweet look he gave her.

"You recognized me, there in that pub, Taryn," he said. "My voice."

"No, it was Fintan. He was the one on stage, not you."

"We are the same. His music, his voice, it's mine."

Shaking her head, she scrunched her eyes closed and covered her ears. The idiotic movement was laughable. With direct access to people's minds, Ardghal didn't require uncovered ears. But Taryn didn't want to hear any more of this nonsense. Yes, she believed in reincarnation, but it was Fintan's soul that hers had recognized, not Ardghal's.

He sighed in frustration and shifted away, tempting Taryn into peeking to see where he'd gone.

He'd selected a spot beside her, but she refused to acknowledge him.

Again, he waited her out.

It appeared Ardghal was the master of patience.

"Only when it comes to you, love," he said absently. A flickering in the pool pulled his focus. "Dissent between us will close the sigils. They require our souls in harmony."

"Who made up that bullshit rule?"

"You did." He whipped back to look at her, and his gaze bore into her. "You've always had a measure of self-preservation when it came to my power." Holding up a hand, he smiled warmly. "No need to defend the action. You were smart to."

"I wasn't going to defend it. I *intended* to say, stop saying it was me. It wasn't." Sure, she didn't want to piss him off, because like his wife, she possessed a measure of self-preservation. Yet hers was likely ten times that of Elizabeth's. Taryn had major trust issues.

"They're ingrained," he said dryly. "I had the devil of a time getting you to trust me the first time."

"If there's a way to murder you, I'm going to take it," she growled, frustrated by his continued insistence that she was Elizabeth.

Ardghal surprised her with his deep laughter. When he sobered, he smiled at her with great affection.

"Should I not say yours was Elizabeth's favorite threat?" he teased.

"Ugh!"

"To answer your question, Fintan in human form, is also me. Reincarnated from the man I was. He chooses to deny it, but he can't when the Siren takes over. That's when I'm in charge."

"One soul, split personalities. Great. I'm back to the whole psycho thing."

"Would you like me to restore your memories of our time together?" he offered, clasping her hand.

Did she? That would mean she believed the ridiculous story of being Mrs. Bloodstone. And if it was the case, why did that fucking necklace hate her so much?

"Objects cannot have emotions, love."

"It doesn't like when I touch it."

"There's a reason for that. You stole it from my neck, where its magic thrived, and hid it. It's designed to protect me."

"Not me. *Elizabeth*," she stressed. "And why would she do that?"

"So I would die."

CHAPTER 22

Fintan was enraged. Trapped, he was privy to Ardghal and Taryn's conversation, and he despised how uncomfortable the creature was making her. If the bastard wasn't careful, he'd scare her away for good, and Fintan couldn't abide that. He needed her in his life, more than air to breathe or food to eat, she was essential to him, body and soul.

The Siren had been spouting shite about Ardghal for as long as Fintan could remember, claiming it knew where those bleedin' artifacts were to boot the ancestors out of his head. But he'd ruthlessly ignored the creature, believing it was a power grab and holding it in check whenever it tried to break free. In addition to pining for Taryn, Fintan hadn't truly desired another woman, so he'd assumed denying himself sex meant denying the Siren, hoping to weaken the beast.

It didn't.

Or if it did, he'd fucked up when he broke his two-and-a-half decade drought. Fintan's fear was born primarily from the skill with which Ardghal could ease her objections. By waiting her out, he gave her the space she needed to see things from his perspective. One of Taryn's best traits was her capacity to reason. If allowed to draw her own conclusions, she'd weigh the information against the facts and see the truth of a matter in due course.

Such was the case now.

Displaying equal amounts of charm and respect, Ardghal fed her information, thereby gaining ground. Taryn's main reason to resist his sway was Fintan. Caring for him held her back.

"I could kill him if that would make you feel better," his creature had said.

Jaysus! Could he? Fintan hoped not. If they were the same person born centuries apart, it didn't seem likely without Ardghal killing himself. Yet, they were of two separate minds at the moment, so perhaps the possibility existed that should he destroy the human, the Siren would remain.

Learning about the sigils taught Fintan one thing, though. His Siren was indeed Ardghal. He hadn't known about the grotto or the artifacts it claimed were beneath it. If the spell was truly cast in the past, and if Peter was taking it as gospel, it must be so.

"Let me out, ya feckin' bastard!" Fintan shouted. He hoped that if he could cloud the creature's mind with noise, it would have no choice but to release him.

"It didn't work in reverse when I tried it. It won't work for you," Ardghal replied dryly. *"Calm yourself, friend."*

"Look, I'll do whatever ya want," he lied. *"Just let me speak to Taryn."*

"Siren's sense intent."

Fecking grand.

"Be patient. It will be over soon."

That's what he was deathly afraid of.

Fintan's attempts at freedom amused Ardghal. Now the shoe was on the other foot, so to speak, his other half was bargaining as if his entire world depended on it. Perhaps he was right, and it did. The future remained to be seen. Ironic for a Seer, but still.

"Why would Elizabeth want you to die?" Taryn croaked, bringing Ardghal back to the present.

"She was tired. Of war, of losing family members and friends, of life." He shrugged and stared at the bottom of the pool. "Of me," he added whisper-soft. "My magic kept her alive longer than any witch would normally live. She wished to end her suffering."

"Why didn't you do it for her? Why draw out her pain?" she asked curiously.

Wonderful question. But Ardghal didn't want to examine the answers too closely. They all boiled down to one, anyway. "I loved Elizabeth and couldn't imagine life without her in it."

Understanding dawned, and Taryn touched his wrist. "You let her take the necklace!"

Meeting her incredible eyes, he absorbed the comfort of her compassion without taking anything else. If he could help it, he'd never steal a drop of her magic.

But he *would* borrow it to open the grotto.

"I did. What was life without her?"

"Fuck, that's romantic," she breathed with stars in her eyes.

"Is it?" he asked softly.

He didn't know anymore. At the time, it had felt right to give her what she wanted, but his soulless energy had drifted around those cursed halls above until Fintan's birth, when it fused with his body. Before then, the days had stretched endlessly, one into the next, until he was on the precipice of madness. And perhaps he'd stepped over the ledge.

Hope came in the form of his soul's rebirth. Or rather, part of his soul. The other half had stayed with Elizabeth, where it belonged. Ardghal had slept for most of the boy's growing-up years, when suddenly the young man's interest in music had sparked life into him. It wasn't until he saw Elizabeth, as Taryn, standing in the audience, that all the missing pieces of his soul clicked back into place, complete once more.

It was also when he remembered he had a mission to perform. But those bloody busybodies controlling Fintan had other ideas. They'd facilitated Peter's death to keep the boy away from Taryn, following it with lies about her role in Fintan's eventual demise.

Fools, the lot of them.

Her restlessness pulled Ardghal from the past.

She shifted, putting space between them. Her wariness sank in, and he cursed himself for an eejit. Without being party to his thoughts, she was subjected to his angry energy and didn't understand that it wasn't directed at her.

"Let me explain." For the next ten minutes, he told how he'd come to be reborn as Fintan's Siren and how the so-called ancestors manipulated everyone to maintain charge of the Seer's ability. "With it, they control the witch community, dousing any fires able to consume them."

"They played him? Using his gift to anticipate danger to their positions? Is that what you're saying?" Her outrage was glorious. The fierce protectiveness of Fintan was a replica of Elizabeth's for him in the early days, when she believed his path was the right one.

"Yes. Just as they played my wife."

Ardghal felt the hammering of her heart through their connection.

Bewildered by the past turn of events leading to his death, she shook her head. "I don't get it," she admitted.

"Elizabeth's brother and father were forming a new council. You may know it as the Authority."

"Holy shit!"

Her cursing grated on his nerves. Modern women sprinkled profanity in their conversation like a heavy-handed chef with spices. It was unseemly. But he had to remember, things were different in this century. People didn't understand manners or the class pecking order in the way they once had. Women weren't soft in his day, but they followed society's rules. In Fintan's shadow, he'd had years to get used to it, but it made him feel ancient and like he never would. Shoving his annoyance away with a resigned sigh, he waited for her to get her disbelief under control.

Taryn rose and crossed to the pool's edge.

Except for her modern clothing, she could be Elizabeth. Her wild mane, with its blend of titian auburn and mocha brown streaked through with natural white-blonde, was identical to his wife's, though not in length. Elizabeth's hair had flowed to her waist, as he preferred it. Still, the soft features, innate kindness, and intelligence were all there, highlighted by the shimmering blue from the water. So was her rebelliousness.

Taryn's brow was puckered as if deep in thought, and he ignored the buzzing in his mind. It comprised her processing of his story and Fintan's demands for release. Eventually, she would come to the proper conclusion.

Peter had been remarkably quiet since they'd reached the grotto, and for that, he was grateful. The man's sarcastic nature would test the patience of a saint, and Ardghal was no bloody saint!

"Peter, I know why I wish to access the artifacts, but I'd like to know why *you* do," he said.

Taryn turned, waiting for Peter's reply. Her mind was racing, and although more input might be overload, it was necessary.

"I'm after shuttin' down the ancestors for good. For what they did to me, and what they're trying to do to me nephew," he confessed.

"But if they're in league with the Authority—and that's what I'm getting from all this—how do we take them down?" she asked.

"We don't," Ardghal said grimly. "Not without your Aether, and I suspect it's not something he's willing to do on a whim."

"Did you meet Damian when you were alive?" she asked, curious about his distasteful expression. "He's the best of men, so I don't understand what you might have against him."

"No. But I met the Enchantress in the early days, before she began her campaign of destruction by stealing and murdering others for their magic."

"But isn't that what Sirens, Succubi, and Incubi do?" she countered with a raised brow.

"Touché." He nodded his acknowledgement. "But our demon form was never meant for one like a witch, and the Darkness was unleashed in the world because of it."

"Wait, what?" She sat down hard, tipped sideways, and barely managed to avoid plunging into the pool. "Are you saying the Darkness that infected Isolde de Thorne was from a Succubus or Incubus?"

"Incubus, and yes. But it didn't infect her first. Through blood-magic, another stole the power from one of my relatives, enslaving and starving them until they were too weak to survive." He clasped his hands, letting the doubled fist hang between his knees, and stared at it for a long minute. "Magic like ours is too much for a mundane witch to possess."

"Mundane?" Ardghal had a way of making others seem inconsequential.

"I don't mean to," he said with a grimace. "I beg your pardon."

"Continue with the story. How did the Darkness break free to exist on its own?"

"It tempted its new host beyond human possibility, driving the man beyond the brink of insanity. It used whatever tool it had in its arsenal: fear, greed, lust, paranoia."

For a heart-wrenching moment, Ardghal seemed lost in the past, and the urge to draw him back to her was strong. He visibly shook himself and met her worried gaze.

"I'm fine." His tight smile couldn't camouflage his sadness.

"Did you know that particular Siren, before he was an Incubus?"

"I did. It was my brother."

"I'm sorry." Her sympathy was more than a platitude. Taryn physically and mentally connected to his pain. Having lost her parents at a young age, she was familiar with loss. Learning about his wife and sibling allowed her to view him in a different light and triggered her desire to comfort him. He wasn't the monster her research claimed, nor the one Fintan had feared.

"Thank you." Ardghal cleared his throat. "With regard to the Darkness, the host grew fevered, his body unable to sustain that level of magic without burning itself out, and he perished, freeing the Darkness to find another host."

"Merlin's balls! That's next-level scary."

"Indeed. But how do you know Merlin? Is he still around?"

"What?" It took her longer than it should've to recognize he was teasing her. "Funny. Go back to the Enchantress, please."

He grinned and gamely continued. "My understanding is that Isolde's husband was infected before she realized the threat and exorcised it from him. Her mistake was absorbing it herself. Despite her Aether status and the power she could wield, the Demon was too strong. Too crafty, even for her."

"The Darkness was why she went insane, right? Its need to feed forced her to do those dastardly acts?"

"Yes."

"Does that mean you're stronger than Damian, than any Aether?" she asked, wonder rounding her eyes.

"I am with the amulet."

Dread churned in the pit of her stomach. "And you want me to help you draw up those magical artifacts why, exactly?"

"To defeat Odessa and get it back."

"And then?" Taryn croaked, sensing his final intent.

"Burn the witch community to the ground."

Her stomach bottomed out. "But I'm a witch."

"You're the exception, love."

There would need to be an obscene number more exceptions if he wanted her cooperation. Picturing Fintan's bedroom, she closed her eyes to teleport. Ardghal's steel bands encircled her and held her in place.

"I can't let you leave. Not before you understand."

"I'll never understand!" she shouted, viciously shoving his marble-carved chest.

He didn't budge, and the only thing she gained was a tweaked wrist.

"Elizab—"

"*Taryn*. Taryn Stephens, *not* Elizabeth!" she snapped.

"Okay, Taryn-Taryn it is."

Her heart pinged. "No! You don't get to use Fintan's endearments. You return him to me, right now. If you don't, I'll blow up this fucking grotto with you in it!"

Clapping sounded from across the pool. "Here, here, you feisty girl!"

"Odessa," Ardghal hissed under his breath. He released Taryn and swept her behind him to face Fintan's aunt.

"Teleport to your Aether and do it immediately," he told Taryn through their bond. *"She'll kill you if you don't."*

"I'll kill her if she does," Odessa replied aloud.

Taryn almost wet her pants. Either way, her life expectancy was nil, but she'd be damned if she was leaving Fintan.

"Fuck," she muttered.

"My thoughts exactly," Ardghal murmured. "If it counts for anything, Fintan is voting for you to escape, love."

"He's not the boss of me."

Other than a snort, he didn't reply.

"Bloodstone, am I correct you've returned for good?" Odessa purred as she sauntered around the pool's edge. "It's why the necklace drew me here tonight, by the way. It sensed your magic."

"Well, it *is* mine. I'd be much obliged if you returned it," he said, as if they were chums instead of foes.

Odessa's laugh rang out, but there was no real humor in it.

"Okay, we're in harmony," Taryn said in a low voice. "Do what you need to get your weapons from the grotto."

The sigils lit, catching Odessa's attention. She frowned. "Your journal hinted at a treasure, but never stated the location. I suspect this pool was charmed by you?"

"You assumed correctly," he replied. Putting a hand behind him, he pressed Taryn backward as he retreated a step for each of Odessa's. "Far enough, woman."

"Not nearly enough," the elderly Sullivan boomed as she began the metamorphosis from human to beast.

Having anticipated her action, Ardghal dragged Taryn against him and clamped his hands over her ears. *"Muteion!"* The single-word spell was foreign, but she recognized its immediate effect as a gel substance filled and cushioned her ear canals like high-quality earplugs.

Odessa's banshee-like cry was bone-chilling, and the unholy wail ricocheted off the cavern walls, haunting and unrelenting. Ardghal's quick thinking had saved Taryn from ruptured eardrums, but she didn't have the wits left to thank him. What came next was a morbidly captivating nightmare. One moment, Odessa was a cane-wielding crone dripping arrogance. The next, she towered at seven feet, all hellfire, hunger, and fully awakened Succubus cloaked in deathly allure.

CHAPTER 23

As their kind went, Odessa wasn't the ugliest Ardghal had seen, but she was damned close. The infusion of magic transformed her body, leaching her dyed hair of color and turning it to the palest white. Her beady eyes glowed an unholy red, and the horns that emerged from her temples to curl skyward were harder than bone, encased in withered leather. A second set of arms grew from her ribcage and were the most useful tool a demon could possess. Long claws sprouted where her fingers should be, and her skin developed a thick rusted-metal veneer as her cells shifted from flesh to protective scales. Her scapula took on the new shape of wings, pushing through the scaly barrier. Resembling a bat, they were human-sized and could encase her entire body twice.

Slack-jawed, Taryn was frozen, mesmerized by the sight, making her the perfect victim should Odessa target her. He gave her a little shake.

"Loan me your magic, love, so that I might defeat her."

His request woke her to the danger.

"Bring Fintan back," Taryn replied.

"Are ya mad, girl?" Peter hissed as he appeared beside her. "She'll just murder ya both faster."

"Odessa wants Ardghal's power, and she can't get it if he isn't here," she snapped back.

Admittedly, Taryn's idea wasn't the worst Ardghal had ever heard, but a Sullivan was stronger in Siren form. And as the first and only of his kind, he was the strongest. Yet his goal wasn't to fight today if he could avoid it. His mission was to take down the Authority and neutralize Fintan's fake "ancestors." But he couldn't do that if he were mortally wounded.

"How many of Elizabeth's journals did you read, Odessa?" he asked as she glided within striking distance.

"Only the one." Her voice was serpentine, as was the calculating gleam in eyes tracking his every movement. "The others disappeared along with the necklace years before I learned of your existence," she said, ending with a hiss as her forked tongue struck her teeth.

Peter surged forward, and if it was to protect him or Taryn, the man was misguided. In his ghostly shape, he was useless as anything but a distraction. But perhaps that was his plan, because he asked, "And how was it ya got your grimy hands on the one, sister? Sure, and I scattered them to the winds when I became the Seer."

A sneer curled her lips. "Did you forget the wealth I possess, fool?" she boomed.

"*You* possess?" Taryn sidestepped Ardghall, avoiding him as he lunged for her. "The bulk of the Sullivan holdings belong to Brenna, Narissa, or Fintan. Not you." She grinned. "But we can easily settle this, right? Peter, why don't you be a dear and fetch your niece and grandniece? They should be part of this discussion, I think."

With a conspiratorial touch of his finger to the side of his nose, he disappeared.

"And then there were three," Taryn said. Hands on hips and

the light of battle in her eyes, she lifted her chin in challenge. "What is it you *want*, Odessa? What will avoid bloodshed and your ultimate demise?"

Ardghal almost choked on his tongue.

Odessa actually might've, considering her purple complexion.

"Ah, Fintan, my boy. She sure is the perfect woman, isn't she?"

"Aye, but watch my aunt. She's as dangerous as a vipers' den."

Her eyes, flat and glinting like polished stones, locked on him. Cold and unblinking, they spiked Ardghal's unease. Odessa's head swiveled to measure Taryn's worth as a magical meal, and his fear coiled at the base of his spine. His back grew clammy. Was the cunning bitch baiting him, or was the lure of Taryn's untapped power too mouthwatering to resist?

As if sensing the dangerous atmosphere brought on by the subtle shift in Odessa's stance, Taryn inched closer to him. "Uh, you can't just"—she twiddled her fingers—"like her?"

"If I bring forth my Incubus without the necklace, it will kill everyone present. You're friends included."

Without removing his focus from Odessa, he subtly gestured toward the far side of the cave where Peter had returned with Brenna, Eoin, Narissa, and Creed in tow.

"Why the blasted fool brought those deadweights is a question for the ages," Ardghal said. "Brenna and Narissa are backup enough."

"They're already shifting," Taryn murmured.

"They recognize the threat, and their protective instincts are engaged," he replied. "It may be good for us all."

Odessa honed in on the newcomers and licked her lips.

A single thunderous clap from Ardghal snapped her attention back to him. If she let her hunger cloud her mind, she'd become more dangerous than she already was. Siren females were lethal when protecting a mate. A battle between the Sullivan women? It would be nothing short of catastrophic.

The tentacle struck without warning.

It whipped toward Taryn and woke Ardghal's instinct to protect. Grabbing her, he twisted midair to shield her from the blow. The impact against his ribs was brutal, otherworldly, and hurled them both into the pool.

The cold rush of water flooded his mouth and stoked his rage. He'd grown soft and complacent in the shadows while Fintan toiled around this estate, hiding from the outside world.

No more.

With a few strong kicks, he surfaced. Taryn emerged beside him, looking far less rattled. Then again, water was her elemental magic, so drowning was unlikely.

But she was enraged.

So was he.

Their combined energy crackled like a live wire, and the water responded. Around them, it churned. At its center, a whirlpool formed, tossing them like dinghies lost in a hurricane.

"Control yourself," he barked.

"It's not me," she hollered back. "The water, it's aliv—"

A wave crashed over her head, sucking her downward.

Ardghal didn't hesitate. Nor did he think about transitioning; it happened instantaneously when he fell in. His legs fused into a mighty monofin, and with a swish of his tail, he cut through the current. He found Taryn fast and, clamping an arm around her, launched them upward. With one explosive surge, Taryn was airborne, flying toward the far side of the grotto.

Eoin and Creed were already waiting to catch her. Their intervention prevented her from slamming into the boulders along the shore.

Satisfied she was safe, Ardghal turned away. Swift and purposeful, he sliced beneath the surface, fury tightening every muscle. He was ready to tear Odessa's mutated head from her shoulders.

A large portion of his anger was self-directed. He should've seen it coming. Should've warned Fintan that his aunt had a hidden motive for retrieving the necklace. But it hadn't seemed important. The amulet would only work for him, its creator.

Narissa's and Brenna's Sirens had Odessa cornered, fierce and relentless in their mission to stop her.

But it wouldn't last.

She'd fed recently.

Odessa's skin was rich ebony, taut and gleaming with vitality. She was fully charged.

Every time the Sirens advanced, she fended them off with a vicious tentacle strike or a razor-sharp swipe. If she meant to kill them, Narissa and Brenna would already be bleeding out on the cavern floor.

When her glowing eyes flicked from him to the overhead stalactites, he guessed her intent.

He twisted toward Taryn, trying to catch her attention. She and the men were huddled together, with Creed alert and ready.

"Teleport!"

Bless her, she reacted swiftly. Latched onto Eoin and Creed, she vanished just as the first note of Odessa's screech rang out. There was no time to be grateful for Taryn's fast action. He barely had time to brace as the cavern wall behind him rumbled.

Odessa, the clever bitch, had learned to weaponize sound. With surgical precision, she directed her voice to collapse the grotto ceiling.

As the first stalactite plummeted, Ardghal dove deep. His merman body could survive for hours beneath the water, but he hoped like hell someone survived the Succubus and came to dig him out.

"I HAVE TO GO BACK!" TARYN CRIED. "ARDGHAL, HE—"

"Ardghal? Who the hell is—"

"Fintan's Siren," she said, cutting Creed off.

"Fuck that!" Eoin said. "Past experience has taught me to let the Sullivan's fight that shite out. We're no match for those bleedin' creatures."

"You don't understand, Eoin. Ardghal's trapped! I can feel it."

"Trapped?"

"Aye," Peter said, appearing beside her. "There was a cave-in."

"Jaysus!" Eoin grabbed his chest. "I'll be askin' ya to stop doing that, man. Me feckin' heart can't take it."

Creed fisted his hands, and probably would've grabbed the wiry old ghost if he could. "Cave-in? What about Narissa and Brenna?"

"Nah, just the ceilin' above the pool. Me sister's monster is a wily one, able to use her voice as a weapon."

Taryn clutched her head as Ardghal's pain-filled thoughts clouded her mind. "He's pinned under the weight, injured. Guys, I think his fin is crushed."

"You have a direct line to Fintan's Siren now?" Creed asked sharply.

She nodded. "But he's not speaking. It's more like sensation, and he's in so much pain."

"Those rocks weigh a ton." Turning to Eoin, he said, "Do you have the same ability? To speak to Brenna's?"

"I've never tried, though Brenna and I do share a thought-bond."

"Maybe ours is stronger because Ardghal was the first of his kind?"

"Not the first Siren, those existed centuries before him. But he's the first Siren hybrid," Peter corrected. "Feckin' Odessa is intent on killing the man, but she doesn't understand she can't. Not in the way she thinks."

"I don't understand." Taryn shook her head. "He can die. He told me Elizabeth took the amulet and left him in the grotto."

"Aye, but he willed it. His heart was broken." Peter waved a ghostly hand. "None of that's important, girl. The truth of the matter is Bloodstone's necklace isn't for Odessa. It isn't for anyone but Fintan. It's come home to the one who owns it and can only be operated by him."

"So all of the fighting is for nothing?" Taryn's frustration was at a boiling point. That crazy-ass bitch would kill them all for a useless cause. "Why is she doing this?"

"Sure, and if I had to guess, it's because she's afraid of dyin' and goin' to the Netherworld. Me sister has a lot to answer for."

"Sounds like it makes her even more dangerous," Creed said grimly.

"Yes. Okay, I may know how to get the necklace."

Eoin conjured a tray of drinks. "We're all ears, love. But ya best make it quick, yeah?"

"Yeah." She downed the whiskey in a single gulp and slammed the glass down with a gasping cough. The burn centered her for what was to come, what she needed to do, and what she might lose.

Her life.

But Fintan and, by extension, Ardghal, were too important.

"I'm going to attack Odessa," she said.

"You're as mad as a toddler with feckin' glitter and no bleedin' adult supervision!"

Eoin's aghast expression amused her, but her laughter was in short supply.

"Maybe, but hear me out. If I can distract her, you and Creed can don dive gear and help Ardghal. You're an earth elemental, Eoin. You might have an easier time moving the stalactites pinning him."

"And you're a water elemental," Creed said. "I should be the one to distract her while you and Eoin combine your powers to free Ardghal."

"But—"

"No buts." He gave her a roguish grin. "Damian chose me as a Sentinel for a reason, Taryn. I've got mad fighting skills."

"I thought it was because you were a thief?" she countered with an arched brow.

"That hurt."

She rolled her eyes. "Someone needs to call Damian. He—"

"Sure, and he won't come here, not even for you, girl," Peter said with a longing look at the empty glasses. "Ardghal can steal his power when he's in full command of the necklace."

"I thought an Aether's ability could only be stolen if they are murdered, or something like that?"

Eoin picked up on Peter's message first. "As the original Siren hybrid, he's more powerful than most, yeah? Is it that Damian fears him?"

"Damian fears no one!" Taryn said loyally. "If he won't come, it's for a reason. Like Fintan, he's able to see the immediate future. And as the Oracle, Sabrina would tell him all potential outcomes."

The men remained silent, considering what she'd said.

"But I guess we do this alone," she concluded with dread burning her guts. "Whoever survives may want to get the Healer here. I've a feeling we're going to need Jordan in short order."

CHAPTER 24

From atop a boulder at the water's edge, Taryn hesitated to follow Eoin into the pool. She had a bird's-eye view of the fight and it looked to be going sideways.

If Creed were a prizefighter, he'd have lost the championship belt to a knockout in the first round. The vicious blow caught him unawares when he went to Narissa's aid as she went down. The crack of her head against the ground was sickening, and despite his claim of not caring, Creed did. A whole helluva lot. In his rush to check on Narissa, he exposed himself to danger, and Odessa quickly took advantage.

If asked, Taryn couldn't explain how she understood the Succubus's intended move, but she felt it clear to her bones. Closing her eyes, she drew water from the grotto. She reshaped it into five-inch-thick, foot-long spikes by changing the molecular structure of the water to ice.

She'd created five before Brenna's Siren trilled a warning and launched herself at Odessa's back. And when Taryn looked up, it was to see the Succubus bearing down on her.

"Stay back, Brenna. She's too strong," she hollered.

Her warning served to fuel Brenna's anger, and she attacked with vigor. The precious extra minute gave Taryn time to construct two more ice stakes.

But Odessa was done being nice. With one of her lethal tentacles, she tossed Brenna into the cavern wall, stunning her to stillness.

Pulling up her element, Taryn directed the water to chuck her icy weapons at Odessa. But she only managed five before she was facing down seven feet of enraged beast.

"Has anyone ever said that you resemble Ursula from *The Little Mermaid*? But only if she lost a fight with a weed whacker and her glam team quit halfway through," she taunted.

Odessa hissed. Her unwavering, sly-eyed stare slithered under Taryn's skin and stayed there.

Digging in her heels, she held onto the last dregs of her courage. "No? It's just a tragic coincidence?"

"You are insignificant, you fool!" Odessa raged.

Taryn pointed with one of her stakes. "See! That's what I'm talking about right there. I bet you'd manage a passable rendition of *Poor Unfortunate Souls* if you weren't such a tightass." Summoning all the magic she possessed from a cellular level, she threw the deadly ice shard.

Once again, the Succubus effortlessly batted it away.

"I'm going to enjoy killing you, girl," Odessa said in her creepy-ass serpentine way.

A cold fist clenched around Taryn's heart. Was Fintan slipping away? Fear for him reignited her fighting spirit, and she hurled her final stakes.

She never noticed the extra limb. Hell, she didn't know the bitch could sprout so many! But one lashed out, and the fucking thing fileted her like a trout. It sliced through her abdomen with its claw extruding from her back. Sheer agony wrenched a scream from her throat.

Odessa grinned, savage and gleeful. The sadistic cow yanked

Taryn, prepared to deliver the kiss of death. She managed a token resistance, gurgling a feeble protest.

"Did you really think to best me, child?"

Fetid breath gagged her.

"Ursula called. She wanted her look back, but then she realized you're only the budget version—ahhh!"

She shrieked as Odessa twisted her claw, shredding organs, muscle, and bone.

Focus, Taryn. Please, for the love of—

"Why focus?" the Succubus purred. "Ah, you forgot I can read your mind."

The hideously forked tongue slithered between Anglerfish teeth and licked the blood from Taryn's lips.

Internal bleeding. Never good.

Dizziness assailed her, and a haze blanketed her mind. She fought the feeling.

It was now or never.

She blanked her thoughts, gripped the amulet, and ripped it off Odessa's neck in one smooth move. With the last burst of elemental magic, she flung it into the water's waiting embrace, commanding the current to rush it away.

"Find Ardghal," she breathed as one final whisper.

ARDGHAL'S BODY JERKED. ONCE IN RESPONSE TO THE WATER encapsulating his amulet, and again to the abrupt snapping of Taryn's and his bond.

Above him, the remains of the ceiling were illuminated, and Eoin systematically disintegrated the boulders. Through the shimmering waters, Bloodstone's necklace fell, drifting ever closer as Odessa's tentacle chased it.

A gap in the stones provided a view of the scene above water, and with dread in his heart, he looked upward.

A careless toss of Taryn's lifeless body proved Odessa

considered her nothing more than yesterday's garbage. The pain was a thousand times worse than Elizabeth's defection, and it lacerated his soul. It wasn't only his grief or rage; it was Fintan's. Odessa now had to contend with their mindless fury, animalistic in nature, and beyond anything but a need to destroy.

The amulet's chain was almost within Ardghal's grasp, and he curled forward, elongating his arm to reach it first. As his fingers brushed the metal, electricity shot through him, straight along his spine to his tail, healing the damaged vertebrae, muscle, tendons, and tissue. He pressed the disc against his breastbone and welcomed the current. His cells quickly absorbed the amplified elemental magic through the water and earth supporting him.

He was born to a full blooded Siren princess in this grotto's water, and his first physical incarnation died here. The amulet had been crafted by a loving father, Bloodstone. A demigod, who, by hanging the chain around Ardghal's neck, had gifted him the ability to walk on land. Father had allowed him to bridge the divide between the two worlds, sea and soil.

Ardghal was the only *Fiorghin Scairdeanach*.

The Trueborn Surge.

And he was back to full strength.

The energy didn't stop at healing. It surged higher, resonating like a pulse through the grotto, through the walls, the water, the bones beneath. The power of the amulet embraced him and reached inward, where the threads of Fintan's soul still clung to what they had once shared.

For the first time since his death, Ardghal stood alone inside himself.

Whole.

Singular.

Their split wasn't gentle. It was fucking brutal.

Beside him, a muffled gurgle sounded, and he recognized it

as Fintan's scream. It echoed through their bond as it snapped and tore like a sail in a storm.

And then, silence.

Ardghal's jaw clenched, and for a sickening moment, he feared the worst. He sent a feeler through the water, searching for Fintan's heartbeat.

Nothing. The worst had happened.

Reaching inward, he withdrew vitality from his core and pushed it into the chest of the sightless man beside him. The chambers of Fintan's heart pulsed once, twice, and on the third beat, he gasped and sputtered as he sucked in water. When he would've struggled to the surface, Ardghal gripped the back of Fintan's neck.

"Breathe, boy. You've Siren blood. The water is your friend, don't fight it."

Panic receded from Fintan's eyes as he processed the words. "We're separate?" he asked.

"Yes," Ardghal said roughly.

He didn't mourn their separation, because he'd always known it had to come. They had walked as one for too long. Now, there would be two princes to rule again.

His fingers closed over the Bloodstone amulet, fully fused to his chest.

No chain.

No clasp.

It pulsed like a second heart.

And the grotto responded.

Stone fell away. Magic bent to him. And he rose, not swimming but ascending, propelled by elemental reverence.

As his head breached the water's surface, Odessa turned.

Her expectant expression froze as fear claimed its place, and she faltered.

Peter had done him a service by scattering the journals—each laced with ancestral spells—to the four corners of the earth. His action, resulting from his gift as Seer with knowledge of this future event, had prevented his sister's power grab.

The Siren rite of power reclamation was always intended to restore to Ardghal what he'd lost. With his amplified water magic, the resonance-based spells, and ancestral bonds afforded to him by his lineage, he once again possessed what he needed to destroy his enemies. Odessa among them.

"Taryn!" Fintan's anguished cry filled the space and echoed off the rocks.

But Ardghal couldn't let himself be distracted. He had a job to finish.

"Come to me," he compelled Odessa. Into his voice, he wove seduction and royal decree. Her DNA made it impossible to resist. Like a marionette, with movements the opposite of fluid, she stepped upon the pool's stone lip. "For your actions, your life is now forfeit, Odessa Sullivan."

"Your power was supposed to be mine," she said raggedly. Her death was imminent, and she knew it. Yet her anguish left him cold.

"It was never going to be yours," he snapped. "Your mind was clouded by your insatiable thirst for more. But the amulet wasn't made for you."

Father had constructed it of his demigod blood, Siren placenta, and the enchanted waters of the grotto where Ardghal's parents had secretly met. The amulet was always unique to him. When Elizabeth removed it from his chest, she dislodged his spirit and sent his body back from whence it came, resting in its watery grave, waiting to be revived.

With his sacred object returned, he was once more immortal and ruler of his Siren clan, as meager as it was.

"Will ya give me a chance to say goodbye?" she pleaded.

"To whom? No one living or dead will mourn your loss."

"My sisters, my brother, and my parents are all here." She

pointed behind him, and he didn't need to look. The weight of the deaths she'd caused was heavy in the air.

Taryn among them.

"They're here to see justice, Odessa. Not to mourn your passing or guide you to the next life. There will be none for you."

From the corner of his eye, he spotted Taryn hovering beside Fintan, who was bent over her bloody, broken body, sobbing. Ardghal's rage at Taryn's senseless murder boiled to the surface. His arm flashed out, and he gripped Odessa by the neck.

"Jaysus!" Eoin gasped from beside Brenna. "Did ya see how feckin' fast the fucker moved?"

She and Narissa were once more in their human forms, looking worse for wear.

"Return to the house," Ardghal ordered them, not unkindly. "You shouldn't be here for this."

"I'm stayin'," Fintan said dully. "And I'd be thankin' ya to let me be the one to dismember Odessa."

"It'll take more than your anger, boy. Go."

Creed wasted no time lifting Narissa and teleporting away, and after a tearful look at Taryn, Brenna allowed Eoin to do the same. As he waited for his order to be obeyed, Ardghal sensed the struggle within Fintan. He allowed him the time he needed.

"Taryn's here with ya, boyo," Peter said gently. "You've the ability to see her spirit if you're of the mind."

Fintan lifted his head, his gaze disbelieving as it landed on her beside him. "Why were ya so foolish, Taryn-Taryn?" he cried. "I told ya you couldn't fight a Succubus, not as a mere witch."

Tears shimmered in her mournful eyes, and her loving smile was heartbreaking in its intensity. Ardghal's vision blurred, and grief nearly cleaved him in two. He forcefully shifted Odessa to view the tragedy she'd rendered.

"Was it worth it?" he snarled. "All the lives you've taken in your endless quest for more… was it fucking worth it?"

"I—"

He snapped her neck before she could utter another word.

It wasn't, and nothing she could say would right this wrong.

With a deep inhale, he said, "Fintan, I need to finish this, and you need to go now or die here."

"I'll die here. With her."

Frustration at the foolish romantic drivel made him fling Odessa's body harder than he needed, and her skull cracked open on the stones at his feet. Stalking to Taryn's body, he picked her up and carried her into the water. He'd braced himself for the impact of Fintan's expected attack, but still, he staggered under the weight.

"What the fuck are ya doin'?" Fintan shouted.

Ardghal faced him, Taryn locked in his arms. "Think, boy! The waters are enchanted, as are the boulders she helped me spell."

Hope, that ever elusive bitch, flashed in Fintan's pain-darkened eyes. "You can save her?"

"I can try, but you need to go."

"And if I don't?"

A disbelieving laugh escaped him, and Ardghal stared at him in wonder. "Did you get your arrogance from me, then?"

"Aye. Seems likely."

"Remember what I said about ya dying?" He waited for Fintan to nod. "My Siren song is the strongest of our line. It will burn up your DNA as I intend it to Odessa's. You can't survive it, Fintan, not now that we've split in two."

"What about Taryn?"

"She'll be safe where I place her. You won't," he said.

"Was it always goin' to play out this way, then? Were the ancestors right when they said she'd be my downfall? They meant her death, didn't they?"

"No. They fought my resurrection. They always knew it was coming if Taryn handed you my amulet."

"Save her. Please," Fintan begged.

"That's the plan, Fin. Now, for her sake, go."

Ardghal waited long enough to ensure Fintan's teleport before he sank to the depths of the grotto floor and placed Taryn's body on the bed where he was born. Her multi-colored hair floated around her, creating an eerie visual with her too-still visage and bloody body.

"Rest, love."

After returning to the surface, he relied on the water's buoyancy to keep himself afloat as he twisted his upper torso back and forth, summoning what he needed from within the mini-tide he created. The energy flowed through him, building as it joined with the magic inside his cells. Throwing back his head, he released a single note, increasing the volume as his power took hold.

His Siren's song, a utilization of hydro-acoustic resonance, created a soundwave strangulation in Odessa's bloodstream. The vibration shook her body where it lay, gaining in intensity with each accelerando, his voice climbing from baritone to tenor, and then soaring into an otherworldly register, piercing and florid, like a male coloratura, until Odessa's body collapsed under the weight of his final note.

Stepping from the water, he crossed to her empty husk. Dispassionately, he stared down, mourning the loss of her potential as his descendant. The good she could've done in the world would've far exceeded that of her evil self. But that was the problem with greedy Sirens when the lure of *more* was too strong to resist.

Fortunately for him, his father had anticipated Ardghal's nature and added a failsafe into the amulet. Through metal, blood, and stone, Father allowed Ardghal to transition from human to sea creature to Incubus without the demon taking control. He'd instilled his wisdom and patience in his hybrid son, teaching Ardghal the importance of both in addition to empathy and compassion.

All things Odessa had sorely lacked.

"What will ya do with her now?" Peter asked.

"Burn the remains and scatter the ash away from the sea. She doesn't deserve a proper burial for her crimes." Ardghal glanced at him, noting the sorrow and regret. "Do you believe me wrong?"

"No. I'm mournin' me bright, wild-child sister from our youth. After she killed her first, she was dead to me."

"You think my judgment fair?"

"Aye, my liege."

"So it will be done." He touched Peter's shoulder, making him solid. "Prepare her body for the bonfire. I've a need to see to Taryn."

<h1 style="text-align:center">CHAPTER 25</h1>

The wait was endless, and Fintan was about to lose his bleeding mind!

Narissa, having been fully healed by Jordan, paced the library, stopping in the doorway periodically to give him a helpless or pitying look. Brenna was no better and remained tearful within Eoin's comforting embrace.

As for Fintan, he remained on the landing, at the entrance to the caves. He didn't know which way Ardghal would return, whether by teleport or passageway, but he was prepared should Odessa escape her fate.

The image of Taryn, broken and bloody, with her face frozen in triumph, would forever be emblazoned in his mind. She'd risked it all to save him—or Ardghal—by confronting the one monster even the Sullivan Sirens feared.

He wished she'd have saved herself and left them to their fate. She'd still be alive, and his family wouldn't face the wrath of Damian when he discovered what had happened.

"We should go back," Narissa announced from the bottom step. "It's been too long, and I don't trust that rotten sow hasn't talked her way out of a rightful execution. Or worse, gotten the better of Ardghal."

When they'd returned, Fintan explained everything he and Taryn had experienced since Peter woke them. How the grotto had infused its history into his memory, and how Ardghal came to be born, then reborn today.

It was still hard to believe the entity residing in him was the original Siren hybrid.

"Ardghal won't fail," he said tiredly. "He has more to lose than we do."

Except for Taryn... but Fintan had already lost her.

"I'm sorry, sugar," Narissa said gently as she climbed the stairs. Sitting one step below, she placed a hand on his knee. "For what it's worth, I was rooting for you two crazy kids."

His bark of laughter sounded remarkably like a barely held-in-check sob, and he closed his eyes against the agony. Losing her a second time was so much worse than the first. At least before, he knew she was living her best life somewhere in the world.

"It's all my fault," he admitted raggedly. "If I'd just stayed away like the ancestors ordered... if I'd have ignored Peter..."

"She'd have still found my amulet," Ardghall said, stepping from the shadows of the hallway. "And Taryn was always destined to be involved, Fintan. She was my wife in another life, remember? Souls always orbit around each other, crossing paths until destiny is fulfilled."

The weight of guilt and grief crushed him as he stared up at the grim face of his Siren.

"She's dead, then?" he asked hoarsely.

Ardghal's mouth curled on one side, and humor lit his sea-bright eyes. "Oh, ye of little faith."

Fintan's heart skipped a beat. It resumed with a clunky thud, hammering so strongly, it felt like it would come through his chest wall and land at his feet. He surged upward, knocking into

Narissa. When he scrambled to help her, she waved him away with a laugh. "Go on, Fin. Claim the girl!"

He took the stairs two at a time and ended up beside Ardghal in four bounding steps. "Where?"

"Your bedroom."

But before Fintan could leave, Ardghal stopped him with a hand on his arm.

"She's in a stasis. It was the best I could do—for now."

Joy abandoned him, and his knees weakened. "I don't understand."

"She's in a transformation process. From death to life, and human to Siren."

"What?" Fintan couldn't believe what he was hearing. His hands grew shaky, and acid burned his belly. "Siren? Ya cursed her?"

Ardghal flinched as if slapped but recovered swiftly. His cold expression edged toward hostile.

"We are of royal blood, boy, and you'll do well to remember that."

"Sure, and it's still a curse," Fintan spat. "She wasn't born to this and doesn't deserve to constantly battle a power-hungry beast to avoid becomin' a demon."

"The demon curse is activated when a Siren steals what isn't theirs and murders to get it. The purest-hearted rarely cross the line."

Fintan shoved him. "But you did, didn't ya? Tales of your ruthlessness abound."

"I won't deny my history, but until you know the why of it, keep your judgment in check."

Ardghal never raised his voice, but Fintan could feel the power of the Siren prince pulse through him, as he had in the cavern. Denying the unspoken command to submit burned him on a cellular level, but he didn't flinch as he locked gazes with his liege.

After a minute-long standoff, grudging respect shone in the other man's eyes.

"You're a stubborn bastard, I'll give you that," Ardghal muttered.

"How do we undo—"

He held up a hand, cutting Fintan off. "We don't, unless you care to carve her heart out yourself. She's one of us, now. It was the only way to save her."

Fintan cursed himself for a fool. Why had he left her? Ardghal wanted his wife back at all costs. Hadn't he repeatedly tried to claim Taryn as his?

"You did it on purpose, didn't you?" he accused. "To make her the perfect princess to your princely self?"

"If she loved me, as she loved you, perhaps I might have," Ardghal admitted. He sounded tired as he said, "But my Elizabeth turned from me in the end and left me to die in that grotto, not realizing I couldn't, not truly."

"Ya once said I was you, reborn, but we're split souls. Who am I to her, then?"

"You're Fintan Sullivan. The Seer and love of her life." Clapping a hand on his shoulder, Ardghal shook him. "Stop this foolishness, Fin. She'll need you to guide her through the rest of your lives."

Narissa sauntered forward. "He's gifted you a third chance, Fin. Don't waste it, sugar."

She was right.

Here Fintan stood, quibbling over details when Taryn was in what constituted a coma down the hall. He raced to his bedroom and rushed through the door to find her exactly as Ardghal described—in a stasis. Perhaps he'd hoped she'd woken during his confrontation and would greet him with open arms the instant he stepped across the opening.

But she didn't.

Her too-still form was unnatural, as it had been stories below in the cave. Searching the room, he didn't see her spirit, and could only assume she was clinging to her physical self.

Fintan climbed on the bed and stretched out beside her. Resting his head on the pillow, he stared at her profile, as he'd done countless nights when they'd first hooked up. Whenever he was too wired to sleep, he'd watch her, unable to believe his good fortune. Worried that one day his happiness would crumble like an unstable house of cards. And it had.

He wanted to yell at the unfairness of life. But his voice still held power, and he checked the urge.

"It seems I've cursed you just by lovin' ya, *aoibhneas mo croí.*" His vision blurred, and he angrily swiped at his eyes. "The life of a Siren isn't what I'd have wished for you, love. If I can reverse it, I will."

"Like Ardghal said, it isn't the Siren, Fintan. It's those with evil intent."

He rolled to his feet, prepared to fight the newcomer before his conscience registered who it was.

"Jaysus, Dethridge! You gave me a feckin' heart attack, ya did."

"You didn't think to call me when all this began?" Damian asked from the foot of the bed. His tone was chilly and disapproving, making Fintan uneasy.

"It happened too fast, man. And Ardghal—" The Aether's sharp glance stopped him. "Did you know he was me Siren?"

The rigidness left Damian's expression, and he nodded. "I suspected, yes. But I also hoped I was wrong."

"Sure, and that's why you didn't want anythin' to do with Bloodstone's necklace, yeah?"

"I couldn't touch it. He warded it against Aethers."

"Why, if it doesn't work for any but him?" Fintan asked, curious why Ardghal would do such a thing.

"We have the power to gift or remove abilities, and part of them remain with us. Aethers are comprised of all bloodlines, even Sirens, to achieve this."

"He's the original hybrid. How is it you have Siren blood?"

"The Goddess. It doesn't make me a hybrid, though, just as it doesn't make me a Guardian or Traveler by possessing some of their power."

"Sure, and it's a migraine I'm gettin' from all this information," Fintan confessed.

"Or perhaps you need sleep," Damian said dryly. "But to answer your original question, I don't believe Ardghal wanted to take any chances after discovering my mother had absorbed the Darkness, which was born of a rogue Incubus."

Fintan sat heavily on the mattress beside Taryn. "Can you wake her?"

"I can try, but it will take Ardghal's trust in Beastie and me."

CHAPTER 26

Fintan didn't want to leave Taryn, not for one second of one minute. But he needed to broker the peace between the Aether and the Siren prince. Damian had to have unwavering faith in his skills if he intended to bring his beloved daughter into the mix. But then again, Taryn was Sabrina's aunt, and as her father, Damian would want to save her the pain of loss.

Fintan shoved aside the image of her grave, praying to the Goddess, the Fates, or anyone willing to listen that his vision had been wrong. It begged the question: once seen, was the outcome set in stone? He had avoided Taryn for fear she'd be his downfall, as predicted. Yet Ardghal and Peter believed the ancestors fed him a load of shite. Did it mean he wasn't a true Seer? During many situations in the past, he hadn't relied on them, and only when they hijacked his mind were the truly horrendous predictions imparted.

"Fin?"

He glanced up to find Brenna lingering in the doorway.

"Dinner is ready. I thought I'd sit with Taryn while you confer with Damian and Ardghal."

After pressing a kiss to Taryn's temple, he rolled to his feet. And in a spontaneous show of affection, he hugged Brenna. "Thank you. It's a kind offer."

"It's my fault," she whispered achingly. "I should've fought harder. Everyone believed I was stronger than Odessa but—"

"Shh. Taryn wouldn't blame you, love, and she sure as shite wouldn't want ya to blame yourself."

"She'll appreciate becoming a Siren." Brenna drew back and ran a shaky hand across her cheeks, wiping away her tears. "She always said it was a badass gift."

"You always know the words to say to make me heart lighter," he told her. "It's blessed we were the day you walked through our doors, Brenna Sullivan."

She grinned. "I bet you say that to all your cousins."

"Only the beautiful ones."

"All Sirens are beautiful," she said with a frown.

Unbelievably, he laughed. "Aye, but I meant on the inside, love."

"Okay, then, I'll give you that one. Now go. Don't keep them waiting. The sooner we wake Taryn, the better we'll both feel."

Fintan teleported to the hallway outside the dining room. The open doors revealed a lavish setting fit for a king.

Or a prince.

Normally, household chores were left to him as the caretaker, but Brenna had made sure to set out the finest china, light the candelabra tapers, and set out decanters of red and white wines, which he suspected came from his prized stash in the cellar. He couldn't fault her for the care she'd taken. This meeting was too important to fail.

"Are you ready to discuss the next step in Taryn's care?" Ardghal asked as Fintan entered.

"Aye. Are you willin' to listen to the Aether and work together to bring her out of stasis?"

"I am. But if he breaks the truce, I'll do what I must to save myself and my legacy."

"I feel the same," Damian said as he joined them. Summing up Ardghal, he held out his hand, "You're taller than I imagined, Prince Ardghal."

The Siren prince grinned and shook the proffered hand. "Just Ardghal or Bloodstone. And you're shorter than I imagined."

"I believe my height is fairly standard for a human."

Ardghal's gaze narrowed. "But you're not human. Not fully. You're the most formidable creature on this planet."

"Close enough," Damian agreed. "But there are others to watch. The Authority controls many of them."

They chose their seats, surprising Fintan when neither selected the head of the table.

"Was it a test? To see if I'd react to your comment," Ardghal asked as he poured them each wine.

"Perhaps." Amusement brightened Damian's obsidian eyes. "My daughter tells me you'll be instrumental in dismantling the organization."

Fintan halted in uncovering the vegetable medley Brenna had conjured. "Yeah, and what will that mean for the magical community?" he asked. "What are the consequences of such a thing?"

"It remains to be seen," Ardghal replied as he filled his plate. "But I'll not let them continue to manipulate you or Narissa, nor anyone else as they see fit."

"Is that what you believe they are doing, Bloodstone?" Damian asked. His tone was neutral, but his expression held deep curiosity, as if he were peering into the Siren's soul and attempting to figure out his true purpose.

"My wife's family was instrumental in forming the Authority

with the sole intent to control those like me. Hybrids from gods and mythical monsters terrified them."

"How is it you were able to marry her if they knew what you were?"

"They didn't at first." Ardghal nodded at Fintan. "I looked exactly like him and passed for a full-blood. They had no objections to a human warlock. This form"—he waved a hand to indicate his body—"was the one wasting away in the grotto beneath the estate after my wife…" Looking uncomfortable, as if he'd said too much, he dropped his gaze to his plate. Elizabeth's defection had hurt him, and though he forgave her long ago, erasing the pain of her actions wasn't as easy.

"Are you able to transform back to human at will?" Damian asked curiously. As someone possessing an empathic ability, he'd have read Ardghal's emotions and recognized them for what they were. Not delving deeper was a kindness.

"I haven't tried," Ardghal said, "But with the amulet back in my possession, I'll assume it's possible."

"I'm thrilled to see it returned to its rightful owner and Odessa dispatched. She was becoming a thorn in the side of many." After sipping his wine, Damian set it aside and picked up his utensils. "I'd have been happier if a Death Dealer had been present to obliterate her soul. The corrupt and rotten return worse in their next lives."

"To be honest, I didn't give it any thought other than to stop her from hurting anyone else," Ardghal admitted. "But she'll not return. I made sure of it."

"You possess Death Dealer magic?" Damian asked sharply, stilling as he awaited the answer.

Ardghal met his look with a challenge. "From my father's side, yes. I've only ever used it in cases like these. Is that a problem for you, Aether?"

"No." Appearing satisfied with the answers, Damian cut into his steak. "Getting back to your new goal, I've only known the

Authority to be fair for the most part. However, there were some council members, in recent years, who only had their own interests at heart." He chewed a bite in a slow, deliberate motion. Everything about the man was deliberate, as Fintan had come to learn. Ardghal would know this, too, had he been paying attention when his Siren was bonded to him.

A glance showed his princely self to be amused by the act, and he outright grinned when Damian dabbed the corners of his mouth with a napkin. "It's a grand show, but speak plain, Aether."

"All right, I will. I'm not certain I can condone toppling the entire establishment when it means there will be no law in the magical world."

"If you say there are trustworthy individuals, then I believe you. I don't propose destroying it completely, but it needs to be rebuilt from the ground up, with each family represented fairly." With care, Ardghal set his fork down and picked up his wine. "But I want those controlling Fintan punished."

Damian frowned, and he sent Fintan a sharp look. "Controlling? A Seer receives their information from their deceased ancestors, or so I've been led to believe. What's changed?"

"Ardghal and my uncle believe they've been feeding me what they want to influence outcomes and keep me doin' their biddin'." Fintan shook his head, tired of the fucking cloak-and-dagger bullshit associated with working for the Authority. "And they believe it's the Authority that made a deal with my ancestors."

As someone who abhorred injustice, Damian's anger was a living thing. Its energy snapped and snarled like a rabid dog on a chain, eager to be free and bite. The temperature dropped by at least fifteen degrees, as he shoved back his chair and rose to pace.

He halted beside Fintan.

"For how long?" he asked.

"Forever," Ardghal said, watching him warily.

"All the times, when I turned to you after the Fates suspended my psychic ability, those visions were manufactured?" the Aether asked Fintan.

"Sure, and I can't say for certain, but we think so, yeah." He held up his arm, displaying his burning skin. "You might want to calm the fuck down, Dethridge. It's uncomfortable when you're riled."

"Bloody hell." Damian didn't lose his cool often, not without consequence. Regret and compassion were in his expression as he laid a hand on Fintan, healing his burnt skin. "My deepest apologies, Sullivan. I was worried about my daughter's well-being."

"I'm grand." He stopped Damian from moving away. "I don't believe they've purposely targeted her, but I can't say they haven't, either. They've been tormenting me with Taryn's death."

The Aether stilled, and the intensity in his eyes was frightening. "How so?"

"Visions of me standin' over her casket in an open grave."

"We need to get to her. *Now*."

Ardghal was already gone.

Taryn was trapped.

Stillness pressed in from every side, and it wasn't natural. It wasn't the quiet peace of sleep, but something more oppressive. Though not floating in an abyss like Fintan had described, it felt very much like it. The scene around her could've been crafted from a painter's imagination, yet it was too perfect. Trees were too symmetrical, and the sky was a perpetual twilight, never growing darker. But the lack of scents and her inability to touch anything were the giveaways. The air didn't move, which meant no oxygen. And she wasn't breathing, so there was that.

This *place* was a carefully constructed prison, designed to cage her soul. And her wardens lurked in the shadows.

But there was another presence close by. One known to her, though she couldn't grasp who yet.

"Fintan?" she whispered, hoping like hell it was him. The sound of her voice was swallowed by the glowing atmosphere.

Not him, then.

Ardghal maybe? Did she dare call out? What if this was all a construct by the Sullivan ancestors, and by speaking his name, she alerted them to his resurrection? But if they were all-seeing, wouldn't they already know?

Fuck.

She hated the intrigue and landmines waiting for her one wrong step.

With nothing left to do, she floated toward the treeline, yet another clue she was in a weightless mind state. It remained out of reach, moving when she did. If she had a physical heart in her spectral body, it would be hammering right about now.

Sensing the presence behind her, she spun around.

Nothing.

She didn't care for the bug-under-a-microscope feeling she was experiencing. Someone was here, she was certain of it. Fingers brushed along her cheek, and she jerked. But no one stood next to her. They were soft, familiar, and she sought their warmth when they stroked her skin again.

Fintan.

Definitely him.

She'd know his touch anywhere. On the other side of this imagined world, he waited for her.

The crackle of electricity was loud in the air, and blue bolts disrupted the sky, as if the gods were attempting to penetrate the shell surrounding her.

"Taryn."

Her non-existent heart lurched.

He'd found a way to repair their bond.

"Fintan!" she screamed. And once again, the landscape muted

her voice. "Fuckers! When I get out of here—and I sure as shit will—I'm going to sic the Aether on your ass. Don't think I won't!"

Her threat didn't hold water, but it made her feel better to say it.

"Taryn."

The person calling her wasn't Fintan. Yes, the cadence was the same, but he wouldn't call her by name, not like that.

"Who are you?" This time, her voice reached farther.

A chuckle answered her. It wasn't audible in the traditional sense, more of a feeling of movement through her, and his intent accompanied the humorless sound.

"I know you're there. Waiting, like a fucking spider for an unsuspecting fly. Just show yourself and tell me what you want already."

Her warden waited.

She sat down and pressed her hand to the floor. Whatever ether she floated on, it was made up of liquid.

Taryn almost grinned. Suppressing her glee was difficult, but whoever had trapped her here had erred in their planning. With her elemental abilities, she could manipulate everything from mist to ice and pull back the curtain on this charade. A second of doubt stayed her hand. Was it possible to control magic when one wasn't corporeal?

Peter Sullivan had managed to teleport in and out, but Taryn couldn't recall if he'd performed any spells while in his ghostly state. Was that different from her? Yes, she was in a spirit world, but she wasn't dead.

"I can see your mind working overtime," her warden finally said. "You should relax. You're going to be here a long, long while."

"How long is long? Where is this place? Is it the Otherworld?" She'd heard the Otherworld was beautiful, but rumor had it the holding area was similar, still with no other life but those who'd passed with you. If this were Purgatory, she should be grateful no one she loved had crossed in the fight with Odessa.

"If you prefer to see it that way. And you'll stay here as long as the Authority needs to control Fintan Sullivan."

No Purgatory. Her captor's sneering of Fintan's name provided the final puzzle piece.

"Micha."

"Clever woman."

He came into view, and Taryn cursed herself for not noticing the resemblance to Fintan earlier. The coloring had thrown her off. This guy's hair was short and blond, unlike Fintan's multi-dimensional mane. His eyes were a dark shade of brown, vastly different from the sea-foam green she loved. But the features? Yeah, they belonged to her man.

"You're related to him," she said flatly. "How?"

CHAPTER 27

"Why would you believe that?" Micha asked.

Taryn swatted away the question, irritated that he believed she was that stupid. "Don't play games with me, dude. I've had a long twenty-four hours and want to go home."

He studied her, watching, waiting. But she'd be damned if she knew why.

"Are you expecting me to figure all this out?" she snapped.

"I'm sure you could if you thought about it long enough and provided you had all the information."

"Well, I don't. Is it a family grudge? Did he piss in your Wheaties as a kid? Because that sounds like something Fintan would do."

"Ouch, Taryn-Taryn. Sure, and it hurts you'd think somethin' so vile of me."

She tried not to react—she really did—but against all odds, Fintan was there, inside her dream state or whatever the hell this place was. Their bond simply reappeared, like a snap, and through their connection, she could feel his palpable relief.

"You might as well welcome him to the party, Taryn. He should be aware of the stakes."

"What stakes?" Fintan asked, stepping from the shadows.

The urge to run to him was as strong as she could ever remember having, but she couldn't trust that his spirit's presence was real and not some trick. Not yet.

"Micha Forsyth, yeah? My half-brother from da's side?"

Other than a sneer, Micha didn't respond. His disdain, more than anything, convinced Taryn that Fintan was truly there.

"What took you so long?" she asked him.

"I was brokering the peace between my Siren and boss, so it took a wee bit to realize you were in danger, love." He flashed a grin, and she couldn't prevent an answering laugh.

"We've both stepped in it now," she warned. "Apparently, I'm to be used as a weapon against you."

"Not a weapon," Micha corrected. "The fuse to his bomb, and we control that fuse. If we hold you, he has to keep it together and continue to do as he's told. He can start by turning over Bloodstone's necklace."

Fintan was taken aback, as was Taryn.

"And if he doesn't?" she asked.

"We'll take you out of the equation. Permanently," Micha said coldly. "We'll break him one way or the other."

Fintan's cold rage was instantaneous, and all his sweet Irish charm went out the window as he stepped between her and Micha. "You keep sayin' 'we' as if you've an army at your back, boyo. But Taryn has an army at her side. The primary being Damian Dethridge. You may know him as the Aether, yeah?"

"Damian is contracted to the Authority and serves the Fates. He'll do as he's told."

A bark of laughter escaped Fintan. "Have ya met the man?"

Leaning around him, Taryn held up a hand. "Uh, I think you should check your facts, dude. He's agreed to consult. He's not contractually obligated to anyone."

"But this isn't about Taryn, is it?" Ardghal's deep, lyrical voice rang out. "It's about you, Micha Forsyth, descendant of the original founders, and your hatred of those different from you," he concluded on an accusatory note.

"No!" And for the first time, Micha displayed true anger. "No," he said more calmly. "This is about order. There are rules, which the Aether and his motley crew of Sentinels refuse to follow."

"What rules have they ignored?" Taryn demanded. Challenging the man who held the key to her metaphysical cage wasn't smart, but Damian wasn't present to defend himself. She'd be damned if she let anyone malign him.

"It doesn't matter, Taryn," Ardghal said soothingly. "It never did. Elizabeth's family members have always sought a reason to crucify those who weren't human. You've the look of her brother about you, Forsyth. He always wore that pinched expression, as if his shoes were too bloody tight."

Taryn grinned. Call her warped, but if she were forced to be stuck in a mental prison, she was glad to have Fintan and Ardghal to defend her.

"You hybrids are all alike," Micha sneered. "You believe your power gives you the right to do whatever you want."

"Ah, so we're finally getting to the heart of the matter," Ardghal said silkily. "Does your hatred of Sirens stem from Fintan's father straying from your mother's side? No? Not the forbidden affair between a spy and his target?"

The inquiry-turned-taunt was so smooth, Fintan jerked, but he remained silent as Ardghal joined their group.

The Siren prince narrowed his eyes. "I can only assume it goes farther back, and the Forsyths taught you to hate from birth. Their fury was mighty when they learned what I was and that I'd married Elizabeth."

"Your children were an abomination!" Micha shouted, warming to his cause. He pointed to Fintan. "They still are."

"You shut your whore mouth!" Taryn shouted, enraged by his prejudice. "Fintan is all that is good and beautiful in this world. His music was legendary, but your stupid Authority ended his career to make him a slave to their desires. Like a fucking trained monkey, telling them the future so they could manipulate the magical community."

"Whore mouth? That's a new one from ya, to be sure." Laughter lurked in Fintan's question.

"I'm tired and not all that creative at the moment. It was the best I could do."

He chuckled, and the warmth of his amusement washed over her. It was bizarre how a person could spend just a few weeks in another's company, learning their likes and dislikes, discovering the secrets of their body, memorizing certain aspects of their personality, only to miss all of it desperately when it was gone. That's how she felt about Fintan and his humor. How, when they'd first met and for the short time they'd been lovers, she'd absorbed everything about him, celebrating each new facet of him.

But it had been fleeting, and she'd spent a lifetime trying to forget how he'd made her feel. Forever comparing him to others and being disappointed when they'd come up wanting. Perhaps that's why she'd agreed to a date with Micha. Her brain had recognized the physical likeness, even though their coloring and personalities were vastly different.

Thank the Goddess a date with him had never come to pass.

The truth slapped her in the face. "You never wanted to date because you liked me, did you? It was to gain an advantage over Fintan," she accused Micha.

"As if I could be attracted to anyone who'd given themself to a filthy hybrid!"

"You'd better hope this binding of yours holds, buddy. If I ever get free, I'm going to rip you a new asshole," she snarled. "You're going to wish you'd never heard of—"

Ardghall stepped up beside her. "Calm yourself, love. Conserve your energy for what's to come."

"Is it to pop his head off? Because I'm totally down with that."

A wicked grin flashed on his face, and Taryn could easily understand Elizabeth's attraction to this princely man.

"You're not a monster, Ari," she said softly. "You never were. If Elizabeth was confused at the end, it wasn't because of you."

His eyes shone with adoration as he gazed down at her. "Thank you, Taryn."

DAMIAN STOOD ON THE LIP OF THE GROTTO POOL WITH TARYN IN his arms. He hoped like hell that between her elemental abilities and new creature's skills, she could pull herself out of her mental prison. As much as he believed the Siren prince had the right of it concerning the Authority, he needed more time before dismantling the entire organization and rebuilding it with incorruptible leaders. Basically, he required a foolproof plan with gods, goddesses, Fates, and his fellow Sentinels on board. If he couldn't gain collective support, he and Ardghal might create a war among the magical community.

As Damian eased Taryn down into the water, he gave Sabrina a nod.

"All right, Beastie, lend her buoyancy as you did for Fintan and Ardghal."

She swirled a finger in the water beside Taryn. "This will work, Papa. Don't worry."

Ronan O'Connor's snort echoed from the opposite side of the grotto. "Sure, and we're about to electrocute a pool-full of people with the power of two Aethers and a Guardian. How is it ya expect us to be calm, wee beastie?"

She lifted her chin and shot her Guardian a look reminiscent of Isolde, so confident of her gifts. Damian's heart swelled with pride for his fearless daughter. But it also hurt from the aching memory of a young boy's love for his beautiful, doomed mother. More and more these days, he thought of her and how he'd failed her by leaving her in the Netherworld. He should've found a way to free her by now, and as soon as he dealt with the corrupt council members at the Authority, he intended to.

Perhaps Ardghal could help him defeat the Darkness if it hadn't already died off.

He glanced at Noah, who observed him solemnly. Undoubtedly, his brother understood, having gone through life motherless.

"One bolt for each of them, fellas," Damian instructed. "The energy surge will trigger the sigils. Sabrina can channel the rest through Taryn's link to the pool."

"We got it, man. Let's get on with it already," Noah said with an eye roll.

"Bratty little brother making up for lost time," Damian replied warmly, grinning when Noah laughed.

The three of them gathered molecules from the air around them, drawing electrical energy into the palms of their hands. Around them, the cavern echoed the crackle of power, and Damian gave a sharp nod.

"Now!" Beastie shouted, diving into the water.

For a split second, Damian's fear overcame him. She wasn't supposed to enter the pool, but he had to have faith she knew what she was doing as Oracle. Still, Noah and Ronan looked to him for confirmation.

He nodded. "Do it."

The moment their bolts struck, the sigils flared to life in brilliant, shifting hues, illuminating the entire place and glowing like molten etchings on the boulders. The force of their combined abilities ran hot and fast up Damian's spine. But it wasn't just their power. What existed in that water was something more primal, perhaps more ancient than all theirs combined.

Siren magic.

Beneath the surface, Sabrina swam from stone to stone, grabbing and tethering the strands together. From his place above, she appeared as a human spider, weaving an intricate web. She'd yet to surface for oxygen, and he worried she might be pushing the limit. Trusting a child, even one as worldly as his daughter, wasn't easy. They didn't understand limitations like adults, and if they did, they chose to ignore them.

Eoin's sister Dubheasa, Ronan's mate and fellow Guardian, stepped up on the lip, prepared to dive in should Sabrina need saving.

"We'll give her thirty seconds more," Damian said, trying to keep his nervousness at bay for the sake of all involved. When Aether emotions rode high, everyone paid the price.

At the center of the pool, the three bodies floated, each aglow with the voltage feeding them. Taryn's torso arched upward. Limbs dangling, head tilted back, and hair fanned around her in a silky cloud, she showed no signs of life.

"Please, Taryn. Come back to us," he urged. How the hell was he supposed to tell his wife that her sister was in a permanent stasis, or worse, dead? Channeling his anxiety, he directed more force straight at her body and prayed it did the trick.

Tremors shook the ground beneath his bare heels, and a subtle hum rose from the rock itself, growing louder until it became a deafening throbbing one might associate with a pulsing packed nightclub. The vibration was vigorous, enough to awaken a sleeping soul, and he held his breath as he waited for it to recharge Taryn.

Come on, Taryn. Come on!

Sweat beaded along his forehead, escaping to run along his hairline and gather at the base of his neck. He didn't dare shift his concentration off his objective, but he sensed Noah's and Ronan's struggles.

"She's been in there too long, Dove!" Ronan cried. "Get the wee beastie out!"

"No!" Damian shouted, going against his fatherly instincts. "Let her finish. She'll never forgive herself if she doesn't wake her aunt."

"And you won't forgive yourself—or us—if she dies in the bleeding process!" Dubheasa snapped. "I'm going in."

So saying, she kicked off her shoes.

"I'm ordering you to wait, Guardian," he said.

Her expression was as distressed as Ronan's. "Damian, please. Viv can't lose both Taryn and her daughter."

"She won't."

The sigils flared brighter than a solar flare, forcing their group to protect their eyes thereby breaking the current to the three bodies. The lights sputtered, dimmed, but held strong as Sabrina's web rose from the pool's depths to encircle Taryn and her two champions.

Beastie cut through the water faster than a water sprite, and her gasp was sweet relief. He blinked, dispelling his grateful tears.

Across the way, Ronan grunted and swiped an arm over his perspiration-dampened face. "Something's holdin' Taryn back, Dethridge, and I'm after thinkin' it's stronger than us."

Damian nodded. "Yes. If I had to guess, it's a spiritual anchor created by Authority bindings. They've done it before when jailing the strongest threats."

And it was one more check in Ardghal's column of Pros, and another reason to overthrow the institution they'd previously held sacred.

"She can break it," Sabrina assured them. She hopscotched along the boulders, as if she hadn't had the workout of her life, and plopped down by his feet. Sitting cross-legged like she had all day, she propped her chin atop her fisted hands and stared at

Taryn's body. "She'll do it, Papa. Aunt Taryn is more stubborn than *me*."

"Aye, and that's pretty feckin' stubborn, ya wee beastie," Ronan agreed with a grin.

Damian huffed out a laugh and settled down beside his daughter to wait.

It felt like hours, but finally, a shadow shifted in the depths, causing the surface to ripple. Another two followed.

Taryn twitched. Not much, a mere curling of her fingers, then a flick of her wrist. The water around her began to swirl, gaining momentum until it was a rapidly churning whirlpool.

They all jumped to their feet, but Taryn's body was sucked down within seconds. As Damian prepared to dive in, Sabrina clasped his hand.

"No, Papa. Wait."

"Damian," Noah called. "Look."

Glancing in the direction his brother indicated, he sighed in relief.

Fintan and Ardghal were waking. They wouldn't have left Taryn in limbo, this much he knew.

Across the distance of the pool, Ardghal met his eyes. "Take your family and clear out, Aether."

"Taryn *is* family."

"Granted, but she's triggered Siren magic, and it's best if none of you are here for this next part."

Sabrina tugged on his hand. "It's okay, Papa."

Leaving before Taryn was fully awake went against the grain. Yet Ardghal had trusted him to care for them while they joined her in the metaphysical world. The least he could do is extend the favor and trust him in return.

With a nod, he rounded the others up and left.

CHAPTER 28

"You should leave, too, Fin," Ardghal said, after the others had gone.

"No. I've Siren DNA, and she's my mate," Fintan replied. "I'm never leaving her to fend for herself again."

A bittersweet smile curled his ancestor's mouth. "If I haven't said it before, boy, you do our clan proud."

Fintan wouldn't have thought it, but Ardghal's praise touched some long-forgotten need for paternal approval. Familial love wasn't new to him, but his family was small. He extended his arm. The Siren prince reacted in kind, and clasping forearms, they mutually agreed to save the girl.

"Let's go." Ardghal waved his free arm toward the rocky ledge. A flat stone, wide enough to support them both, detached and sliced through the water until it was directly beneath them. In a musical language unknown to Fintan, Ardghal sang, and the water eagerly responded, gathering beneath the stone and acting as an escalator, guiding them to the grotto's bottom. Taryn's whirlpool had made a tunnel from floor to ceiling, allowing for easy breathing.

Fintan was grateful.

Yes, his Siren genes would've helped, but the energy required to survive underwater was great, and he wanted to be at full strength should Ardghal and Taryn need him to be.

"She's awake!" he said, surprised to find her back with them. "Taryn!"

Facing them, she glared. Her visage was twisted with suspicion as her gaze darted between them.

"Why is she actin' afraid?" he asked Ardghal in an aside.

Through narrowed eyes, Ardghal studied her, as warily as she them. With an abrupt laugh, he elbowed Fintan. "She thinks you're trying to trick her, boy."

Through their link, he said, *Why would you believe I'm after trickin' ya, Taryn-Taryn?*

Relief flooded her face, and she shook her head with a snort.

You never call me just Taryn, you damned idiot. I was worried Micha stole your body or something equally outrageous.

Her smile was luminescent as she held out her hand, and Fintan was quick to grab it.

"What are we doing down here, *aoibhneas mo croí?*"

"We need to work in harmony to open Ari's treasure trove. I want those fuckers at the Authority stopped." An evil grin curled her lips. "And if we can make Micha pay in the process, even better."

"You'd be the perfect Siren ruler, love," Ardghal replied. "You've only to say the word, and—"

"Zip it, Ari. I'm Fintan's."

With a chuckle, the Siren prince gripped her other hand. The water separated, granting them access to the boulder they approached.

"This is it," he said. Glancing down at her, he raised a brow. "Do you recall being Elizabeth, or do you need assistance?"

"What would that entail?"

He grinned. "A kiss."

"If it's from anyone but me, she'll not be rememberin' shite," Fintan growled. He'd damned well find another way to break the spell hiding their treasures.

Taryn laughed. "We needed to work in harmony, remember?"

"Work, not snog."

"Would it help to know you're my favorite snogger?" she teased.

"Sure, and that's grand. But just so ya kin, you'll not be snoggin' anyone but me," Fintan said with a warning glare.

"He's a sore winner," Ardghal quipped. "Come, we need to get this done."

RELEASING FINTAN, TARYN STEPPED UP TO THE FIRST BOULDER and examined it.

"Here goes nothing," she murmured, pressing her palm flat against the surface.

Ardghal placed his hand over hers, and she gasped as his collective magic, Siren and Demigod, flowed through her. The churning water picked up speed, toppling over itself from the center outward. It was a living entity, like his life force prior to latching onto Fintan to be reborn.

Bolts of blue and white streaked from all the stones at once, twisting together and forming a helix around their bodies. As the coil lit, so did the symbols on the remaining stones. One by one, they ignited, climbing to the top of the boulders, displaying ancient ancestral runes known only to purebloods.

Taryn didn't know what they represented, but she didn't need to. This place recalled her spirit from her time on earth before, and it knew Ardghal.

The ground rumbled, and she had a momentary pause, fearing they'd screwed up. But Ardghal's smile was reassuring, and she held fast as the helix swirled around them, gaining speed with each spin.

"What now?" she hollered over the howling wind it created.

He didn't answer, and his knitted brows concerned her.

"We need Fintan. He's my other half, and this won't work without him," he relayed through their link.

As if he'd heard, Fintan was pushing through the coil to get to them.

"What does it need from him?" Her shout became a scream as Ardghal's hand transformed into a claw, and he cleaved through Fintan's chest, shredding his heart. *"No!"*

The wind died.

"No! No, no, no, no, no! Fintan!" Taryn dropped to her knees, catching his head before it impacted the ground. She couldn't catch her breath and hiccuped her sobs.

"Why, Ari? *Why?*"

"Sorry, love. It required a blood sacrifice."

"You could've used me instead," she sobbed as she straddled Fintan and applied pressure. The gesture was useless, and his heart pumped no more.

"I am."

The talon piercing her back was as brutal and painful as when Odessa gutted her earlier. But Ardghal's betrayal cut deeper.

Ardghal scored his wrists next, opening the vein. As his blood mingled with Taryn's and Fintan's, he called it to him. Working quickly, he raced against the clock and the weakness beginning in his limbs. Ignoring Taryn's accusing eyes, he dipped his fingers into the precious store of blood.

The first symbol belonged to Taryn, and on her forehead, he drew a spiraling wave intersected by a rising flame.

"Solmara," he sang. "My flame. The one who creates storms in calm waters. Rise up, love."

She rolled to her feet and awaited his command.

On Fintan's forehead, he sketched a crescent harp entwined with vines, creating an infinity loop.

"Vaelthorn," Ardghal sang. "My twin soul. The tethered one no more. You are the voice of our people. Rise up."

Fintan climbed to his feet, prepared for whatever came next.

And finally, relying on feel, he drew a trident encircled by a serpent chasing its tail on his own forehead.

"Drekharn. The sovereign tide. One who rises and falls for love."

All three of their wounds sealed with a sizzle, and the images he'd created melded into their skin, leaving only a red mark that would fade when their ceremony was done.

"Find your symbol and claim your birthright," he sang in his birth tongue.

In a trance, they moved, each to a different boulder. Once there, they knelt, awaiting the grotto floor to relinquish its prize.

Solmara's box appeared first, delivering to her the Ember Pendant. Shaped like a teardrop mid-fall, the aquamarine stone would produce a faint ember glow when activated. Moving forward, Taryn would be protected from both the ancestors' mental abductions and the Authority's machinations. As long as she wore the charm, she'd be able to manipulate any spelled threshold, breaking through enchanted doorways, wards, prisons, or veils.

Vaelthorn's relic was the Songblade. An obsidian dagger etched with voice-activated runes not visible to the naked eye. With his weapon, Fintan could disrupt magical influence and cut through illusions or constructs meant to control him. He was a Seer without chains.

Drekharn's key arrived last. Tarnished with no teeth, it was smooth and cold to the touch. When they returned to the house, he'd work the metal into a ring, never to be removed. With it, he could access any charmed "locks," including minds. When pressed to skin, the key would unlock the truth, revealing deception and those beneath a glamour.

He sang the sigils closed, waiting as they burned first gold, then green, then a blinding white before they were snuffed for good. If he needed them, they'd be here, but this sacred place deserved a respite from the centuries of guarding Elizabeth's and his treasures.

The minute they were all rested and had conferred with the Aether, a reckoning would begin.

But of utmost importance was the apology he owed Taryn and Fintan for the attack they hadn't suspected from him. He waited impatiently for them to recover their will. As strong and as stubborn as the two of them were, it didn't take long.

"Come," he said, as soon as their eyes were focused and their actions were their own. "We should get topside before the Aether and his friends become nervous."

He held out a hand to help Taryn stand, but she knocked it away.

"That! That right there is why I left you back then, dickweed." Her voice had reached banshee-level rage, and Argdhal winced at the disagreeable sound. "You could've let us in on the plan."

"It required sacrifice, as I stated before," he replied with a patience he was quickly losing. "It meant sacrificing the two things I loved most. You and Fintan."

"You've a shit way of showing love," she snarled, delivering a stinging kick to his shin.

"Leash your woman before I strangle her, boy," he ordered through gritted teeth. "I swear—"

His head snapped back under the weight of Fintan's first blow. Getting struck by him was less punch and more an act of God. Ardghal wiggled his nose, suppressing a groan when he discovered it was broken.

"For fuck's sake!" He barely managed to keep his voice in

check. The ground rumbled with his anger. "Are you two done beating me up?"

Taryn and Fintan gave sullen nods.

"Lovely. Now, wait here while I dip into the water and heal my face."

"Fuck all the way off," they said in unison, teleporting away and leaving him alone.

The whirlpool dissipated, and the resulting tidal wave dragged him under. But he didn't mind. This enchanted pool loved him, was bound to him, as he was bound to it. The current stirred the bottom, and a gleam caught his eye.

He swam for the spot and brushed aside the sand. When he saw the jewelry piece, his heart spasmed.

His signet ring.

The one he'd given to Elizabeth on their wedding day as a promise to love her always.

Ardghal slipped it on his pinky and kicked for the surface. Though the desire to grieve his lost love consumed him, he couldn't rest until the Authority and Fintan's ancestor problem were resolved. By then, if witnessing the love of Taryn and Fintan became too much, he'd return here for a permanent sleep.

CHAPTER 29

Taryn strolled through the Dethridge gardens for the fourth morning in a row as she tried to gain perspective on what she'd become. It felt impossible. Another physical part of her existed, and she had to be cautious. Raising her voice could hurt those she loved.

The crunch of gravel caught her attention, but she didn't need to turn around to know who had joined her. It wasn't as if she could evade Fintan forever.

"You've been avoidin' me since you've returned from the ancestors' abyss, *aoibhneas mo croí*."

Taryn was no closer to reconciling all that had happened over the past week. She'd discovered she was the reincarnated wife of a Siren prince, essentially died, and was resurrected with his Siren DNA. Upon her return to the land of the living, her spirit had been held hostage to be used as a weapon against Fintan. She endured electrocution, and having been rescued, she was once again stabbed. This time for a sacrificial rite to collect ancient magical artifacts, by a man who claimed he loved her.

But none of that bothered her as much as how quickly she'd

escaped her prison. She was a novice, and while she had help, she did the bulk of the lifting. Yet it had taken Fintan twenty-four years to rebel against his psychic captors and finally admit he loved her. And the more she thought about it, the angrier she got.

Their day of reckoning had come.

She faced him, and crossed her arms.

"Yes. I've been avoiding you."

"If you're willin' to tell me, I'm after knowin' why," he said softly.

When they returned, she built a wall to keep him out so she could work through her feelings. The second it was completed, she told him she was moving in with Damian, Viv, and the kids. Her family's joy provided a welcome distraction while at the same time helped reaffirm her life.

"Why didn't you fight harder for me?" The question was packed with her anguish and poured from her mouth. Embarrassed by her lack of control, she presented her back to him. "I'm sorry, I—"

"I should have, to be sure."

She felt his approach and the wave of masculine energy he brought. This was new to her, this *feeling* of things, especially men. Her Siren senses, she supposed. The damned thing felt everything. Craved what it shouldn't. Who it shouldn't.

"It was cowardly to hide the way you did," she said coldly. Purposefully. Better to drive him away now than to eventually be his downfall, as predicted. Although how anyone could've seen that she would come to be a Siren when she was born a regular witch was a mystery. It definitely wasn't on her bingo card as a possibility.

"Aye," he agreed quietly. "But I was a broken man, Taryn-Taryn. I love you that much."

She blinked against the stinging tears. "If you love something, you fight for it."

"Sure, and I agree." He stepped in front of her and tilted up her chin. "I'm after fightin' for you. Until me dying day, *aoibhneas mo croi.*"

"Maybe I don't want you to. Not anymore." How she'd forced those words past her emotion-clogged throat and made them sound as chilly as she had was beyond her comprehension.

Fintan narrowed his eyes as he traveled over her set features. It seemed like a year had passed when he finally nodded and said, "Too feckin' bad. You'll not be rid of me so easy."

She scowled.

He grinned.

"You don't know how to take a hint, so let me spell it out for you, Fintan Sullivan. I. Don't. Want. You!"

"Sure, and you're a feckin' liar, all the same."

"Are you thick?" she growled.

"Aye. But I'm not wrong."

"Well, come see me in about twenty-four years or so. Maybe I'll feel like giving you a second chance."

He winced.

"It's deserving of your scorn, I am, but I'll have the why of its suddenness, love." In a stunningly fast move, he wrapped an arm around her waist and dug his hands into her hair, fisting it as he hauled her close. "Should I use my five-note skills to soften your mood?"

Her surly Siren perked up, forgetting to pout at being denied another's magic, and she clapped her hands with enthusiasm. *Yes! No! Bad Siren!*

"No," Taryn squeaked. "And women like agency, Fintan. You can't go around singing them into an orgasm."

One dark brow shot up as his mouth twitched, but he wisely kept his thoughts to himself.

"I'd not do it for anyone but you, love."

"Did you merge with Ardghal again? Is that how you're able to do the whole singing-O thing?" Yes, she was growing suspicious in her old age, but if his original Siren had separated from him, how did he retain the power?

He chuckled, and the sensation against her neck sent delightful shivers along her spine.

Gripping his hair, she tugged and forced him to look at her. "I mean it. If your Siren is gone, how can you manipulate others with your voice?"

"My Siren isn't gone."

"What? How is that possible?"

"Ardghal's energy split from mine and returned to his body at the bottom of the grotto. The water was blessed by both his mother's magic and his da's, who was a demigod. It regenerates life. His, yours, and mine." Fintan fought her hold and kissed the hollow of her throat, then trailed his lips along her neck to her ear. "That's why he was able to sacrifice us for the artifacts. Sure, and he knew our bodies would regenerate."

"I'm still salty about getting stabbed twice in a day."

His mouth curled, and because the sensation wasn't at all unpleasant, Taryn didn't object when his hand slid down to cup her ass.

"Aye, as you have a right to be," he assured her. "But gettin' back to your question. Me Siren still exists, but with me at the helm. I've control of it."

She shifted closer, angling her head to give him better access to continue his lovemaking. "Didn't you before?"

"Aye, but my grip was never as firm as it should've been. Not like Narissa, Brenna, or Ardghal."

And it finally clicked.

Taryn gasped and framed his face between her palms. "That's why you were afraid. And why you didn't break free of the ancestors when you so easily could've with Ardghal's power!" She shook her head, amazed she'd missed it before. "It was never truly about me being your downfall, was it? You were worried you'd lose control of your Siren and kill me one day."

"Aye. And if that happened, I'd have become an Incubus. Feral and power hungry. Whatever human bits were left would live in a state of grief forever. Unable to move on."

"Like Ari letting Elizabeth have the amulet," she murmured.

"Just like that," Fintan agreed, revealing his memories of their previous lives were alive and well.

In her mind's eye, she formed a wrecking ball, demolished the wall she'd built, and dusted her hands.

"How is it we both recall their past when we couldn't before?"

He toyed with her new pendant. "I'm guessin' our rebirth at the grotto."

"Fintan." Taryn stilled his fingers. "What if your initial vision wasn't wrong? What if I'm still to be your downfall?"

"What's this, love?"

"I don't think I'm strong enough to keep a leash on my creature like you were. She fights me at every turn."

"And what is it you think she wants?" he asked gently. "You should see."

"Is it as simple as asking her?"

"Sometimes."

Turning inward, Taryn faced her creature, surprised to feel Fintan enter her mind through their link. His show of support was both terrifying and calming.

"What is it ya desire?" he asked her Siren.

"You."

"And if I said you could have me, what then?"

Taryn jerked within his embrace, unprepared for him to offer himself up.

"No!" she cried.

"She's selfish," Taryn's Siren counterpart told him sullenly. *"Unwilling to share magic. To share you."*

"Just as I'm unwillin' to share," he said aloud. "You have the answer you seek, *aoibhneas mo croí.* You're stronger than she is. You always will be."

"It can't be as easy as that. Can it?"

"Aye. If you want it to be," Fintan assured her.

Relief coursed through her, so strong, her knees went weak. Luckily, he was there to catch her. Scooping her into his arms, he strode to the nearest bench and sank down with her cradled on his lap.

"Are ya satisfied we're safe together, Taryn-Taryn?"

As she peered up at him, his eyes full of quiet reverence, she smiled, positive they would be. "You've grown wise," she teased.

"Aye, and it's about feckin' time, yeah? I was a proper eejit for not returnin' for you sooner."

"Hm. I'll give you that one."

He grinned at her sass. "And now our fears are out of the way, can I snog ya, then?"

"Snog?"

"Kiss. I've a powerful need to kiss ya, love."

She didn't hesitate until her mouth was less than an inch from his, and a giggle rent the air, followed by an aborted, *"Ewww."*

"We have company," she murmured in his ear.

"Why isn't Ronan babysittin' the wee beastie?"

"Baby!" Sabrina's indignation kicked up the wind.

"Did that plonker just call us weens?" another young male voice demanded.

Shifting toward the hedge, Taryn did her best to keep the laughter from her voice when she called out, "Your mother would serve you a bar of Irish Spring for dinner if she heard you say 'plonker,' Aeden O'Malley!"

"Shite!" the boy whisper-exclaimed.

Their hasty retreat was hilarious.

"Sure, and how did ya know that would work to give us privacy?"

"I have three sisters, Fintan. We always used the threat of

punishment against each other." Taryn ran her index finger over his upper lip. "Now, where were we?"

"Discussin' me powerful need to snog ya, but I'm rethinkin' our location," he said with a glance at the hedge.

"We'll be free of prying eyes in your bedroom."

"Sure, and it's like we share one mind, it is."

She laughed during the short teleport to his home. With a quick glance around, she wrapped her arms around his neck. "Let's get to snogging."

EPILOGUE

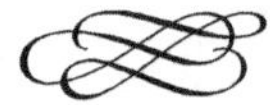

FOUR MONTHS LATER...

"*D*o you still have reservations?" Ardghal asked.

Taryn's full-length mirror displayed him in all his finery, and she inhaled sharply.

"Ari, you need a warning label."

He grinned as he approached, his hot eyes raking the length of her. "I'm not half as dangerous as you, love."

"Pfft. I bet you say that to all the girls at the pub."

His expression sobered, and his smile turned bittersweet. "Fintan is a lucky bastard."

"I'm the lucky one." She smoothed a hand down his shirt, straightening the buttons. "To earn the love of two good men. Once as Elizabeth and again as me."

"You've always been easy to love, Taryn," he assured her. "Fintan is hopelessly smitten."

"So am I," she said with a soft smile.

"Here. I've brought you something old for your human-wedding tradition."

Staring down at the velvet box, her heart tripped. Without

needing to open it, she knew what it contained. "Those jewels were a gift from your father to your mother, Ari. I can't take such priceless items."

"Mother has long since returned to the sea, love, and she gave them to you—uh, *Elizabeth*—on our wedding day. They were meant for a woman in love."

Flipping open the lid, she sucked in a breath. There was a king's ransom in emeralds and diamonds, but the setting was all new.

"Dude," she whispered. "If your mother were here, she'd kill you for doing that."

He chuckled. "Both pieces are charmed and will change shape to suit the woman whose neck and wrist they adorn."

"I'd forgotten that little party trick."

He grinned as he handed her the box. After removing the necklace, he held it up before her.

"May I?"

Facing the mirror, she met his admiring gaze and became overly warm. "You've *got* to stop looking at me like that, Ari. Fintan's, remember?"

"How can I forget? You take every opportunity to remind me," he replied dryly. Leaning in, he pressed his lips to her ear. "Would you like one last—"

Spinning around, she clamped her hand over his mouth.

"Don't you dare!"

His eyes crinkled with laughter, and with sudden clarity, she recalled the first time he'd laughed at Elizabeth. For a moment, their gazes locked, and her heart ached for their loss.

"I'm sorry I wasn't a better wife to you."

"I'm sorry I wasn't a better husband," he said huskily. With a tender kiss on her forehead, he cleared his throat. "Fintan will make up for my wrongs. He's not nearly as arrogant."

Taryn let that one slide.

"Do you think it's possible to love two men?" she whispered.

"No."

"Oh." It depressed her to think she wasn't normal, that perhaps she was sabotaging her relationship with Fintan by caring for Ardghal, too.

He tapped her nose. "We're the same man, love, meaning you love only me."

"Fintan," she corrected. "And someday, I'm going to need a further explanation of how the two of you can exist at the same time if you're the same soul."

"Yes, well, as soon as I channel my inner genius and work it out, you'll be the first to know."

She pressed her palm to his chiseled jaw. "Thank you for everything, darling Ari."

As she gathered her train, a stray thought implanted itself in her brain and began to grow wildly out of control.

Taryn paused in the doorway. "Ari?"

"Yes, love?" Amusement shone from his bright eyes as he patiently held the door for her.

"Do you already know what I'm going to ask?"

"I suspect, but please, voice your question."

After a warning glare, which made him grin, Taryn sighed. "If you and Fintan can split off, what's to stop Elizabeth and me from splitting off? Is there a second chance for you crazy kids to get it right?"

"And if I had the answer, you might not be wearing those jewels, Taryn." He winked and ushered her down the hallway. "Don't keep Fintan waiting. I can't take another broken nose. The first one hurt like a right proper bastard."

"Do you still have your psychic ability? Like Fintan?"

"Yes, but like him, it's sporadic and ever changing. It will be there when it's important."

"Why did no one see Odessa stab me? I'd like to have avoided that incident."

When he remained quiet in the face of her question, Taryn stopped short. "You *knew*? And you let me die anyway?"

"Don't scrunch your nose at me. I'd always planned to revive you."

"Every time I feel bad for you, shit like this pops up."

He laughed as he swept her, cradling her in his arms. "Stop stalling. I'm not dealing with Fintan's wrath."

"I'm afraid," she admitted, staring into his understanding eyes. "Love always goes wrong for me."

"Not this time, *aoibhneas mo croí*," Fintan said from the landing below them. "I'll make sure of it."

As she looked down at him, calm descended, sweeping away the shadow of broken dreams she had lived in for so long.

His eyes locked on her necklace and matching bracelet. "I'd wondered where they'd gone. I've spent the last twenty minutes searchin' for the feckin' set."

"Ari beat you to it. Something old."

A wry smile curled Fintan's mouth, and he bounded up the steps two at a time to relieve Ardghal of his burden.

"I've written you a song for the new," he said. "We just need somethin' borrowed and blue."

"The sky over the garden is as blue as I've ever seen," Creed said as he joined them.

"And Brenna has your something borrowed downstairs, sugar," Narissa added.

Just as she settled into Fintan's embrace, she gasped and stiffened.

"What?" There was a thread of panic in his voice, indicating he wasn't as cool and collected as he pretended.

"You saw me in my gown before the ceremony!"

"Oh, for fuck's sake! Ya almost gave me a feckin' heart attack over a bleedin' superstition."

"It's bad luck," she moaned.

Ardghal huffed a laugh. "You're safe. That silly superstition stemmed from arranged marriages. Not love matches."

"Really? Why?"

"It might create doubts about a match, especially for the groom if he didn't find his bride-to-be beautiful enough. To allay doubts and keep the marriage on track, men were discouraged from seeing their future wives before the nuptials."

"A superstition born of practicality and not real." Fintan grinned. "And you have two Seers here, Taryn-Taryn. We'll be on the lookout for problems."

"I know I will," Ardghal said with a devilish smile for the double meaning.

"Aye, and I've no problem plantin' you another facer, ya feck."

"Come on, sugar." Tucking her arm through Ardghal's, Narissa led him away. "Taryn will be upset if the two of you come to blows."

Creed checked his watch. "I'll buy you five more minutes with the crowd downstairs, but then I'm sending up Damian."

"You're the best of friends, man."

"Us boy-band members need to stick together," he said. His evil laugh drowned out Fintan's curse.

When they were alone, Fintan gave her an amused look. "Sure, and you put him up to that, didn't ya?"

"No, but I don't hate that he said it," she replied with a giggle.

"I've a powerful need to snog ya when ya look at me that way, Taryn-Taryn."

"Mm, and I've a powerful need to let you," she purred. "But if we get started, we'll be late, and Bridget is catering this event. You know how she gets."

"Feck."

"Exactly."

A wicked gleam entered his sparkling sea-green eyes. "I'm after takin' me chances."

"I was hoping you were. And that maybe you were up for a five-note song, while you're at it."

Love this book? Please leave a review!

And if you've got a powerful urge to snog, we've got the merch for you. Aye, it's grand. Visit our Irish collection here.

Turn the page to learn more about upcoming stories.

BOOKS BY T.M. CROMER

Get your printable list at https://www.tmcromer.com/printable-booklist/

PARANORMAL ROMANCE

The Sentinels of Magic Series:
THE AETHER
THE DEATH DEALER
THE SEER
THE TRAVELER

These Boots Are Made For Witching:
WICKED WITCHMAS
WANTON WITCHMAS

The Thorne Witches® Series:
SUMMER MAGIC
AUTUMN MAGIC
WINTER MAGIC
SPRING MAGIC
REKINDLED MAGIC
LONG LOST MAGIC
FOREVER MAGIC
ESSENTIAL MAGIC
MOONLIT MAGIC

ABOUT THE AUTHOR

T.M. Cromer is a multi award-winning, bestselling author, who loves to craft wildly entertaining stories designed to keep you glued to your seat, turning the pages to find out what the hell happens next. She specializes in kickass heroines and the men who adore them.

Genres she writes include romantic fantasy, paranormal romance, and romantic suspense.

If you want to stay up to date on what's happening in the world of T.M. Cromer, please subscribe to her newsletter or text JOIN to 1-877-795-1526 to receive release news and promo alerts.

You can also join her VIP reader group on Facebook to chat with her, participate in polls, or keep current on what's happening. Become a member today!

FOLLOW T.M. CROMER:

facebook.com/tmcromer
instagram.com/tmcromer
tiktok.com/@tmcromer
pinterest.com/tmcromer
amazon.com/stores/T.M.-Cromer/author/B011QK3WXY